W9-BFA-051

Sins of the Mothers

Sins of the Mothers

PATRICIA ANGADI

LONDON
VICTOR GOLLANCZ LTD
1989

First published in Great Britain 1989
by Victor Gollancz Ltd
14 Henrietta Street, London WC2E 8QJ

© Patricia Angadi 1989

British Library Cataloguing in Publication Data
Angadi, Patricia
 Sins of the mothers.
 I. Title
 823′.914[F]
 ISBN 0-575-04433-0

Typeset at The Spartan Press Ltd
Lymington, Hants
and printed in Great Britain by
St Edmundsbury Press Ltd, Bury St Edmunds, Suffolk

For
Kiran, Tara, Tavares, Kalyan,
Clovis and Eloi
with love

PART ONE

Present Tense

1 *Last Will and Testament: 1987*

This is the last will and testament of me, Iphegenia Esmeralda Daly of Holland Park, London. I wish expressly to emphasise here the deep debt that I owe to and the affection that I feel for my dear friends Rosemary and Hilary Donovan, by willing to them my three Picasso drawings and my four Henry Moore maquettes, always supposing that these friends outlive me. Should they predecease me then it is my wish that these same works be passed to their daughter Sally.

Everything else of which I die possessed, I pass to my most beloved son, partner and devoted companion, Caesar Simeon Daly.

I've made wills before, but they've always been cold, formal things written by the solicitor, and I wanted this to be *my* will rather than his. Also, I thought it important now to mention Sally individually in order to show that I do look on her as a part of the family. Of course I'll get it all done up legally, but I particularly wanted the affection bit said. You try to make clear, all through your life, just what you feel about those close to you, but do you ever really succeed I wonder? No one can ever be quite sure what other people think about them. There's so much we keep hidden isn't there? My own story is built up on things I have kept hidden; on things I haven't admitted to, sometimes even to myself; on deceptions, lies and half-lies. And yet I consider myself an honest person and a great lover of the truth. Odd, isn't it?

I still can't work out the rights and wrongs of many of the facets of my life, and that's after nigh on eighty years of trying! I've done what I've done, and presumably I'll be judged accordingly. I can't even remember half the wickednesses that I've committed; quite a thin dividing line between good and bad when you stop to look at it. I mean, supposing someone wants your opinion on a really appalling piece of work they have spent

9

their life completing, do you tell them the truth? Or even half the truth? Of course you don't! You say that's fine, that's great, that's terrific, and send them on their way rejoicing. You deceive them, in fact (just like I've deceived my dearest friend for most of my life), because it would destroy them if you didn't.

At my time of life, I can't really be bothered to sort out the moral from the immoral, much easier to leave it to the Almighty; but I do find myself thinking about death quite a bit, now that it can't be all that long delayed. Can't say I welcome the idea. Thank God, I'm pretty healthy still, and I don't pee the bed or anything like that. The memory's a bit of a bugger of course, but even that can be quite a laugh at times.

On the whole, I've been very lucky in my life, hardly ever been really *down*, because something good's always seemed to pop up before I got desperate. Even my weight, though a burden and an embarrassment, isn't a total disaster, and being what nowadays is known as black, but which, in my young days, was called (*sotto voce*) half-caste or coloured, well, that has been a bind sometimes. At the beginning it was, when I was very young and didn't understand what it was all about, but now it's a positive asset, because it means I'm not run-of-the-mill ordinary, which I would hate to be.

To be honest, though, I have to admit that being overweight is not, and never could be, any sort of asset. I think I've probably always deceived myself about my size. It was really the only way I could come to terms with being over six foot tall and seventeen stone in weight practically all my adult life. Can you just imagine that? All you people who glory in that splendid averageness of being the correct weight those horrid little tables tell you for your age and height, and when even tiny deviations of a pound here and a pound there will send you into agonies of anxiety, can you imagine what gross overweight really does to your ego? The only way I could deal with it was to pretend I gloried in it; to act the clown in order to induce people to laugh out loud before they sniggered behind my back at my grotesque shape. The knowledge that you cannot be taken seriously because you are a funny fat lady does things to the soul, because being fat is, of course, your own fault. You eat too much; you're a greedy fat pig and a figure of fun. The only thing to do is to join in the laughter and act the part.

I don't know who my father was or where he came from. You see Mother was a black prostitute and, when I was born in 1908, she was working for a high-class Madame in a high-class brothel somewhere off Park Lane. At least this was what I was told much later by her old accountant, Edmund—Uncle Eddie I always used to call him—who was one of her more devoted lovers I think. Was he my father? Somehow I don't think so, though that may be because I prefer to imagine that I was the daughter of this mysterious aristocrat who, I gather from Eddie, set Mother up in a flat of her own in the centre of Mayfair soon after I was born.

I remember sessions when Bessie, my big, black nurse, brushed my hair and tied it up with pink or blue bows, and then took me into my mother's drawing-room, "To meet the Duke," she always told me, "so you just mind your ps and qs." I puzzled long over what ps and qs might be, even asked Bessie, but never got a satisfactory answer.

The Duke was a rather fearsome character with sandy white whiskers and moustache, who smelt of a mixture of what I now know were cigars and bay rum. But he was gentle with me and showed me such things as his repeater watch and usually gave me a gold sovereign to put in my money-box.

After I had been in his presence for about five minutes, Bessie used to appear at the door and hover there to whisk me back to my nursery as soon as Mother gave her the nod. I would have liked to stay longer, and I would always sulk a little on the way upstairs, and then stare out of my nursery window to watch the Duke's liveried chauffeur drive him away from the front door of our mansion block. I wanted to ride in that splendid motorcar that looked so tall and stately with its brass headlamps and bodywork that imitated a cane chair seat, but I never got the chance.

"Don't you take no liberties with him lovey," Bessie warned me. "He's a very kind old gentleman, but we don't want to chance our luck do we?" Again, I tried to press her on why riding in his motorcar might chance our luck, but she became vague in the way she often did when she talked of the Duke. And then again, was he really a Duke? Or was that just a title he was given by Bessie?

Dear, dear Bessie, what a lot of security and confidence I owe to her presence in those first eight years of my life, and what a traumatic shock to my system it was when Mother decided that I should be sent to boarding school. Poor Mother, thought she was doing right in extricating me from the comfortable den of vice in which we were living in order to give me the chance of respectability. It was the only possible thing she could have done with me I now see. In those days, the half-caste, illegitimate child of a prostitute — however well set up she might be — didn't stand much of a chance of happy childhood in London society.

Before I went away to school I was, of necessity, almost completely isolated from other children, because whoever heard of a frizzy-haired piccaninny, with a big black nursemaid, being pushed out in a pram in Kensington Gardens in those days before the first world war? Black women, yes, you saw a few: prostitutes, music-hall artists, and servant girls brought over from the colonies, but I never knew any children of my own age before I went to school; their nurses kept them firmly away. I remember thinking at the time that I was somehow special, Bessie told me I was. "You don't want to get mixed up with them common children my darlin'," she said. "You are ten times better than them, what with your background. Your mammy's family come from great chiefs. She's a great lady, baby; don't you ever forget that my lambkin. Me, my grand daddy was a slave in Alabammy my darlin', but your mammy, now she's different, no matter what she do now, my honey; she's royalty. Oh yes, darlin', for sure, she's royalty."

I had every reason to believe her, and grew up with the certainty that I had a princess for a mother. This belief helped me to get over the bitterness of saying goodbye to Bessie, and the resentment I felt towards the mother who could leave me alone, that black day, in the charge of a smiling, voluminous nun, who told me that she was Reverend Mother. Whose mother? I wondered. To me she was like the cackling witch in Hansel and Gretel.

My spirits rose as she led me by the hand to meet the other children. Was I at last to be allowed to mix and play with the common lot Bessie had kept me from? They were certainly a mixed bunch: tall, short, fat, thin, fair, dark, but none so dark as me. They had all been trained, as I had been, not to make personal remarks, so there were only a few stifled giggles, which I took as friendly welcoming smiles.

"This is Iphegenia," said Reverend Mother, "who comes from a far-away country where it is very hot and the hot sun makes your skin brown."

"No, no," I said, surprised at her ignorance. "I come from London and I'm not allowed to sit in the sun because it gives you sunstroke."

There was a great deal more giggling, which Reverend Mother silenced rather sharply I remember. "Look after her in the way we always like to look after strangers within our gates," she added, before billowing silently away out of the room.

"I shall call you little black Sambo," one of the bigger girls said.

I had never heard the title before and was not at all put out. "Oh but that's much too long," I said. "If my name's too difficult for you to remember, you could call me Iffey. Can I call you Carrots? Your hair is like the colour of carrots. It's very pretty," I added with admiration. "It must be nice to have hair that colour. I like it very much." Poor little things, I thought, I mustn't make them feel bad because they probably haven't got beautiful princesses for mothers nor important dukes for fathers. Bessie always said I didn't have to show off even though my Mummy and Daddy were particularly special.

Thus I was cushioned and quite oblivious of any prejudice that might have come my way. Being a different colour to these lesser mortals was not a problem at the time. Much more of a problem was being fat, because then you seem to get it from everyone, and you're so physically disadvantaged as well. Can't run as fast as the others, nor do any of the physical things like climbing trees and any of the sports things that are so important when you're a child. I suffered quite a bit from that when I was young, because I was fat from the word go.

I met Rosemary the first day that I arrived there. Such a little thing she was, only six years old, and a helpless pulp of tears and crying.

"Don't cry," I said. "I'll write to your mother and tell her to come and take you away." But this only gave rise to louder sobs.

"She can't, she can't," wailed Rosemary. "She lives in Africa with Daddy who's a soldier and I can't live there any more because it makes me ill."

I didn't think to ask her if she had any aunts or uncles or grandparents. I didn't have any that I knew of, so thought it unlikely that anyone in boarding school would have any either.

The staff were kind though strict, and made us as happy as possible. A motley little lot of deserted children, most of whose fathers were in the army overseas, and some who had no fathers or no mothers at all.

"We're like the lost boys," I told Rosemary. "And we're in The Never Never Land and Wendy will come and rescue us."

But she had never heard of Peter Pan and the lost boys, so I had to tell her the story there and then, and that's really what started our friendship, seventy odd years ago. What an age, and we are still inexplicably attached in an odd sort of way.

That first encounter was one of those milestones that trigger off a whole set of circumstances, a chance meeting that in the end would be responsible for the pattern of our subsequent lives.

First words: "Hallo. Why are you crying?"

Rosemary: "Sob, sniffle, moan."

Iffey: "What's your name?"

Rosemary: "Sob."

Iffey: "My name is Iphegenia Esmeralda Daly. I am eight and three-quarters and my mummy is Princess Gladys Emily Mary Daly and my daddy is the Duke of Park Lane. Will you be my best friend?"

All sound behind the sodden handkerchief ceased immediately.

"Is she a real princess or only pretend?" Rosemary asked.

"Real of course. I mean she isn't magic or anything."

"Does she wear a crown?"

"No," I paused to consider this rather extraordinary fact: princesses should wear crowns. "Only when she goes out late at night, but I'm always asleep then, so I don't see her wearing it. But my daddy does." I thought the story could do with a little embellishment to make up for my mother's lack of dress sense. "He wears a long red cloak with fur and gold boots."

"Like Father Christmas?"

"No," I was a little annoyed at her lack of imagination. "Father Christmas doesn't wear gold boots."

"My name is Rosemary Celia Anne Robinson and my daddy is a soldier and my mummy is a soldier's wife," said Rosemary.

14

So I took on the caring role of Peter Pan — brave, masculine and competent — and perhaps translated Rosie into the domesticated, dependent female that she was later to become. Occasionally I feel a bit guilty that I maybe led her into that sort of situation, because I certainly did my share of protection in those early years. We played out the whole Peter Pan drama at that time, which satisfied my current fantasies of being on the stage when I grew up, and gave her the comfort of having a protector. We were inseparable, and cocooned against the injury of banishment.

In the end I relied on her as much as she did on me, and we developed a real kind of love for each other during the school years. I suppose we were more like sisters than anything else. Being deprived of any other sort of family, a kind of kinship bond took its place. Why else should we have remained so close after all these years? We should have grown apart, but we never did.

It probably had something to do with the hideous day that Uncle Eddie arrived at the school when I was just twelve years and two days old, with a face as long as a boring Sunday, to tell me that beautiful, fairy-tale mother was dead. Syphilis, I learned much later, along with all the other details.

Eddie was crying when he told me, and Mother Superior was busy with the handkerchief at the other end of the room.

"But you won't be alone, Ginny my dear," he said.

I had forgotten he called me Ginny. What did he mean I won't be alone?

"Shall I be living with Bessie?" I asked. If that were the case things wouldn't be all that much changed.

"Bessie has moved on since you grew up and went to school."

I was afraid of that. I'd said goodbye to Bessie when I came to school. I had *known* that, when I found she wasn't there in the holidays. So what was to become of me?

"We will arrange something for those holidays which you cannot spend here at the school," Eddie said. "You don't have to worry, Ginny, your mother left you very well provided for, and I will always be here as a friend and adviser, like a father would be."

I looked at him in total despair, and started the great storm of weeping that went on for hours, days, weeks — I couldn't tell how long, nor do I remember much about it.

It was then that my role as protector of Rosemary became metamorphosed into her role as protector and organiser of me.

"But Iffey, you can live with me in my home," she said, and in due course, and without my having to think about it, it was all arranged. In moments of crisis, Rosemary proved herself to be the tower of strength. When I look back, it surprises me to this day to realise what organising ability Rosie had, even at the tender age of ten.

When the time came for us to leave school, we both became rather desperate at the thought of being parted and made a solemn, schoolgirl pact never to lose touch.

"Don't think I could exist if I thought you weren't going to be around, Iffey." We were both crying I remember.

"Don't be a silly ass. I'm coming home with you, aren't I? Like I always do."

"But being at home is different."

I knew what she meant. Back at the Robinsons', Rosemary at once became swamped in the family circle, and I was the poor little black orphan child they were being kind to. Not that I minded that particularly, but I minded that Rosie was swept out of my care into theirs. Jealous I suppose, though it didn't seem like that at the time. Rather that I thought they were treating her all wrong, and that she would do much better under my guidance than theirs.

"We'll make a pact," I said.

"What sort of a pact?"

"We'll solemnly swear that circumstances will never divide us."

"All right." She paused, with her eyebrows drawn together in anxiety, "but anything might happen, I might marry a soldier and live abroad."

"So it will have to be a proper commitment, like we'll contact each other at least once a month: letters, telephone, visits. Something like that."

We made out a document, signed it, and mixed drops of blood from both our wrists with the sealing wax we sealed it with. I still have my copy in the ivory and silver-gilt casket I always keep by my bed!

Oh we were very much in love with each other in those days, in the way schoolgirls often were. If we hadn't been so innocent and lacking in any sort of sexual knowledge at the time, things might have turned out differently for both of us. Odd that we never mention all that nowadays. Has she forgotten? Is she embarrassed by all the sentimental emotion we indulged in then? That is very possible, because she's become absurdly conventional with age. Perhaps she can't admit to ever having those sort of feelings. It would probably make her feel uncomfortable if I reminded her, so I don't.

As it was, we moved off on our separate paths, but linked always by that odd strand that binds the most diverse characters together in friendship or kinship against all odds. I moved out of Rosie's parents' house, as soon as I left school. It was much too claustrophobic and they were far too caring and always wanting to organise my life.

"We think you ought to go somewhere where you could learn domestic things like cooking and sewing, Iffey dear," Rosie's mother said to me. "It's so important for a girl to know about all these things, whatever she intends to do with her life."

Can you imagine that? Me learning to cook and sew and lay tables and make beds and be polite! I knew they meant it kindly; wanted to make me a little more ordinary, more normal, so that I could blend in better with London society in spite of my size and colour. They probably thought I should end up being a companion to some rich old lady, or perhaps a governess, the sort of thing unwanted spinsters had to fall back on in those days. Poor old things, they must have worried about me; I expect they thought they'd failed in their efforts to help me to fit into society when I refused.

But I knew what I wanted to be; had done ever since I was five and Mother got me to sing to all her friends. It seems I was a natural and could imitate the best of the day — Tetrazzini, Florrie Forde, Melba — the lot. I used to listen to Mother's gramophone records and then sing along with them, evidently pretty accurately. I suppose the voice was quite something from the very beginning, and at school they recognised this, thank God, and encouraged it. So it was grand opera for me from then on.

"Darling Mrs Robinson," I said, because I'd never agreed to call them Auntie Julia and Uncle George, which they'd always wanted. "I'm going to be an opera singer, so I have to start training straight away and that means I have to live where I can practise my scales without upsetting too many people. Thank you, thank you for all that you've done for me. You are the kindest people I know and I shall be eternally grateful, but you don't have to worry about me any more, I shall be all right." And off I went, there and then, to demand some of my money from old Uncle Eddie, and to find myself this studio in Fulham Road where I felt free, and where I was able to meet the arty Chelsea types with whom I felt much more at home.

Eddie grumbled like anything, and said I was far too young to live on my own, but I got round him. Poor old Eddie, he didn't want any trouble, so he agreed, providing I employed a housekeeper-cum-chaperone until I was at least eighteen. He found a nice old body called Mrs Gamp, who managed me beautifully, but whom I could twist round my little finger. I told Eddie he could come and visit whenever he wanted to, to see how I was getting on. The Robinsons were very shocked — though probably relieved to see me go — and didn't think it safe to allow Rosie to visit me much but we went to concerts and exhibitions and the theatre, and somehow or other, we hung on to each other and stayed friends in spite of everything — the proper and the improper; the conventional and the unconventional; the odd couple. Later on in our lives we always seemed to land up living next door to each other in more or less the same street.

As individuals, I don't think two people could be less alike. To look at, for instance, she was always the gentle English rose type with sandy hair, bright blue eyes and a complexion like peaches and cream. Quite breath-taking she was when she was young, and she is still one of those old women that people look at twice and say either, "She must have been beautiful when she was young", or, "What a strikingly handsome woman". And she is: just slightly plumpish with a mass of burnished white hair that still looks gold in some lights.

As for me, well, I'm big, black and I hope, still beautiful! I can't say that I have ever come to terms completely with my size — who could? But I suppose I'm resigned. Same sort of thing with age; it really does depress me sometimes, all these lines and wrinkles and disgusting bulges, and the gradual loss of faculties; it's pretty bloody grim. But there's nothing much you can do about it is there?

I suppose I would have been very happy to have looked as pretty as Rosemary did (and still does), but then I wouldn't have been me. I wouldn't have had to do all that adjusting which I'm sure was very character-building, and that would have made me a different person altogether. Better to make the best of what you've got I always say. Even though I may have rather more to make the best of than others. Makes you laugh really, when you stop to think about it.

2   Sir Hilary Donovan

Sir Hilary Donovan does not at all enjoy old age. Although there are perhaps certain compensations in the respect and acclaim that are accorded to him these days, he is deeply unsatisfied with the lamentable onslaught of deterioration and decay that is for ever creeping up on him so insidiously. It is humiliating and disgusting and an abomination.

"There's a great deal to be said for euthanasia," he says over his breakfast *Times*. "If only there was an untraceable instant pill that one could swill down with the morning coffee, or, perhaps better, with the last whisky and soda before bed."

"And would you take it now?" Rosemary asks him, "or would you wait to see what the day brought first?"

"I should have taken it at four o'clock this morning," he says, "so that by now I should be blissfully ignorant of all the aches, pains, insults, disappointments and rejections I shall probably have to face today."

"You talk such nonsense." Rosemary slits open three letters neatly with the tortoiseshell and silver paper-knife they had had as a wedding present fifty-odd years ago. Slitting envelopes like this always gives her a shiver of pleasure, something like walking on nutshells or ice puddles or popping fuchsia buds. "You know you'd never actually do it, any more than I would, because there always might be something better round the corner; and there usually is of course. And anyway, you needn't think you'll go sailing up to heaven straight away, you're much more likely to be getting yourself in a terrible state wondering how we shall ever manage without you."

"I shouldn't ever worry that you weren't going to be able to manage perfectly well without me."

She looks over the top of her half lenses and the letter she is reading. "You are well aware," she says smiling, "that I should collapse and die without you." She puts the letter down and takes off her glasses. She notices that her hands are shaking quite visibly.

"I have a very startling piece of news for you," she says. "If you are quite awake and ready to hear it, because it will need talking about."

Hilary puts down *The Times* and spreads butter on his toast. Rosemary's startling pieces of news are often rather dull, and follow-up discussions sometimes quite boring, but perhaps he is being unfair, her life is not particularly exciting, so ordinary, dull occurrences might well appear startling and exciting to her.

"I'm all ears."

Rosemary is irritated. There are occasions she finds Hilary condescending, so she contains, for the moment, the turmoil into which the contents of the letter have plunged her.

"Sally's coming home," she says in a flat, matter-of-fact voice that denies the earth-shattering importance of the statement.

"WHAT?" Hilary is agitated. "What do you mean, coming home? You mean coming back to England? For a holiday you mean? Has she written? Where is she?"

Rosemary picks up the letter and feels remorse at having given him a shock like this. How could she have been so unkind over something that meant so much to both of them? She is astounded at her own insensitivity. Tears start forming, and she takes out a handkerchief as she hands the letter over to him.

"According to the postmark — because naturally there's no address given — she seems to have come back already. The postmark says Manchester."

The feeling of hurt wells up in her throat and stops her from continuing until she can take a hold of her emotions again. The astounding cruelty of her own daughter towards her is unforgivable.

"Everything seems to have gone wrong for her again. Terry was obviously as great a disaster as Andy, so she actually wants to come home. After all these years, she actually wants to come home." The tears run unchecked now. "Those poor darling children — and wretched Sally adrift again. I suppose we must be grateful that she feels she can still come home to us. I thought we had been rejected as completely useless." And she allows herself to cry as Hilary reads the letter.

"Oh God," he says, trying to adjust thoughts and emotions. Sally had become a lost cause and pushed to the back of his mind. Something he had had to adjust to, years ago. He was not good at adjusting. "The children too?" he says, trying to make the whole thing a reality.

"Of course it will be wonderful," says Rosemary, recovering a little, "to have them here with us again, but why couldn't she have told us sooner? Such a shock, that's all." She forces a smile that merely stretches her mouth without giving any hint of pleasure. "Just think though, to be able to meet our grandchildren! Just wonderful!" She tries, without much success, to make her words sound convincing, at least to Hilary, if not to herself.

Marvellous woman, Hilary thinks to himself; she can whizz through a whole gamut of emotions in less time than it takes to think them. For himself, he needs far more time to accept the frighteningly altered circumstances this news is bound to impose upon their lives.

He gets up from the table, unable to face a discussion as yet. Must sort out his own mind first.

Rosemary is shocked. "But we must talk about it, Hilary, there are arrangements we must make." He surely can't leave her on her own to arrange everything? There is so much to say. talking to him would help to straighten out anxieties. To be alone in a crisis is lonely and frightening. He surely could understand that?

"Give me time, my dear," he says. "We'll talk about it this evening, plenty of time to talk about it then, and I have to get in to the theatre this morning. Got business to attend to there. We'll talk about it this evening." And he kisses her with great tenderness and makes good his escape, fearful of an emotional scene. Much too shocked to deal with that at the moment.

He walks quickly through the park towards Iphegenia's flat, thinking about Rosemary. What an extraordinary woman she has turned out to be. How she manages to call up and dispel emotions with such astonishing speed. Could be called superficial if you didn't know better. Much more an ability to deal with situations, especially upsetting ones, by turning them into everyday events. She seems to be able to take everything in her stride while insisting on his making the decisions. Manages to make him feel responsible all the bloody time. He feels vaguely put upon and yet guilty for feeling so. Can't really find fault anywhere.

Life with Rosemary could be considered a little boring he supposes, but that would be a churlish suggestion. It might, though, have been difficult for Sally to live up to Rosie's standards, he thinks. Not that any blame could possibly be levelled at Rosie for that, because she would have checked any signs of superiority that Sally might have picked up. She was certainly one of the kindest and most thoughtful people imaginable. Always thinking of others, never of herself.

The other two children never had Sally's sensitivity. An uncomfortable pang of distress shoots through him. Something had obviously gone wrong somewhere; difficult to see where to put the blame — if blame had to be put somewhere. True, he had not had much time to share in the kids' upbringing, but at least he had always been there, and naturally had supported everything Rosie had done; relied entirely on her where the kids were concerned. That was just it, she *was* always so reliable; there never seemed to have been any worries in that direction.

So why were all three children such disappointments? Genes? Most unlikely, he thinks, Rosemary is a saint, and he doesn't consider himself to be a particularly self-centred, unfeeling sort of individual. And yet together they had produced Sally, who has run away from them, Jonathan, unsuccessful and alcoholic, and Tim, highly successful, but ruthless, with no time and, seemingly, no affection for his family.

Doubts nibble tentatively at Hilary's conscience as he strides through the cold, brisk air that usually acts like a charm on his anxieties and depressions. Not today. Is Sally his fault? For being a successful actor and yet not being able to help his own daughter get a decent part after drama school? But then Sally had been so adamant that she wanted to do it on her own, changed her name so that his fame should not be allowed to rub off on her.

And when that bastard of a husband had walked off with someone else, she didn't even tell them until years later; just rejected them as she had been rejected, and disappeared into oblivion for years. Cut herself right off from them all. She had only contacted them fairly recently with the news that she'd taken herself abroad after the failure of her marriage — would never tell them where — and now had two kids with someone called Terry.

He can't really forgive her for the suffering her alienation has caused Rosemary though. And now fresh disaster it seems. Hilary's emotions tangle themselves into inextricable knots as he is forced to dig them out of limbo. Bloody kids, one can never free oneself from them.

He walks easily and fairly fast. His lean strides eating up the distance, and his intense expression sorting him out as a handsome, lithe, slightly eccentric old man wearing a large, soft hat, and the sort of clothes that could only have been made to his own design or bought somewhere where up-to-date fashion had not penetrated.

He begins to feel irritated to realise that he will have to slow down slightly because his breath is coming faster than is altogether comfortable, and the hip is starting to twinge every now and then. Blast this inevitable decay.

Iffey's flat, a vast, Edwardian studio, attached to the opulently panelled and spacious ground floor of one of the larger Holland Park houses, is full of what she always tells them is the best possible taste. Packed, one could say dripping, with an excess of everything that has ever appealed to her. One must suppose that some things have worn out or been broken and discarded over the years. That there must have been jumble sales to have profited from her overflowing good nature and generosity, but it is difficult to believe that Iffey could ever have disposed of anything when one surveys the excess of riches that is displayed here.

"Hallo my darling," she greets Hilary with an effusive hug that envelops him in swathes of Indian silk scarf and Yves St Laurent's Opium, and rouses a small amount of sexual excitement in him

23

immediately. "Just about to embark on the morning ecstasy of coffee, cream, soft brown sugar and exquisite and expensive Danish pastries. Come and share the bliss." She moves into her studio with the grace of a whale scything through water, and it is as though the hangings and the furnishings she passes are swept a little from their places into her swirling wake.

The studio is behind the house, built in the garden, and joined by a paved courtyard, one side of which is enclosed by glass and is thick with trailing greenery, jasmine, passion flowers and plumbago. There is a small aviary in the centre with finches and canaries.

"Smell the jasmine," Iphegenia says as she wafts through, but Hilary only catches the Opium, and feels like a Bisto Kid, following her through to the studio.

"Sally's finally coming home," he says, sinking down among the cushions on the sofa. "Coming home to mother with two grandchildren."

Iffey's laugh always seems to come from the depth, working its way upwards through the rolling plains to emerge finally in a lazy, but musical sound that is very contagious. "You're not going to like that," she says, as the laugh continues to shake her whole body. "And it's going to be too much for Rosemary, who will drive herself into the ground for the little darlings and get precious little in return."

"No no. Rosemary likes the idea. She adores the thought of seeing those kids. She'll take it all in her stride."

"Rosemary is nearly as old as we are, and it *will* be too much for her, you mark my words. That daughter of yours is trouble."

Hilary is offended. What right has she to condemn his daughter when her own son . . . ? Thoughts fail him. "There's nothing wrong with Sally. It's the bastards she shacks up with that are the trouble."

Iphegenia bites into a pastry. No use arguing. She wonders how she can help Rosemary. "Well Sally will have to find some work if she's to feed two kids." If she's not going to live off Rosie and Hilary, she thinks. "Have a bun darling, it will give you energy to cope with the situation."

He smiles and shakes his head. "I have to watch my figure."

Again the deep rumble of a laugh. "Poor starving, Oxfam child," she says. "One bun would quite possibly show up as a bump in your under-nourished stomach, whereas one tiny little bun will get lost among all this and won't show at all." She caresses her stomach. "I have this wonderful new Jessye Norman record," she says. "I will let you hear it before I demonstrate how well my voice blends with hers. I have learned so much from that woman, not only in my singing technique but also in understanding how beautiful big women can be." She is disappointed that he does not respond to the request for a compliment. "There," she sighs, taking the record out of its sleeve, "but for the inhumanity of God go I. Born some twenty to thirty years too early; it could well have been Iphegenia Daly's name on this disc singing Dido's Lament. But instead it's an old 78 of Iffey Daly singing *Blues in the Night*." She gives an explosive bellow of laughter, and takes a further bite into the bun.

Iffey's voice had been outstanding at school, and had evolved, under later tuition into something that was quite exceptional. But the times were not ready for her. The daughter of a black prostitute was not, at that time, the kind of material from which opera singers were fashioned, and all her attempts at recognition were unavailing. She had to support herself by other means, and because she had learned sufficient technique from her mother, she had, over the years, been able to earn a great deal of money in other ways.

She moves over to her grand piano. "Perhaps a little sentiment is in order first though," she says and launches into Liszt's Sospiro.

"God, that takes me back," Hilary says with a great deal of relish. "You played me that for the first time all of sixty years ago."

"You actually remember? And here was I, imagining you to be an unfeeling, unsentimental selfish old bastard."

"As you constantly remind me."

"Oh I don't, not constantly; only now and then. So when did I play it to you for the first time?"

"Just after the war, when I came back to London after that season in Exeter rep. I thought it was the most romantic music I'd ever heard."

"That was because you were in love."

"Still am; what about you?"

"Me? Perhaps, a little. So many aspects of that over-used phrase, and such a lot of make-believe intermingled that I never have been able to make up my mind."

"You really should have come to some conclusion after sixty-odd years, my darling."

"I disapprove of conclusions," Iffey says. "They never get you anywhere."

3 Rosemary and Iffey

"Strange," Rosemary thinks, "how competent I feel when Hilary is here, and yet as soon as he walks out of the house my confidence is immediately dealt a death blow." When she is on her own, there are no egos to boost but her own, and her own ego is the one that remains obstinately unboosted.

She sets about doing something useful and practical. Mrs Clarke will be waiting to clear and do the dining-room; the day's meals are organised, so nothing to do there. She was going to arrange a dinner party next week for some of the cast of Hilary's new play, but that will have to be postponed until the *bouleversement* of Sally's return has been absorbed. She climbs to the top of the house to start organising the rooms there. Mrs Clarke will have to come an extra day to help clean them right out. Hilary will have to give up his study for the time being. He won't like that, but it's really such a waste of a room, he hardly ever uses it, and Sally is bound to move on before too long.

Her mind pauses for a moment on the disaster of Sally, until she pushes it resolutely forward again into the rearrangement of furniture — the sofa bed would do for one of the children; what a good thing she decided against giving that to jumble last year. Hilary never liked it. Poor darling, he won't like this invasion at all; so set in his ways these days. His files and books can all be moved down to his bedroom, quite cosy she could make it, he might even like to have all his things together in his bedroom, make it into a sort of study-bedroom for him. She sees in her mind the desk facing the window and the bookcases ranged along the left-hand wall. It would need different curtains of course.

Searching in the linen cupboard for the extra bedclothes for Sally and the children — duvet cover for the sofa-bed and blankets for the two single beds in the spare room — she is reminded of Iffey's real linen sheets and real fur bed-cover. Such absurd extravagance! Linen sheets cost a fortune these days when cotton and Terylene mixture do just as well. Linen was horribly cold; her mother had never had real linen sheets because they were so cold. But then Iffey has no sense of economy, never did have. There always seemed to be an unending supply of cash from that dreadful old accountant of her mother's — what was his name? Edward? Egbert?

Poor dear Iffey; it really isn't fair to blame her for her shortcomings; with all the disasters that had struck her in her lifetime, there is no wonder that she has turned into the extravagant show-off that she is today. Such a shame, when she should have become the revered opera singer she had wanted to be.

She remembers the early days when Iffey's mother died and the tables had seemed to be turned so that Iffey's role of carer and minder of Rosie had become transformed; Rosemary and her parents became guardians of Iffey the orphan. Where was the grand duke then? Rosemary often wondered but never liked to ask. Had he really been a duke? It had dawned on her very slowly that the whole set-up had probably only been in Iffey's imagination. She could never bring herself to burst the bubble, it would have been far too painful for Iffey to admit to.

But when Rosemary's parents had returned to Aldershot from abroad, Iffey had spent all her holidays with them.

"Poor, wretched child," her mother, Julia Robinson, had said. "It's the least we can do for the disadvantaged little creature. Bring her into a safe, respectable home, and hope that we can influence her away from all the vulgar, ostentatious trappings of her late mother's style of living."

"You're wonderfully unselfish," Captain George Robinson had told his wife. "I am sure you will work miracles with the poor child."

27

Rosemary remembers now, as she lays out blankets and sheets upon the beds, the bewilderment she had felt on realising the daughter of the Princess and the Duke was, from then on, to be pitied and cosseted as a disadvantaged unfortunate. It had sometimes been a little upsetting, having her parents show such kindness and generosity to someone other than herself, but she had gradually come to be convinced that Iffey was unfortunate and unlucky and to be pitied and indulged.

Iffey, on her own after Hilary had gone home, puts on a record of Kiri Te Kanawa singing *Depuis le Jour*, wishing to indulge herself in sentimental nostalgia, and tries to remember her mother. Tall, willowy, regal (she was a princess wasn't she?) and unapproachable. But who was this mysterious creature really? The whole thing was shrouded in mystery. Was she the daughter of some romantic African chief, as Bessie had hinted? And if so, what was she doing as one of London's wealthy and respected courtesans?

When Iffey felt the need to probe further, she surmised that Mother was probably the daughter of faithful family retainers, brought from Africa by paternal Brits, retiring from Colonial Service. There had been occasional talk of a large estate, with memories of rolling English hills; but further than that, Princess Mother would never venture. Grandpa and Grandma were dead, way back, she gave that much away, but Princess Gladys Emily Mary reminisced only of English oaks and rain, and never of palm trees and heat. Born here? There were no answers from Bessie either. Past swept away in ambition for the future.

Iffey visualises Mother clearly, with the elegance of the huge sloping shoulders of the time, draped in wide stoles with fringes and tassels, or sable wraps, or shawl collars, and low tapering hips, tightly clinging hems, and plainly visible ankles encased in buttoned kid boots.

Then there were those mountainously large hats; Iffey still has one of Mother's mountainous hats, treasured over endless years, together with an ostrich feather fan, and several very early sepia photographs of Mother in elegant poses in that distant, and altogether unbelievable period when Iffey was born. The hat, embellished through the ages with new and decorative adornment, is now worn by the marble bust of some eminent Victorian which stands in the hall. Iffey likes marble statues and has collected many over the years. There are nymphs in the courtyard and cherubs, emperors and Greek gods scattered in corners everywhere. The walls are hung with a disorderly collection of paintings of every period from Sargent to Hockney, interspersed with hangings and curtains of damask, brocade and velvet. Iffey has brought her mother with her into her own life, and has added more of the mixture as before.

She let her thoughts drift to the anxious years after school, when Rosie, being three years younger, remained the schoolgirl, while Iffey found herself frighteningly adrift in an adult world. She failed to get into any music academy, and finally persuaded Eddie to engage a singing tutor for her: a handsome Italian who promised great things for such an impressive voice.

He seduced her in the third lesson, and thereafter preferred to teach the techniques of sex to the techniques of singing. Iffey enjoyed the lessons greatly, but made no headway in getting herself accepted into opera circles.

"Not even the chorus," she told Rosemary. "Just because I'm black, all I seem fit for is a female production of *Otello*. And even then they'd probably prefer to black up a white singer."

It was a blow that took time and heartache to subdue, but it somehow seemed undignified to fight. If they could not accept her singing abilities because of the colour of her skin, she was not going to attempt to barge her way in. A life full of fighting did not appeal. There was so much living to enjoy.

Iffey met Hilary and Rosemary married him. Not in any sense of competition as Iffey hastened to insist.

"Of course I don't mind, darling Rosie." The sonorous, oscillating laugh was already a hallmark of the mountain of a personality that Iffey had become. She was, to all but her closest friends, a huge, overweight embarrassment who overflowed everywhere she went, like some windblown black tent. It was difficult to accept Iffey without being swept up into her folds, and carried, regardless, along the way on the crest of her particular wave.

Rosemary was still her devoted friend, attached for life. She could do nothing that would hurt Iffey.

29

"Well you got to know him first, he was yours, and I don't want to trespass."

She was engulfed by a laughing, enveloping embrace. "I may have dallied a little," Iffey boomed, "but I didn't tarry. I was much too much for him. And I'm only half white, don't forget, he's too conventional and successful to be held back by me."

"Oh but I'm sure he . . ." Rosemary hastened to defend, "he isn't prejudiced or anything like that. He loves you, he really does, he says so all the time."

The laugh reverberated. "Of course he does, darling, but I'm really not suitable, and you are absolutely suitable — added to which he loves you too, and I think it's just wonderful that you should be going to marry him. One word of warning —"

"What?"

"Don't let him overwhelm you completely."

Rosemary laughed at the very idea. A more thoughtful, gentle man she could not imagine. "He could never overwhelm me," she said. "He is far too considerate."

"Ah, but so are you my dear Rosie. You lay yourself out to be overwhelmed. You enjoy being overwhelmed."

"Perhaps I do, so I shan't suffer from it shall I?"

"All my blessings, girl, Hilary is not mine and I would love you to love him."

Did she envy Rosemary at that time? Did she in fact wish that she had been able to do more than dally with Hilary — or anybody else for that matter? She could not remember needing to be permanently attached, even in the adolescent romantic years. The only time she was, had been a disaster. Her men, and there were many of them, had to make do with short, voluptuous bursts of love, passion and affection at irregular intervals, so that they did not interfere with her independent, extraneous existence.

She has been discussing the past with Rosemary only recently.

"I find it hard," Iffey says, "to decide when I actually launched myself into the real world, but I think we have to say that it was after my disastrous marriage to that dreadful Sydney Weekes rather than before it. It all seems so long ago, quite another world."

30

"As indeed it was," Rosemary agrees. "It was so full, wasn't it? Hopes, beliefs, excitements. Much more exciting." She at once feels guilty for the statement. Iffey's life, at that time, had been horrifying. She is mortified at her own tactlessness.

"And agonising," Iffey says, without recognising the embarrassment or the need for it. "More fear, wasn't there? Because everything was so new and untried. I suppose we come back to the good old cliché that life is what you make it. God, that's such a boring statement. But was then really so much better than now? I can't actually remember it being so. Age does have its inevitable limitations, but I seem to be enjoying life as much now as I did then."

Rosemary's uncomfortable guilt subsides in the face of her own feeling of resentment against ageing. "Can't say I am," she says. "I may like the increased peace and security and not having to strive, but I hate the limitations, specially this awful loss of memory. It makes me feel so stupid. And then everything seems to annoy me a great deal more than it did, I'm not nearly so patient as I was."

"You're the soul of patience, dear Rosie. For ever putting up with situations and making the best of things. As for security," the booming laugh comes rumbling up from the depths. "I think I should probably atrophy if I ever felt completely secure."

"You haven't done badly for someone who thinks herself insecure." Rosemary glances round the opulent surroundings, reverting instantly to uncharitable thoughts, and missing the point of Iffey's statement. "You can't really complain, my dear. In spite of all the hard times you have had to go through and the bad luck you seem to engender wherever you go, you must be about as secure as any woman I know."

Iffey suffers the strange notions of calamity that Rosemary always conjures up for her; she has got used to them over the years. There seems no point in trying to convince Rosie that she is not, and never has been, an unlucky person, the very opposite in fact. Poor old Rosie; it probably gives her a sense of satisfaction that she herself was not so unfortunate.

"Of course," Rosie goes on, "one can never feel completely secure, but I seem to worry about it less nowadays. There was a time when I was neurotically insecure about Hilary for instance, but now I seem to be able to take it all in my stride."

31

There is a frozen moment of tension between them. What exactly did she mean by that? Iffey wonders. What was she actually referring to? Iffey finds it remarkable that she still is not sure whether Rosemary does or does not know about herself and Hilary. She slips quickly to the original subject of age and ageing.

"I must admit," she says, "I am not always sure how one deals with the disgusting infirmities: sans teeth, sans eyes, sans everything. I don't like being so ineffectual, Rosie. The idea that I may just be a hanger-on and no longer a doer. It narks me."

"I don't consider I've ever had any influence over anything that goes on in the world," Rosie says briskly. "Not the type to be a leader of men, that's Hilary's role. I'm the efficient drone."

Irritation jars Iffey's nerves; what a negative character Rosie is at times. Far more comfortable to be like that of course; just accept what comes, but God how *boring*.

"Meaning that in the end you'll smilingly wait in your chair to be fed, watered, washed and potted? What a ghastly thought. I shan't wait for that Rosie. I've got the book and the plastic bag and I shall steal the pills. They do say that hanging is the most foolproof method, but where should I find a rope strong enough?" The laugh explodes this time and fills the room with its reverberations.

Rosie sits upright and unsmiling, looking straight ahead. It is impossible to tell whether she is showing disapproval of Iffey's philosophy or whether her thoughts have switched to another topic altogether. She is, in fact, turning over in her mind the reasons for her being here at all this morning when there is so much else to do. All that arranging of the house to accommodate Sally and her brood, and here she is, just wasting her time with idle surmising.

She finds the opulence which surrounds Iffey has a slightly stupefying effect on her. Occasionally lulled by it, she more often finds herself whipped up to a fever of irritation that Iffey should have wasted so much money on overloading her home and herself with such a display of riches. It's so — well — so *vulgar*. She should, by now, have grown out of the crude milieu she was probably born into.

But in spite of all the irritation, in the midst of all the rearranging and bedmaking at home, she had suddenly felt the ever-recurring desire to be with Iffey, to talk to Iffey, to share coffee with Iffey.

32

She's like a drug, Rosie decided, if I go for any length of time without seeing her, I get withdrawal symptoms. Anyway, she wanted to discuss the earth-shattering news of Sally's imminent return. Hilary did not seem to want to talk about it at all.

"We don't know the details," she tells Iffey, as she sinks back deeply into the ridiculously soft sofa cushions, "because of course Sally's like a closed book as ever. But this Terry person she's been with for the past few years seems to have been a total disaster and, I would suspect, violent into the bargain." Her voice momentarily loses control and wavers upwards. "I can't really believe she's actually coming home. We'll be like strangers after all this time. Twelve years you know."

"Really? As long as that?" Iffey tries to imagine being parted from Caesar for that length of time, but finds it impossible. "And two ready-made grandchildren. It will be exhausting for you, you know. She'll probably take advantage of an on-the-spot baby-sitter."

"No no she won't," Rosie leaps to the defence. "She has far too much understanding of what woman's role in the home already is; she would never impose."

"You old fool, of course she'll impose because you will invite her to. You will stand there, taking all her insults and jibes, and you will positively insist on looking after her children while she goes out enjoying herself."

"Be fair now, Iffey. She's not going to have time to enjoy herself if she is to earn her living."

Iffey's shout of laughter makes her jump. "But Rosie, to work shouldn't necessarily mean you are not enjoying yourself. You know you don't believe that attitude for a moment."

Rosemary smiles slightly because it's true. Hilary had always enjoyed his work, and if he can get Sally into some show, then there is no reason why she should not enjoy herself. She had been remembering Sally's bad-tempered adolescence. "Well — yes, I suppose I was thinking of Sally as she used to be before she'd grown up properly, I'm sure she must have changed a great deal. But in any case she will need to be comforted a little won't she?"

"Not in the way you comfort darling, which is to lay yourself out to be her willing slave and supporter for the rest of her life, or yours, whichever ends first."

They both laugh. "Considering how much life I'm likely to have left, I can't think that the strain will kill me any quicker."

"Don't you believe it my darling Rosie. Those children will chase you to a much earlier grave than you would otherwise grace. Kids of that age would finish me in a week if I didn't finish them off before that."

"But I shall love having them to myself. I've never had a chance with my grandchildren. Timothy and Donna were always so rich and efficient that their three never needed grandparents because they had *au pairs* and nannies all over the place. Now they only come on duty visits, I never had time to get close to them."

"And a good thing too."

"Rubbish, you know you adore having Caesar's offspring here."

"Ah but I am extremely firm to point out continuously that I bear no real responsibility. Not even sure that Caesar does either. It makes for quite a different relationship. I don't mind betting that you will take these two completely under your wing, and wear yourself out with responsibility. I think we should give a grand-children's party for them all, what about that?"

They discuss the idea with enthusiasm.

Dear Rosie, she had been so much help when Caesar was born. There had been the initial reaction to the unexpected pregnancy, which was, by Iffey, passionately welcomed. Caesar was created in the most unlikely circumstances, so Iffey felt that the whole thing was a God-given stroke of good fortune, coming, as it did, in spite of all reasonable efforts to prevent it. It was obviously meant to be, so who was she to fight it?

Rosemary had considered Iffey's pregnancy to be yet another one of Iffey's calamities; worried because Iffey was forty-five and far too fat, she had even suggested an abortion. The doctors were also worried and warned of the possibility of some mental retardation, but Iffey had been equally sure that all would go according to plan. She had even insisted on producing him in her own bedroom with only the assistance of Rosemary and a district nurse.

"It's a woman's right to be among her own at such a time," she boomed. "There'll be no complications, you'll see." And sure enough, Caesar Simeon Daly arrived two weeks early and with the

34

least possible fuss at eight o'clock in the morning in time for breakfast.

That was the beginning of the miraculous, magical period in Iffey's life called The Love Story of Iphegenia and her Son Caesar. Of course it is still going on but she believes that now she must consider herself to be in a later phase of life, which she supposes might be known as Old Age and Death. Could be considered a depressing period to the uninitiated; but to the uninitiated, a love affair with her son could be considered shocking, as could an affair with the husband of her dearest friend. All taboo subjects, along with prostitution, that we don't talk about in polite society.

Iffey brushes the insoluble problem out of her mind for the time being. Might just as well pass the solving over to her maker, now that she's bound, by the law of averages, to be meeting him before too long. Let him decide whether she should go up or down from the pearly gates.

PART TWO

Past History

4   1930 Meeting

Iphegenia Esmeralda Daly met Hilary St John Donovan in a bar in Jermyn Street in 1930 when they were both twenty-two years old. At that same time Rosemary Robinson had just started at a drama school in Leeds, to the astonishment of both her parents.

Iffey was then in the fourth year and at the lowest ebb of her disastrous marriage to Sydney Weekes. For the first and only time in her life, she felt trapped, defenceless and quite without hope.

"Disaster period," she told Hilary as they drank together in what was termed a hostess bar, one of the several projects into which Sydney had invested her money. It was not that she had consciously considered Hilary to be any different from any of the other men it was her job to approach. In fact to this day, she could never understand why she should have chosen that particular moment nor that particular brash youth as her father confessor; but as soon as he had bought her the obligatory drink, she launched into an impassioned and emotional account of her problems. It was possible that she was too unhappy and too frightened to keep her miseries to herself any longer.

"I'm frightened," she told him, "and I just have to tell someone about it, because I think it quite likely that I shall be done away with any moment and I really would like someone to know."

Why had it been so impossible to tell Rosemary anything about the predicament she was in? She was, after all, her oldest friend, but she had deceived Rosemary over the whole period of the marriage. It had always been impossible to tell Rosie unpleasant truths because she was so without guile, and usually over-reacted to situations. She asked to be deceived. And there could have been a sense of humiliation for Iffey at having made such a mistake, an unwillingness to admit perhaps.

Rosie was not enthusiastic about Sydney, though she had never said so. Iffey remembered the first time she had introduced them, that look of disapproval on Rosie's face — she was quite hopeless at covering up her feelings — and the resulting offended resentment that started up in Iffey's mind. She tackled Rosie later.

"You didn't seem over-impressed with Sydney," she said.

Rosie blushed and floundered with embarrassment. "Whatever makes you think that? I only met him that one time, how can you say I wasn't impressed?"

"It was obvious. Of course I realise he's not the ideal you might have in mind for yourself, but he's perfectly all right for me; kind, dependable and with lots of ideas to help me with my singing." Because who else would be likely to take such interest in her to the extent of wanting to marry her? It was an ideal arrangement; living alone in London wasn't easy, and she was beginning to feel the first surges of panic concerning her career. She had the money and he had the ideas.

"We're getting married immediately."

"Immediately? But why, Iffey? What about all the arrangements? Mother and Father would love to do the reception for you, only you must give them a little bit of time. Can I be bridesmaid?"

Iffey didn't laugh, because she knew that it would upset Rosie still further and, if the truth were to be known, she was a little disappointed herself that Sydney should be so insistent on an immediate marriage.

"Caxton Hall," she said sharply. "As soon as he gets the licence. Has to be quick because he's got some business in Paris next month. And he knows someone in the Paris Opera and thinks he can get me in there if he moves fast. Sorry about the bridesmaid thing." Because she was sorry, particularly for Rosie; she felt she had let her down.

Sydney had seemed undeniably kind, and dependable during the months of their rapid courtship. Admittedly much older; admittedly, as Eddie warned her, without obvious means of support and therefore possibly after her considerable inherited wealth. But that had appeared so unlikely at the time; he was never short of money and was always over-generous with her. Said he'd lived in America over the last few years but now wanted to settle in London. Said he'd see to it that she would get to sing at all the biggest opera houses in the world. He personally knew people in the Met and would take her to the States or to Italy to continue her training there.

"How could I ever admit to my friend how wrong I was and that Sydney was a pimp?" she asked Hilary at that first meeting in Jermyn Street. "Told me I'd have to start off being nice to some of his friends who had special influence. Took me out everywhere, and I was so pleased and proud to be shown off like that at all the big night clubs and bars. Can you imagine my stupidity? Said if I wanted to be famous, I'd have to give in return. Said everyone who got somewhere had to do that. Didn't mean anything, he said. And for a long time I believed him." Controlled fury was apparent in her eyes as she looked at the startled Hilary. "Rich, sexy *and* black, oh he had certainly found a prize hadn't he? And so he married me to make the money secure. No fool, my Sydney."

Hilary was aghast, and yet astonishingly, felt a kind of exhilaration at being involved in a real-life drama. He felt he was taking part in an outstandingly good play. To be sitting in a bar, talking to an attractive black woman who was also a prostitute it seemed, in danger of her life. It was heady stuff.

"Monstrous," he said furiously, working himself into a stage rage that such things could be. "You must get away from him — tell the police."

"Useless, I'm his wife, remember. He's holding all the cards through my own stupidity." The tears overflowed. "Can't make a fool of myself here," she said. "Will you come back to my flat?"

"But won't he be there?"

"No my darling innocent, he won't be there. I have to have privacy for the sort of work he wants me to do. He arranges a seedy flat for me in Lancaster Gate and lives in my nice studio in Fulham Road."

"Oh yes, of course." Hilary blushed and forgot his lines.

"We don't have to do anything at all," Iffey said when they entered the Lancaster Gate flat. "But I shall have to charge you because he will know you've been here. I'm really sorry, because in actual fact I should be paying you for listening to my difficulties like this. I just had to have someone to talk to, but the trouble is, he's got control of all my accounts somehow and leaves me ridiculously short. Oh what a fool I was, and I wouldn't take advice of course. If poor, darling Mama had been alive, she would never have allowed me to get into this ridiculous mess because I would have listened to her."

Hysteria was very near the surface all the time, and there was something about Hilary's silent presence that hinted at confident strength. He was, as it happened, probably more hysterical than she was herself, but was dealing with it in the same way that he dealt with stage fright. As long as he concentrated on a particular object as soon as the panic started to overpower him, then he was usually able to stop himself from running away. It was generally something on the set, like a table or a chair, but this time it was Iffey's breasts, so it was not long before he found himself enmeshed in passionate love-making of an intensity that he had never before encountered. Even Iffey was caught unawares by the unexpected pleasure, but put it down to her emotional state of the moment.

Hilary recovered slowly while Iffey poured drinks for them both. He rejoiced in the exultation that accompanies first experiences and forward steps into what he considered to be adult life. The increased physical enjoyment could have been due to her being his first prostitute — he had no idea of this being her profession until she had told him of Sydney being her pimp — or his first black lover, or his first voluptuously big lover. He was amazed at the delight with which he had luxuriated in all that mountainous flesh. Something he had never imagined doing. When he considered the few taut, neat little actress bodies he had enjoyed previously, he felt he had not really experienced sex at all before this moment.

"I just don't know what to do," Iffey was saying. "If I was in the States, I suppose I should hire a hit man and get Sydney bumped off. But somehow that isn't really done over here is it?"

"It probably is," said Hilary, thinking what a good idea it was, "but it's done more discreetly I would think."

"Do you think so? Do you think I could find someone who'd do him in?"

He wondered if she was serious. In a situation like hers it was just about the only way out. "Wouldn't mind doing it myself," he said, feeling suddenly brave, incensed at the evil depravity of this odious man, and filled with a desire to rescue the helpless Iffey from a fate worse than death. The heroism died immediately in a shock of horror that the thought had actually formed itself in his head at all. "People like that should be eliminated," he said. "Unfortunately I'm not really the murderous type." It sounded rather tame and feeble, but a character as eccentric as Iffey might just take him seriously.

Iffey smiled at him. The thought of this pink and white English public schoolboy adopting an American gangster role made her want to laugh in the midst of all the despair. "It's such a melodramatic situation isn't it?" she said. "So unreal — how did I get myself into it?"

Hilary pondered on the same question as he made his way back to his Bloomsbury digs late that same night. How, he thought, did I get myself into such a situation? A casual drink in a bar, and all at once I seem to have stepped into another world. As Iffey said, it's all so unreal.

Even now, as he walked home through the rain, feeling the cold damp seep through his thin coat, he could scarcely believe he had been caught up in that situation a short time ago. Much more he felt as though he had stepped off the stage, taken off his make-up, and was now back in real life again.

But Iffey's presence did not melt away so easily. That stayed with him, disturbingly, through the next few days, and during the time that he decided to accept the Rep company's offer of a short season in Exeter. At least keep him fed until something better turned up. There was not enough money, nor did he have quite enough courage, to meet Iffey again, but most nights, before falling asleep, he imagined the various ways he might solve her difficulties and have her undying gratitude heaped upon him. The whole incident became more of a fantasy than ever.

Hilary's winter in Exeter rep gave him experience in how pleasant theatrical landladies can be; how difficult it is to live on local repertory company wages; how boring it can be to act parts you don't like; how bitchy other actors can get on occasions; how much the adulation of the public can restore one's self esteem, and how wedded he was to the acting profession.

Iffey remained, like a bright star, in his sex fantasies, but comfortably beyond his means. It was better that way, he decided, because she would obviously never be able to come up to the image he had by this time created in his mind. He kept her as a treat for when he should make it in the theatre; when he could approach her at her own level with "What about dinner at The Ivy?" or "I thought supper at the Berkeley after the show". A weekend at Skindles, perhaps? Endless exciting possibilities.

Anxiety began to creep up on him towards the end of his contract, not so much that he would be out of a job, but that he might have to accept another six months where he was. The dread of getting stuck; that success might just be an illusion.

But being blessed, it seemed, with a larger than average share of good fortune, he received notice of an audition for a film from his agent. Hilary regarded auditions with a mixture of exultation, stifling excitement and terror. Selling oneself by way of interview or examination is never a pleasant experience, but as an actor, the pitfalls were greater than in any other profession. You lay yourself on the line, make a fool of yourself, submit yourself to rejection and humiliation. How is it possible to indulge in such masochism in order to earn one's living? Hilary pondered as he approached the interview. It was like going to the dentist.

Once launched into his set piece and the requested reading, the whole mood changed, as though the dentist had said "No cavities today, just a scale and brush up". It would be all right, they liked him; he really was quite good at these things, knew how to handle them. Not such a bad actor actually when all was said and done. And he got the part. Though he was not to know it at the time, the film was the first rung of the ladder; his progress was pretty meteoric from then on, the cold, uncertain, hungry days were over.

But he was in Exeter playing in *Rookery Nook* when Iffey's problems were so dramatically solved, and he never saw the newspaper reports.

"MURDER IN MAYFAIR".

The body of a rich company director with gunshot wounds was last night dragged from the Thames. Sydney Weekes aged thirty-six was the director of a firm of estate agents, but was

44

thought to have connections with London's underworld. Police have not ruled out the possibility of a gangland killing.

Rosemary rushed round to Iffey's Fulham studio when she read the news.

"Iffey, how ghastly. Darling Iffey whatever happened? And what does it mean — connections with London's underworld?"

She saw that Iffey was not crying, and in fact seemed extraordinarily self-composed. Probably the shock of it all. "What *happened?*"

She did look dazed, Rosemary thought, sitting there like a queen among the satin cushions of her sofa, but when she turned her rather bemused gaze on Rosemary, a slow smile spread over her face, and to Rosemary's distress, her large frame started to shake with laughter.

"Oh ha-aa-ah, haa-ah-aa," she roared. "To imagine the schoolboy possibly being a gangster after all — haa-ah-aah!"

Hysterical, Rosemary thought. What should I do? In books and films you throw water over them or slap them, but I can't possibly do that to Iffey. "Stop it Iffey!" she shouted. "You can't laugh at a time like this."

Iffey made an effort, and managed to control the worst of the onslaught. Still gurgling, she wiped tears from her eyes and hugged Rosemary to her. "Oh I know, I know," she said, her voice uneven with the strain of trying to control it. "You must forgive me, I'm not myself."

"Of course you're not. How could you possibly be? I'm so dreadfully sorry for you, poor darling Iffey. What an awful shock it must be, with the police and everything. Do they know what happened or who did it?"

"You don't have to be sorry for me, Rosie. I haven't been quite honest with you about my marriage. It was a disaster. He was a skunk. This is just a blessed relief. The most remarkable release from a ghastly situation."

Rosemary felt her jaw, quite literally drop as she sat back on her heels and stared at Iffey in amazement. Iffey was her best friend, how could she not know all about her? "What are you saying? How could you not have been happy? You always seemed to be — well, bubbling really. I mean like you always are. What was wrong?"

"Just about everything was wrong. I just didn't want to burden other people with my own silliness; thought I could extricate myself somehow, only of course I couldn't."

"But it says he was shot before being dumped in the Thames — Iffey, you didn't — ? No of course you didn't, but who did?"

"I don't know who did. Mind you, I probably would have done it myself if I'd had a gun, but luckily I didn't have, so the police don't suspect me. They think they know who did, only they aren't saying yet. I like to think it was my lovely pink public schoolboy; that's what made me laugh."

"Who on earth is your lovely pink public schoolboy?"

"Oh just someone I met. You'd love him, he wants to be an actor." She paused for a moment to think about his being an actor. In heavy melodrama? The laughter started to surface again. "I shan't ever see him again though, because he was just a chance acquaintance, so I can't introduce you. But with luck, Rosie, when this blows over, then I shall be able to start this phase of my life all over again, and this time I'm going to do things right."

Rosemary felt uncomfortably put out by the matter of factness of the situation which only a few hours ago had seemed like one of the most shocking tragedies she had encountered within the circle of her life. Almost, she thought rather guiltily, as though she had been deprived of the horror she had experienced and acted on when she first read the news, and was now left feeling silly at her over-reaction.

"I know it's difficult for you to understand what's been going on," Iffey said, taking her hand and thinking, how ridiculous this is, having to comfort my friend because this *isn't* a tragedy. "My fault for not telling you all from the beginning. But I was pretty fed up with myself for making such a mess of my life and I thought I ought to try to solve it without involving anyone else."

Rosemary turned accusingly sad eyes towards her. "Iffey how could you not think I would want to share your troubles? You surely know I would give my life to help you?"

Of course she would, of course she would. One of the reasons why she couldn't be burdened. Rosemary was someone who would always have to be shielded.

"Forgive me," said Iffey, considering again the absurdity of asking forgiveness for protecting Rosemary in this particular situation. She felt the laughter welling up inside her again and decided it must be hysteria and had to be firmly controlled. "Would you get me a drink, darling," she said to get her mind on to serious, everyday events, and Rosemary gladly grasped at the opportunity to be of service.

"I'll tell you everything from the beginning," said Iffey.

5 Iffey's Story

So there I was at twenty-two, with one colourful childhood, one squalid marriage and one opportune murder behind me. I should, I suppose, have been a sadder, wiser woman, but I don't think I was. I don't think things would have been so different if I had married a nice sensible husband like Rosie did. Because of course Hilary might just as well have married me as Rosie, and that would have been a disaster. Much as I loved him then, and as I love him now, I would have been bored to death with him as a husband after a very short time. And he would have been exasperated to death with me.

They caught the man who finished off Sydney Weekes, presumably a hit man just as I had suggested to Hilary a month or so previously. Ironic how it worked out. He was hanged for what he did. Poor man, I was really sorry for him because he had done me such a good turn after all. He did the whole world a good turn because nobody regretted Sydney's passing. All wrong that someone should have had to get hanged for it. Someone who had just been paid for the job and wasn't involved one way or another. He settled someone else's score in a thoroughly efficient and premeditated way, and I for one was eternally grateful to him.

It seems to have been a mafia-type killing — something hardly imaginable in England at that time: rival gangs, about which I knew nothing. I was much too frightened of the whole set-up to ask questions in those strange days. The entire period built up into a kind of vacuum, which I moved through in a state of shocked coma; couldn't think what to do — couldn't even think, in fact.

I wasn't even aware of anything until I read it in the papers. It seemed that Sydney had married me bigamously anyway, because there were pictures of some other woman they said was his wife. So I didn't even come in for any publicity.

The whole thing was looked on and written up as a common or garden underworld killing, and I could not seem to relate it to myself. It was all happening to other people. I had never been known as Mrs Weekes anyway; such a ridiculous name that never seemed to bear any relation to me. Some nefarious character did try to claim my money, but dear old Eddie was more than a match for them and only too delighted to get his hands back on the loot. He took his whack, stands to reason, but who am I to begrudge him that? His interests were my interests and he was a remaining link with my dear Mama until he died. So I came out of the whole thing well and thanking God for my good fortune.

Rosemary was far more upset about it all than I was. She could never quite get over it, and even now sometimes refers to 'that dreadful period of your life'. She thinks I'm some sort of miracle woman. "So resilient you are Iffey," she sometimes says. "I do admire you for your great strength. Anyone else would have been submerged by all the disasters that you have had to contend with through your life. You're like some great rock."

Dear Rosie. Little does she know that I would have been submerged utterly by the sort of life that she has had to lead with Hilary all these years. I occasionally feel quite guilty that I was the one to introduce them!

"Don't quite like the idea of being some great rock," I told her at the time. "I had a bit of a rough time, yes, but to get it solved like this, what tremendous luck! What a godsend! Not many people would have such good fortune fall into their lap."

"I wouldn't call being mixed up in a murder case good fortune."

"Oh Rosie, Rosie, it's no good dwelling on what's gone. What's now is what we have to grasp, and now, for me, seems full of good cheer. I'm so *lucky*. Now I can get straight back to the voice training and get a new flat and really get down to the business of succeeding in the operatic world."

"But can you afford a new flat Iffey? Hasn't he used up most of your money? You could easily stay on here couldn't you?"

"In a flat that Syd has been living in? Not bloody likely darling. And I'm sure Eddie has managed to hold on to a good proportion."

I didn't really know how much I had still got, didn't want to, in fact, just rushed out and spent a great deal of money getting a splendid new studio flat in Chelsea and furnishing it. Couldn't bear the idea of using anything that Sydney had been remotely connected with, so I got rid of a lot of things for next to nothing and bought a lot more for a great deal. Dear old Eddie tried to restrain me, but he was getting old and I wouldn't take notice of his warnings. Sydney had run through quite a lot before his demise, so I wasn't as well off as I used to be, but I didn't want to accept that and I didn't think about it much. Didn't want to waste time poring over figures I couldn't make sense of anyway and, after all, Eddie was there to see to all that side. Let him worry over it.

I was in Florence having singing lessons when Eddie wrote me a really stern letter. "You cannot go on in this way," he said. "You are running through your money like water and I am all the time having to cash in your investments. You must think about earning something, Ginny, your money is not going to last for ever, and at this rate it probably won't last more than another year or two. I would suggest that you stop these expensive singing lessons, come home, sell this wildly extravagant flat and buy something much smaller, preferably in the country where you will not be tempted to be so extravagant. You could give singing lessons."

I didn't really believe him, but it gave me a jolt to think that there was a possibility of the money running out before I was a famous opera star. The ridiculous idea of my giving up that beautiful flat, just when I'd got it more or less how I wanted it, made me laugh. But I did decide that I'd have to do without the Italian singing lessons and that I would have to go home, so I did.

London was fun at that time, and I gave some parties and a recital at the Wigmore Hall in order to herald my arrival in town. I got rave notices and a lot of influential friends, but no offers from Covent Garden or even from the provincial companies which I had quite seriously expected. I was never absolutely sure if it was because I was black or because of my size, or because they knew about Mama's profession. I couldn't really believe that would have made a difference, but they were still pretty stuffy at that time. I suppose it must have been because I was 'coloured' as they put it then, black was quite a rude epithet in those days.

As far as my size was concerned, that shouldn't have been a disadvantage because Kirsten Flagstad was no fairy and she and Lauritz Melchior could never approach within arm's length of each other in any of their love duets. I could probably have done all right in cabaret, I mean Josephine Baker and Hutch were all the rage, but I was full of high falutin ideas at that time and thought that sort of thing was beneath me. Thought I was meant for better things: grand opera or nothing, sort of thing.

So in order to keep the wolf from the door, and to get back to a bit of the luxury I had always craved, I thought I would follow in Mama's footsteps for a while until La Scala came to its senses and sent for me. In the most high-class way of course, even if I couldn't immediately lay my hands on a Duke of Park Lane, I made sure I moved into society in a big way by becoming an upper-class tart. It wasn't too difficult; I was quite sought after, being fairly unusual and a bit outrageous I suppose, and the typically British education and high-class accent helped in those snobby old Thirties. You see I wasn't prepared at that time to allow myself to fall in love, and I was being extra cautious about not getting myself into the sort of mess I'd got into before, so I made a point of concentrating on the ones who had money. I set my sights on darling Mama's career, and was quite determined to be as good at my job as she was. I have to admit that I don't think I let her down.

Old Edmund was a bit shocked. "But Ginny," he would say. "What would your mother think? She was so insistent that her work would mean that you could live like a lady in respectability and pride."

"Stop fussing Eddie," I told him. "You know she would have been inordinately proud of her daughter carrying on the trade in the high-class manner which had been her own forte. I'm a good tart, Eddie, very professional and in great demand. I can take who I choose. It isn't as if I'm on the streets. I work for myself on recommendations."

I saw quite a bit of Rosie at that time. And you know she never cottoned on to what I was doing! Crazy isn't it? But, as I said before, Rosie is not someone you can tell blatant truths to. She somehow was always able to overlook the inelegant and see only the elegant. She is a darling and I love her. By 1934 she was having a mild but reasonable success on the London stage in domestic comedies and small bit parts in English movies.

"I'm so lucky Iffey," she would say, bursting in to tell me her latest news, "the maid in the latest Tom Walls-Ralph Lynn comedy. I never thought I'd get it, don't know why I did."

"Because you're so pretty," I would tell her, "and because you're a first-rate actress into the bargain."

It was at this same time that I started to see Hilary Donovan's name up in lights as well and was vaguely interested. I had remembered his name for some odd reason, and had also remembered the sharp physical pleasure he and I had shared on that occasion, four years back, when I was at a very low ebb. He had restored quite a bit of sunshine to my bleak existence on that particular day before the unknown stranger relieved me of my problems. I felt I owed him, but could summon up neither the enthusiasm nor the time at first to do anything about it. But then I noticed he was playing Romeo and had had rave reviews, everyone was talking about him, so I finally went to see it and was completely bowled over. I couldn't believe that the young boy I had known a few years back could have changed into the stunning creature I saw performing on the stage.

Afterwards, when I went back-stage to see him, I realised that it was all a performance. He was still the young, brash boy I remembered. But my God, what a performer! The crowd of young fans outside the stage door clamoured for him, and the dressing-room was filled with high society. I was amazed. As soon as he saw me, he just leaped over to greet me.

"Iffey!" he said. "I so hoped you might come one of these days. I didn't know where to contact you." So we had supper and ended up at my place at two in the morning.

"I've never forgotten the time I spent with you all those years ago," he said. "You did so much to restore my confidence that day. Changed my life really, and sex has incidentally never been the same since. And I have worried about you too, because of the mess you were in. What happened?"

I was really glad to see him. "You don't mean to say you didn't read about it?" It was quite a relief to retell the whole story to someone who didn't know anything. I had kept it inside because there had been nobody I could talk to other than Edmund, and he had been more of an adviser than a sympathetic listener. I hadn't realised how much I had needed to talk about it in order to get rid of it once and for all. So I found myself using the pink and white schoolboy yet again, and finishing off the session with riotous, frenzied love-making of a type quite out of keeping in its spontaneity with my profession.

"And this time I can really afford you," he said afterwards, "because I'm not doing so badly."

But of course I wasn't having any of that. "Darling boy I *owe* you, don't you remember? I used you that day to pour out all my troubles to. You did me the world of good and I never would have charged you if I'd had the option. I would suggest we make today the beginning of a beautiful friendship unsullied by financial transactions — however well you're doing. What do you say?"

It was a great arrangement, and though at the time I was absolutely determined not to become emotionally involved with any man, we both started to find ourselves tangled up with each other more than was comfortable. It tended to make him regard me too possessively.

"Before long," he said, "I shall hope to be earning enough to take you out of all this squalor and degradation. I'm sick that I'm not yet in the position — but I shall be, don't you worry. I can't stand sharing you; it drives me mad." And his well brought up public school nostrils quivered with the wickedness and depravity of a whore's sad life.

I just laughed at him. He was so upright and so upstanding, it made me want to hug him to death. "So let's have some squalid champagne in my disreputable flat, so that we can drink to that long-awaited day."

He squirmed with discomfort. "Oh Iffey, I didn't mean . . . I'm so tactless, I'm sorry."

"You're such an idiot, dearest boy. Like any job, being a call girl can be a really worthwhile occupation if you're at the top of

52

the profession and in charge of your own finances. I work when I want to and with whom. Singing is my true métier and always will be, but it needs money to help it thrive. However, you must realise that I am never again going to be under the protection of anyone. I shall not allow anyone to take me out of this squalor — if I make enough money with my singing, then I won't need to earn more any other way. But I will be my own saviour — I shall not be beholden to anyone ever again."

"You are a courageous spirit Iffey."

What sentimental rubbish the man talked! But it was no use trying to get him to see it my way. "Come now, let's not go mad," I said, trying to suppress the giggles. "But don't go thinking I shall be persuaded to give up all this glamour and live with you in actor's digs, because I shan't." It was then that I thought of Rosie. "You need a nice young thing to share your life," I said, "and I have just the very one. I shall bring the two of you together at the earliest opportunity."

"I do not need a nice tame wife now or ever," Hilary said stiffly. "And if I can't get anything else, then I shall have to be content with the crumbs you are prepared to grant me — for which I will pay," he added angrily, "the same as everyone else."

I couldn't be cross with him, he was obviously hurt, and I was a bit of a shit to laugh at him. "I'm the one who decides on the pay," I said, but I said it gently. "You have to grant me that privilege."

Well of course it worked out amicably; we were much too fond of each other and far too overwhelmed by the genuine sex euphoria that we enjoyed together to quarrel over details. I suppose I was quite a little in love with him, though I would never have admitted it at the time, and I made a concrete effort to safeguard that precious feeling by ensuring that we met only at regulated intervals. I decided, also, that I would have to get him interested in someone else if we were not to head into disaster.

"I have a devastatingly attractive young man I want to introduce you to," I told Rosemary. "Just your type."

"I haven't got a type," she said. "And anyway, I'm much better off without a regular boy-friend now that I'm beginning to get decent parts. I have got to concentrate on my acting if I want to succeed."

"All work and no play," I said, "makes Rosie an extremely dull girl," and I brought the two of them together for a drink.

I can't say that it was an instantaneous success, they were both too much on their guard because they thought I had designs on them, which I did. But Rosemary was tremendously impressed because she knew about him and evidently admired him greatly.

"I loved your Laertes at the Old Vic," she said with far too much reverence I thought, and he was duly flattered.

I hadn't seen his Laertes but, having basked in his Romeo, I knew he was an outstanding actor, more of an outstanding actor than an outstanding man I thought. I often found it difficult to believe this rather pompous and not fearfully intelligent person was the whirlwind of emotion and power I had seen on the stage. Rosemary was obviously going to worship the ground he walked on. I was not sure how good that would be for either of them. I saw that he had never heard of her as an actress, and did not show a great deal of interest either. That annoyed me a little, because it was so obvious that she could have done with encouragement.

In spite of her initial caution, Rosie was overboard within a week of having met him. Her eyes shone, she looked startlingly pretty and she talked of no one else. I was slightly worried by her reaction.

"A little less worship would be in order," I suggested.

"Oh but he's such a wonderful actor," she breathed in an infuriatingly intense manner.

"Actor be blowed, he is a *human being* Rosie, and should be treated as such."

Rosie laughed, "I know, I know, but I can't help thinking he's wonderful."

"Well all right, but try not to show it so obviously or he'll get too big for his boots."

Her adoration made its mark, and Hilary began to appreciate the difference it made to his life.

"She's a very sweet person," he said to me. "I have to admit I am growing very attached."

"She is also extremely attractive, which you must have noticed. Why don't you do something about it?"

Hilary wriggled a little in his chair and fondled the ears of my cat, Sheba. "I can't just waltz out of your bed into hers," he said.

"I can't see why not, the situation being what it is."

"I would feel I was being completely disloyal to you."

"Darling Hilary, you are now being absurd. Though we may be made for each other between the sheets, I am really not what you need out of bed. I will miss our occasional dalliances inordinately, if we have to give them up altogether, but I am not sure that we are good for each other at the moment. I am in danger of becoming too fond, and this worries me because I don't want it to happen. You deserve something better than an outrageous black tart who would do your career no good at all."

"Don't be silly."

"I'm not being silly. I don't think you would do my career any good either. I am selfish and have no wish to give up any part of my life to become a wife and mother."

"I could do without that part."

"No you couldn't, you're much too conventional and well behaved, so why don't we behave like sensible grown-ups: call it a day, and announce to the world that we're Just Good Friends?"

Hilary sat on the sofa still tickling Sheba's ears and looking morose.

"We will do it in true musical comedy style, and then you'll feel it's all completely unreal," I said, moving to the piano and playing some flamboyant runs and trills. "Don't mind if I'm blue, I love only you," I sang to a suitably lugubrious refrain, making up the words as I went along. "If our affair ends we still can be friends and remember the dream of the sweet might have been. . . ." He started to laugh then: "That's cheating, been and dream don't rhyme." So we ended up in a final, tear-jerking love session, and said goodbye, both of us crying our eyes out.

Rosemary told me all about the most magical moment of her life two days later.

6   Rosemary Remembers

Why, thought Rosemary, should some people get all the good things in life, while others are handed out the disasters? It doesn't seem at all fair. How could Iffey have deserved the sort of

55

bad luck that had always dogged her, whereas Rosemary herself had always enjoyed good fortune?

In view of this, Rosemary had always found it difficult to understand why there seemed to be this streak of jealousy between herself and Iffey; it could, she supposed, be understandable that Iffey might be jealous of her — but she of Iffey? That was ridiculous. She had had the stable childhood, the successful student period, and now the felicitous marriage — all she could possibly hope for in life; what room was there for jealousy? And what a despicable emotion jealousy was anyway. It was for ever goading her into inexcusably petty behaviour.

"Why did you choose me instead of Iffey?" she said to Hilary out of the blue. Now why on earth bring that up at that moment? Just after they had become officially engaged, Hilary had taken her to the Savoy Grill after the show, which was a much appreciated treat.

"Because —" Hilary paused, fork aloft, before the first mouthful of the tournedos steak which had already caused anticipatory juices to form — "you are beautiful, sweet, loving, affectionate, intelligent — shall I go on?"

"And Iffey isn't?"

Hilary put the fork back on his plate and wiped his mouth with the napkin. "Omit the sweet," he said. "I have to admit she's everything else."

"So you chose me because I'm sweet?"

"You could say that."

"Stop making a joke of the whole thing, I'm serious."

"Sweet and silly."

"Not a very good reason for wanting to marry me. I mean I suppose Iffey is marvellous in bed and I won't even let you try me out, so how do you know I'm going to be any good?"

"Must be my animal instinct."

So he had been to bed with her, because he didn't deny it. Rosie died slightly in a sudden fear of losing him, but better to opt out now before it was too late.

"I suppose she turned you down?"

"If I had wanted to marry Iffey, I would have done so, but I happen to want to marry you if you don't mind. Please?"

She relaxed. Of course it was all right. Iffey would have been a disaster as his wife because she would never have given him the love and cosseting he needed. He could never have coped with her rough, rumbustious nature. The freeze-up in her solar plexus melted with irrational immediacy. "Since you ask so nicely I can't very well refuse. I think you do probably need a sweet, silly wife to look after you."

Later, as she stirred coffee and drank cointreau, she returned to the subject of Iffey. "Couldn't we do something about her?" she said. "Don't you know anyone in Covent Garden or the Met or somewhere? There might be more chance that they would accept her abroad. It's such a terrible shame that she's not succeeding, because she has a fantastic voice."

"She has a lot to contend with. There are so few coloured people who make it over here in that sort of environment, and Iffey's a bit tactless. She tends to frighten people off. They don't take her seriously." Hilary thought out his arguments as he spoke. He had never really considered the idea that he might be able to help Iffey become an opera singer. Always imagined that he would take care of her in the end, that she wouldn't need to have this difficult career. If she had married him, she certainly would not have had to work. He pulled up his thoughts sharply. Had the idea of marrying her ever actually entered his head?

"Such a waste," Rosemary said. "I hope to God her money doesn't run out. She seems to have no idea about money, the way she throws it around. Her mother must have left thousands. Shocking, really, isn't it? She was a prostitute you know. Poor darling Iffey, she never had a chance, but I wish I could get her to be a little less extravagant. Her mother's money won't last for ever at the rate she's spending it, and she doesn't seem to be any nearer earning her own living."

Dear Innocent, thought Hilary, long may you retain that innocence. "I think she earns a little here and there," he said. "I don't think we have to worry too much."

"But how? How does she earn money? She's never told me about any jobs. Doesn't even seem to be looking for anything. Just aims straight at the top all the time. I mean she ought to try the BBC and get into radio. Physical appearances don't matter there. I keep telling her that."

"Not very tactful."

"Well, I mean, she's got to face facts, hasn't she? If only she'd go on a diet or something, that would at least make her a bit more presentable. She's so — so overwhelming somehow; I'm sure she puts people off."

The idea of helping Iffey seemed, to Hilary, very unnecessary and could be deemed patronising in the extreme. You could not presume to be able to help Iffey do anything, because she could obviously do everything better and more efficiently than you could yourself. Strange that Rosie did not see this. Strange, and rather appealing. Made him want to kiss her gently and affectionately. Made him, in fact, feel masculine and pleasantly superior, not the sort of sensation he had ever felt with Iffey. He and she were two jousting partners, with her the more skilled performer.

"I think the time has come, my darling," he said, at the end of the evening, being filled with the beneficence brought on by good food and drink and the knowledge that life at that moment seemed remarkably satisfactory, "for us to move in together so that we don't have to face these eternal sweet sorrows of parting, don't you agree?"

"You know I agree," she held his hand over the table. "In fact I've been busy making all the arrangements so that they're pretty well ready for your seal of approval. You can't imagine how busy I've been these last few weeks. I thought a summer wedding would be perfect, June I thought, because then your play will have finished and we can get in a honeymoon. I've made out a list with Mummy last week of people to ask because of course there are aunts and things. You'll have to give me your list, and then I'll get the invitations ordered, and I know exactly what I want for the bridesmaids' dresses. We could leave a list of presents we want at Harrods I thought, because you can get everything there. I think we can get it all done by June if I organise it properly."

He adjusted his thoughts fairly quickly to fit in with hers, feeling subtly rebuffed and ashamed of so feeling in the face of such artless misunderstanding.

"A positive miracle woman," he said, lifting up her hand to kiss. "Roll on Summer."

So in June 1935 there was the big and fashionable wedding of Hilary Donovan, the well known and highly praised actor, named as London's most eligible theatrical bachelor, to rising starlet

Rosemary Robinson (stage name Rosie Robin), at St George's Hanover Square, and afterwards at the Hyde Park Hotel.

Crowds of weeping fans watched their stage idol, Mr Hilary Donovan, being spirited away by charming little Miss Rosie Robin, who has appeared in many West End roles and shown great promise as a sympathetic and talented player. The bride looked stunning in oyster satin with a veil of Nottingham lace and a long train. There were four child attendants in apricot taffeta with wreaths of rosebuds on their heads.

Iffey attended in floating white chiffon down to her ankles, wearing Mother's hat, decked for the occasion with white doves' wings and a trailing scarf. She caused a furore at the reception, being constantly surrounded by members of the large company of stars of stage and screen, and managed to embarrass Mr and Mrs Robinson by her panache.

"My goodness Iffey, you *have* grown up. It seems hardly any time since . . ."

"Not lost the puppy fat yet I see!" Mr Robinson said it jovially, digging a finger into one of the rolls round her waist, and making Iffey feel like strangling him there and then.

Rosemary had asked her to sing at the reception some time before, having already suggested that she should also sing "O for the Wings of a Dove" during the signing of the register. "Such a good chance for getting people to notice her," she had told Hilary. "You never know, there might be someone there who could be useful to her."

"I'm sure there will be darling."

So at the crowded reception Iffey sang *I Only Have Eyes For You* and *Night and Day* and several encores which were demanded by the delighted, and by that time, convivial guests. She was an undoubted success.

"Wonderful wedding, darling," she told Rosie as she helped her into her going-away clothes. "I enjoyed it so much, it made me want to have one myself. With a send-off like that, you're obviously going to be the happiest couple that ever lived."

"Do you really think so Iffey? Oh God I do hope so. You do know I shall be eternally in your debt for bringing us together, don't you? You're the best friend anyone ever had. What should I do without you?"

Iffey waved them goodbye as they took off for Madeira, and thought how glad she was not to be in Rosie's shoes.

7 War

Whenever Hilary thought about his wedding-day, an amused air of indulgent nostalgia crept over him, as pleasurable as the moment when the water gradually engulfed him in a very hot bath. That was always one of the most satisfying moments of his day, and a time when life appeared particularly congenial. So he often did think about the wedding, and quite often when he was lying in a hot bath which made the experience doubly enjoyable.

He found it slightly humorous that he should have indulged in such a conventional charade that was much more a part of his stage life than actual existence. To Rosemary it was all part of real life, which was one of the things he found so beguiling about her. Everything was a reality to Rosemary, she believed earnestly in anything with which she came in contact. She was at once beguiling and vulnerable. His desire to protect was a boost and safeguard to his own morale.

He remembered how his and her theatrical friends had delighted in the whole wedding production and reception held to wish them a long and successful run. He had sensed the unreality of the show, but to her it had been an essential part of the whole.

Rosemary's sincerity was like the evening star, shining brilliant in an indifferent sky, and Hilary loved her for it. She was the perfect companion, as Iffey had pointed out right at the beginning of their relationship.

"She is absolutely suited to your conventional tastes," she had said all those years ago, and he had been incensed at the idea of his being conventional and therefore probably despised by Iffey.

"What makes you sure that I am a conventional idiot?"

"Who said anything about your being an idiot? Dear Hilary, you are wise and wonderful and can be relied on for doing the right thing, whereas I am the idiot, who invariably puts her foot in every bit of shit that's going."

He remembered the shock he had felt at the use of the word in those far-off days. He had never heard it used in ordinary speech before, and the added affront that it should have been said by a woman made it seem all the more shockingly crude. His whole attitude towards Iffey at that moment had frozen into a solid block of disapproval. His own upbringing had rebelled as it had been trained to do. So perhaps he was a conventional idiot in those days. Perhaps he still was.

"Well I love your unconventional shitty foot," he had forced himself to say, and they had both laughed, he, because of the bravado of attempting to throw out a part of his orthodoxy.

"You love it because it's a novelty," Iffey had said. "But Rosie is the one for you, believe me. You get your kicks from me, but Rosie will provide what you need in life."

He had become furious again at her insistence on deciding what was or was not what he wanted in life and had retreated in angry disagreement until her physical presence had, without a great deal of difficulty, swept away any resistance he might have felt.

She had been absolutely right, of course, Iffey usually was. He could never have withstood the shocks she was continually presenting him with, not in everyday life at any rate. She was the eternal pick-me-up that one grasped with relief in moments of despair or boredom; she was the restorer of balances, the haven of relaxation. The perfect mistress, in fact, not the everyday sharer of hearth and home.

Rosemary was an angel, and he never stopped appreciating the fact. He swore to himself early on in the marriage that he would not be guilty of taking her for granted. That was a habit that was easy to fall into with someone who laid themselves out to please as Rosemary did, and her selflessness only occasionally cloyed. She was the out and out Good Woman, Hilary decided, of this there could be no doubt.

"She's no doormat," he told Iffey.

"Maybe not a doormat," Iffey quibbled, "but I sometimes think you use her as a hearthrug; you know, off with the outdoor shoes and let the warmth of the wool seep up through the soles."

"But I do appreciate the warmth," Hilary said.

"Maybe you do, but you still put your feet where your heart should be."

"This is carrying metaphor too far, added to which, it is completely untrue."

"But you do tend to forget that she's a human being. A paragon of virtue, a perfect wife, kindness personified, but is she actually human?"

Hilary became irritated. "Stop angling me into defensive positions," he said. "I love Rosie and she loves me. I like being spoilt and she likes spoiling. We are ideally suited."

"She probably likes being spoiled too. You don't do overmuch of that do you?"

"That's not fair. You know I'm not a very demonstrative person and she is, we can't change our natures, and anyway our natures complement each other. We fit."

Iffey often tended to make him uncomfortable. She was so much in control and he felt mildly resentful that he never seemed to be the one who made any decisions when she was around. She made him feel inconsequential on occasions, but Rosie needed his back-up at all times.

He did not see much of Iffey in the years following marriage. At first he had felt unsure that the physical affinity they had shared might remain an embarrassment, but again Iffey seemed to have taken charge. Without letting up on the easy intimacy, she had placed a taboo on their relationship which he could not imagine breaking through. He again felt nettled that she had erected the barrier before he was able to do so. Made him seem an ineffectual drip.

Contemplating all these early enigmas from the distance of six years, he realised, with an illogical sense of regret, that they seemed to have faded in the ordinary progression of existence.

Two children had made their standard appearance, Timothy in 1936 and Jonathan in 1937.

"Much too close together," Rosie complained to Iffey. "We didn't mean it that way, because I really needed far more time to recover. It's dreadful being continuously pregnant and then continuously feeding; quite dreadful, makes you feel like a production line, get one out of the way and there's the next one waiting."

Iffey had reached an uncomfortable stage in her life at that moment, when she had begun to consider the whole business of child-bearing and her own reason for living. Approaching thirty, there was the panic that she had perhaps reached that dreaded rut from which there was no escape. If marriage was not to be and a singing career was not to be — then what? Was child-bearing a possible way out? It was, after all, one of the Great Experiences; was she mad to reject it out of hand?

"Do you think I shall feel deprived for the rest of my life if I don't have a child, Rosie? Shall I live to regret it?"

Rosie thought very quickly. It seemed most unlikely that Iffey would ever get the chance of having a child. Who was there who would marry an enormously fat lady who had the added disadvantage of being half-black? Partners would not be easy to find. Mustn't make Iffey feel that it was a disaster to remain childless.

"Oh no," she said, "I'm sure you won't." How to say this convincingly, when she actually thought it would be a disaster? Not that having children was a wonderful experience in itself — it was bloody agony — but for Iffey, to have a child would be an ideal solution to her difficulties. She could put all the energy and enthusiasm she possessed into bringing up a child and then she would be far less likely to feel the pain of not succeeding in her ambition.

"Of course," she added, "bringing up a child is quite the most satisfying thing in the world. But it doesn't have to be your own child, you could adopt one. Single people can adopt children these days I believe, if they have the right credentials."

Iffey bellowed with laughter. "Oh Rosie, dear Rosie, you always get me wrong, don't you. It's not that I want the patter of tiny feet round me — God, with due respect to your blessed state of motherhood, there's nothing much I would dislike more — no darling, I'm thinking about the actual experience of giving birth. I hate missing out on anything, and this giving birth thing is, I understand, the experience of a lifetime. So people tell me; I wouldn't want to exclude one of the glories of womanhood from my otherwise all-embracing life."

63

Rosie felt snubbed and angry. She did *not* always get Iffey wrong. It was Iffey who was not able to appreciate the subtleties of a helping hand. "If that's all you're worried about, don't give it a second thought," she said. "Giving birth is a ghastly business, as is being pregnant. I wouldn't recommend it to anybody."

Iffey was sometimes so crass. There was a tremendous satisfaction in the task of bringing up a child. Pity Iffey couldn't realise that; but it wouldn't be the same if you had no one to share the experience with. Rosie revelled in the joy of a complete family life. She felt herself fulfilled and Hilary was both proud and caring. Rosemary gave up the stage, for which she insisted she had no real talent, because she wanted to spend all her time with her family. Hilary spent all the time he could manage within his increasingly successful career, rushing back to the family womb to be loved, cosseted, appreciated and refreshed.

But neither he nor Rosemary could get used to the fact that Iffey was now an outsider. Though it was all so seemingly idyllic, there was, Hilary thought uncomfortably, a definite void in a part of his life, a certain air of unreality about the set-up; almost as though it were being acted out — a scene in a play — occasionally he felt that he knew the next line:

Enter husband r. Hangs up coat and hat and places umbrella in stand.
WIFE: Hallo darling, had a good day at the office/theatre/on the farm? (Kiss kiss) Daddy's home boys!
Enter Timothy and Jonathan l.
TIM: Hallo Daddy, will you come and see my tree house? Will you come up into my tree house Daddy? It's very strong. Have you got any sweets for us Daddy?
Husband ruffles Tim's hair, then picks up Jonathan and kisses him.
Hallo my big boys; I would love to see your tree house Tim, and what about you, Jonny? Have you been in the tree house too?
JON: Tim wouldn't let me because he said I was too stupid and would break it. Will you make him Daddy? Have you got any sweets for me?

There was a lazy kind of inevitability about day following day which Rosie enjoyed because she did not expect more, but which Hilary found vaguely unsatisfactory. The only real highs and lows for him were connected with his career; his home life was relaxation and contentment, and all rather boring.

For Rosemary, life had become fulfilling and thoroughly satisfactory. She was in her element, confident and happy in her role as wife and mother. She felt she was achieving something worth while: being answerable for creating two new beings! What an awesome opportunity! So important not to make any mistakes.

"It's such a responsibility," she said to Hilary. "So imperative to do the right thing *now*, while they are still young. You know the Catholic maxim — give me a child until he's five, or was it seven? I want to be certain of giving them all the advantages."

"I don't think you should worry so much. It might be better to have a nanny don't you think? Mine gave me the best start in life possible."

Rosemary laughed at him. "Oh darling, you're so old-fashioned. My nanny was wonderful too, but I wouldn't like anyone but me — well, us I mean — to have control over our children's formative years. I wouldn't want their future to be jeopardised by the mistakes of others."

"A thoroughly worthy objective, my love. Anyone brought up by you could not be anything but sweet, conscientious and exemplary in every way."

"Now you're teasing me."

"Of course, but I nevertheless agree whole-heartedly with your methods. If that's what you want to do, then I back you all the way." What a splendid person she was; so dedicated to what she believed to be right.

Rosemary basked yet again in the pleasure of having a gentle, understanding husband, who, at the same time, managed to be an acclaimed public figure. Public figures were so often difficult to live with; she was remarkably fortunate. Only the anxieties of the times wrecked her peace of mind.

"We have been so lucky up till now," she said to Hilary as they sat together in their well-kept garden listening to summer gnats and droning bumble-bees. "Why can't the world leave us alone to enjoy our happiness without plunging us into a ghastly war?"

"At least we have the relief that the boys are too young to fight." He thought with growing dread that, like the baby bear, he was neither too young nor too old, but just right.

"But not too young to be destroyed by bombs," Rosemary answered, trying to control the panic that was just about stifling her. It would not be fair to show Hilary how frightened she was, he would only worry and be anxious for her. It must be far worse for him, knowing that he would be called up and thrust into a bloody conflict.

"We'll rent a place in the country for the duration," he said. "You could take Iffey too, she won't want to stay in London in a studio which is not only at the top of the house but full of glass into the bargain. She'd be only too glad of the opportunity to help you with the children and the running of the house in peaceful surroundings." He saw a comforting picture of his loved ones all together and safe from harm. And with Rosemary's organising ability, it was easy to imagine such a haven of peace.

"I don't somehow think Iffey would appreciate a country life," Rosemary said doubtfully.

And of course Iffey did not.

"What?" she roared, heaving with laughter, when Rosie reported the suggestion the next day. "Become a flaming land-girl? Not bloody likely."

Rosie had taken the children round to Iffey's before their dutiful afternoon walk in the Park. The two boys tore up the stairs at that moment, and into the studio where she and Iffey were discussing the war possibilities.

"The whole situation is so terribly depressing," Rosie said. "I just want to get as far away from London as I can. The thought of keeping the children near any sort of danger is just about killing me."

"Pow — pow — pow!" yelled Jonathan, aiming his gun at Iffey's stomach.

Rosie was embarrassed. Talk of war had obviously affected the boys. They had become tiresomely aggressive, and she had for so long tried to instil a balanced view of the necessity of standing up for one's rights without having to use violence to do so.

Tim imitated a machine gun with ear-splitting accuracy. "Eh-eh-eh-eh-eh-eh-eh. Put your hands up you German pig."

"I can't," Iffey shouted angrily. "You've just shot me."

How revolting children were. She felt she would like to take both these two and plunge them into a bath of ice-cold water to punish them for shattering the peace of her home like this. They always managed to inject nastiness and aggression and bad smells whenever they came over. Her caged birds fluttered and squawked in a frenzy of panic as they were peppered with a fresh hail of imaginary machine gun bullets, and Sheba the cat fled for cover. What particularly abominable little sods these two were, thought Iffey with venom.

"Sh-hh darlings," Rosie said gently. "You mustn't frighten the birds like that." She smiled apologetically at Iffey. "Real boys I'm afraid. They're going through a bit of a phase at the moment. I think all boys do."

Iffey, Hilary and Rosemary all fell naturally into their respective vocations when war actually came. Rosemary joined the WVS and ran the British Restaurant in the Wiltshire town near to the house they had leased for the duration. She organised work parties for the Red Cross and took in large numbers of London evacuee children to be brought up with her own two.

Hilary joined the RNVR, went briefly to sea in a destroyer where he was hopelessly and continuously seasick and of little use. He was subsequently seconded by ENSA to entertain the troops and later took part in the making of propaganda films. His was an exciting, heart-warming and sociable war which he looked back upon with pleasure, while feeling guilty at the idea of having a good time in the midst of catastrophe.

Iffey flung herself into anything and everything that was going, managing somehow to be at the centre of several disasters. She was bombed three times, once in the Café de Paris and twice in her studio, but only suffered cuts and bruises each time. The blitz on London made her intensely angry, and the fear that was constantly present during the time of the bombing served to stimulate her fury and consequent reactions. She sang in bomb shelters, restaurants, army camps, aerodromes, naval training centres, factories and later went abroad with ENSA to entertain anyone who was in need of entertainment. She dispensed other favours where and when they seemed required and was an undoubted asset to the war effort.

"It takes a war to make you feel truly appreciated," she told Rosie on one of her many visits to the Donovans' country retreat, usually to recuperate after a bombing episode or an exhausting trip to the Far East to sing to the troops. "It's marvellous to experience so much love and companionship everywhere. People are amazing in times of crisis, aren't they? Why can't we be like that always? Why do we have to go through a war to discover our better natures?"

"It isn't only our better natures we discover in a war," Rosemary complained. "Some people round here delight in making things difficult just because there's a war on. Don't you know there's a war on they say when you ask for anything. Not everyone is loving and giving like you are Iffey. I wish you wouldn't take so many risks. You could give lots of concerts to the troops down here and be safe. Why don't you stay?"

It was useless to try to explain, Iffey decided. "How's Hilary?" she said instead.

Rosemary glowed immediately; talking about him made the separation easier. "Oh he's wonderfully cheerful," she said. "Don't quite know where he is at the minute, probably Malta or somewhere. But he thinks he's going to get involved with something Noël Coward's doing, so I'm hoping he'll get out of the danger zone. He's ridiculously brave and never complains about being in the thick of things."

Because he's damn well enjoying himself, Iffey thought. The same as I am. The responsibilities of life are swept away in war; you do what you're told, keep yourself alive and enjoy what you can. But Rosemary is different, she has adopted responsibility as her war effort. I wonder if she will find it as easy to revert when it's all over.

And when it *was* all over, they spent VE Day together in a splendid confusion of wild excited delight at the relief of tension.

"A bloody period at an end," Hilary said with his arm round both of them. "Now we can get on with our lives." The relief was overpowering; he had the satisfactory feeling of a job well done, and of vistas of endless possibilities stretching away into the future.

The champagne flowed, friends, acquaintances and strangers thronged through the London streets in jubilation and Iffey felt a twinge of regret and anxiety that her life might possibly now retreat into the ordinary and the humdrum.

8 *Peace*

So the roar of guns and the crash of bombs died away into the distance and the euphoria at the cessation of horror invaded their lives. It became, fairly quickly, a commonplace companion that aroused little or none of the original joy with which it had been greeted. At least this is how it seemed to Iffey. For the first time in her life there was the suspicion that yesterday was probably better than today.

"I don't seem to be able to feel the same enthusiasm about things," she said to Rosemary, on one of the very few moments that she brought herself to voice the anxieties that kept cropping up in her mind. "I feel let down, in a state of anticlimax."

"It's the aftermath," Rosemary said. "Reaction after all that tension. I've got it a bit too. I mean I got 'flu as soon as Hilary got home. Sort of sheer relief I suppose."

Only of course it wasn't that at all. Iffey knew that Rosemary and Hilary would now pick themselves up, brush themselves off, and start all over again. And for them things would proceed from where they had left off.

"You'll go from strength to strength," she said. "Life is going to be wonderful for you, I feel it in my bones."

Rosemary appeared to sparkle. "Do you think so? I do think Hilary is going to be a fantastic success in this new film. I always knew he would get right to the top. Thank God this ghastly war is over so that he can get on with his career."

"And you Rosie? What about your career?"

"Oh darling, you know I never had any ambitions other than

to have a family. I am so completely happy with that. When I think how lucky I have been I just can't get over it."

She glanced rather guiltily at Iffey and cursed herself, as usual, for being tactless. So insensitive to brag about her own good fortune when Iffey had still to struggle against the odds with no one to share her life and the dice being invariably weighted against her. No wonder she felt let down and unenthusiastic about everything.

"You mustn't get depressed," Rosie said. "Things will get better for you now that the war's over. I'm sure you'll be able to make your way now, the war's swept away all that prejudice."

"Rosie, you're unbelievable." Iffey's gloom lifted at the charm of Rosie's credulous simplicity, and the laugh started to heave itself up from the depths. If there was a wrong end to the stick Rosie would be sure to grasp it.

Rosemary was pleased that she had at least been able to cheer Iffey a little. "You must find yourself a nice husband so that you can sit back and not have to worry any more. I shall be on the look-out for someone who will look after you for the rest of your life. You found me one, so the least I can do is to find you one now. I owe it to you."

It was still just not too late for her to get married and have a child, but after forty, child-bearing was unwise; she should really settle down now and not become a lonely spinster. Rosie's heart actually quavered with the anxiety of desire for Iffey's happiness.

Iffey swept her into an effusive hug. "You're the best friend a girl ever had. But you'll never get me to put up with one man for any length of time, they're much too selfish and pleased with themselves. I'll go solo thank you very much."

Rosemary shook her head, "You're wrong you know; just because you had a terrible experience once, doesn't mean you wouldn't be happy with a good man. Someone like Hilary I mean, and then you could have a family and be complete."

"I don't suppose you'll ever give up, you boring old nag, however many times I tell you that I really hate kids and I don't want a husband, not now, not ever."

"Rubbish! Everyone does *really*, deep down."

Iffey probed into her mind to discover if perhaps she was being defensive. Was there really a need for love in the clichéd sense?

Was she just afraid of losing her personality to someone else? Was she frightened of the responsibility of children? Was she afraid of another failure? Not possible; life was good as it was; could easily be spoilt by having to share it. But you'd never get Rosemary to see that.

Hilary and Rosemary, with the boys, had moved back into London when the war was over, and soon after found another impressive house on the river near Maidenhead for weekends — spoils of Hilary's successful film career.

Timothy and Jonathan had taken an active part in the choice of the new house.

"We can't have this one Pa," Tim said of one, "there's no separate games-room for us. Johnson Major's got a room where he and his brothers can do absolutely anything they like — there's a sort of gym with a trapeze and rings and room for the train set to be laid out permanently. There's no room in London to lay it out like that. What's the good of having a train set if you can't lay it out?"

Hilary saw his point; having started them off with Hornby trains from the age of five, as his parents had done for him, he found it difficult to give enough time to help them set it up, let alone play with it himself.

"I'm not a millionaire," he said. "Perhaps Johnson Major's father is."

"No he isn't," Jonathan said. "He just makes sausages. He's not nearly as famous as you so you ought to have a much bigger house than him."

"Being famous doesn't always mean being rich," Rosemary said, feeling that a lesson on relative values was indicated.

"I can't see the point of being famous if you aren't rich as well," Tim said. "I'd much rather be rich than famous."

"Oh I wouldn't," said Jon. "I'm going to be famous and have people fighting for my autograph. But not many of the boys at school know you're famous," he said to Hilary. "Can't you go on at the Palladium or something? Or do something on the wireless like Arthur Askey or Tommy Handley? Then my friends would want your autograph."

"Couldn't you be someone like Winston Churchill?" Tim suggested. "He's rich and famous."

71

"I would be much happier," Rosemary said, "if you were *nice* rather than famous."

"I might be both. Pa is."

"But he isn't rich enough," Tim said sadly.

Rosemary had to admit to a slight disappointment in her children. She was surprised that they did not seem to be becoming the loving, well-mannered little boys she imagined that her careful and well thought out upbringing should have made them.

"Children learn more by example than anything else," she had pointed out to Hilary when they had first started school during the war. "You don't have to be clever or well-versed in psychology to realise that. They have a splendid example in you my darling: kind, wise, clever and successful, and I don't think I'm too bad a model myself. Just have to remember not to get irritated or anxious in front of them. Don't you agree?" she added when she noticed that Hilary was not listening.

"Absolutely darling," Hilary said immediately, without bringing his mind back from contemplating the incompetence of his then commanding officer.

"It's very sad," Rosemary had continued, "that they cannot see more of you because of this dreadful war. But I talk about you all the time and tell them how lucky they are to have such a father. I only hope they won't suffer too much from the lack of a father figure during these formative years."

Hilary had had no such doubts at the time, being perfectly content to leave the whole of the actual upbringing to the competent Rosemary. She could not imagine, surely, that he was more than a secondary influence, knowing so little about children and what made them tick. Always felt slightly ill at ease with them as a matter of fact; never knew what they might say next, though of course he loved his own with a deep affection, that went without saying; no doubt at all about that.

Rosemary could only suppose, now that the war had ended, that the boys *had* suffered from Hilary's absence, even though they had been sent off to prep school early, at seven, so that they should learn to fend for themselves, and have the benefit of some male influence in their lives. Coming back for the holidays, they were now, at nine and ten years old, like rather distant and noncommunicative strangers. She found them usually rude and aggressive whenever they did speak, and supposed that the choice of teachers in wartime had, of necessity, been restricted and therefore less than satisfactory. She determined to press the theory of education by example more strongly than ever.

"I sometimes feel," she complained to Iffey, "that they don't even *like* me very much, and that they look on Hilary as an ineffectual foreigner rather than the father who loves them."

Probably because he gives them that impression Iffey thought. What sort of inhibited stereotyped upbringing had *he* had to make him so stilted where children were concerned, she wondered.

Towards the end of the war, she had bought herself a vast and derelict studio in Holland Park, after her Chelsea flat was virtually destroyed, and when large, neglected, London properties were going for small amounts. She had then found herself thwarted by restrictions on rebuilding and redecorating and had to exist in cold squalor for a time. It was another cause for Rosie's concern.

"You *can't* live there Iffey. Why ever did you buy it? If only I'd been with you, I would never have let you waste your money on such a white elephant. You must live with us until you can either sell it again or have all the repairs done, and that won't be for ages with restrictions as they are."

"You are blind Rosie." Iffey felt sorry for Rosemary, that she should not be able to see the possibilities of this stupendous abode. Attached by a conservatory to a large, Edwardian mansion, it still boasted the luxury of mahogany doors, panelled walls, spiral staircase out of the studio into the upper-floor gallery, and an entrance-hall with a tiled floor. The conservatory joining the house to the studio had most of its glass missing. The courtyard and garden were overgrown and surrounded with trees that seemed to reach the sky. Iffey was transfixed as soon as she saw it. It had to be hers.

The reparations took time, a great deal of money, and some fairly devious strategy by Iffey. One of her younger clients was already immersed in the business of buying up wrecked houses with a view to doing what repairs were allowed before selling them off again. It was he who introduced her to the corruptible builder whose fortune had been made on the black market. He was really quite a nice man in many ways, just had a blank where morals were concerned. And after all, thought Iffey, I am not so far removed from that myself in the eyes of most people. It was a mutually beneficial situation and one that she found satisfying if physically rather unedifying.

She began to enjoy an unexpected *succès fou* in cabaret. An agent who had managed her wartime performances to the troops kept phoning with offers of engagements in night clubs and at private parties.

"I'm being sought after," she told Rosemary. "They like my sexy songs and my sun-tanned complexion. I'm a hit at last."

"But Iffey, you're prostituting your talent," Rosemary complained. "You'll ruin that wonderful voice if you belt out these dreadful songs in these dreadful places."

"I'd be putting more strain on my wonderful voice if I was belting out Brünnhilde or Isolde instead of *Deep Purple* or *Red Sails in the Sunset.*"

"But you may be ruining your chances, you'll never get serious offers if you accept this sort of thing."

Iffey shrugged. "It's all entertainment, after all. If they want Jerome Kern or Gershwin, why shouldn't I give it to them?"

"Hilary doesn't think you should."

"Drat Hilary. He's never even heard me. Tell him to come to the Café de Paris one night and hear my act, and then let him criticise." Iffey was incensed. Sweet, silly Rosie could criticise in her uninformed way, but Hilary had no right at all. The self-righteous bastard.

"But Hilary never goes to night clubs."

"Well he should. See how the other half lives."

"Oh Iffey, he doesn't think he's superior, it's not that at all." Rosie tried to remedy the situation. It was so important not to let Iffey feel her lack of success. "He just feels you are so tremendously talented and that your voice is so wonderful that you should only have the kind of work that's worthy of you."

Iffey was not mollified. Hilary was a bum and she would not let him off lightly. "Tell him to come to one of my shows, I've been to every one of his. Tell him to bring you to one of my shows before he starts to criticise."

74

"But Iffey he wasn't criticising, really he wasn't." How stupid of her to get herself in this position. To upset Iffey was the last thing she wanted.

"I got myself in a horrible mess," she told Hilary afterwards. "I never seem to say the right thing. I think we must go and hear her sometime. Or at least you go, I should simply hate to go to one of those places. I don't like drink and I find the whole atmosphere so false. You go one evening will you? I think she's really very depressed at having to sing at places like this only of course she doesn't want to admit it. Poor Iffey, she just doesn't have the luck does she?"

Hilary took her hand and smiled at her. "Your heart's much too tender," he said. "I don't think you have to worry so much about our Iffey. She gets along all right."

"But not as well as she should. She ought to be a famous and wealthy opera star by now and look at her. Singing in sleazy clubs and living in an old ruin. She would love you to go and see her act."

"I give in, I give in. I will sacrifice a few hours' sleep and I'll take our new producer to have supper there. It's a pretty expensive sleazy club so he's bound to be impressed."

Rosemary laughed. "I suppose it isn't as sleazy as all that, they charge the earth for those sort of places these days, even though it's all dark and hot and uncomfortable. Thank you, darling, for being so sweet and self-sacrificing, but Iffey deserves it."

"Sure you won't come?"

"Will you forgive me if I don't? I always feel so out of place in those haunts. I can never stay awake for one thing, and anyway, it upsets me to hear Iffey wasting her voice like that."

Hilary and his producer had supper at the Café de Paris later that week.

"Been required by my wife to check up on the performance of this singer, hope you're not averse to a cabaret turn, but she's a great friend of ours."

"Iffey Daly?" The producer seemed surprised. "Didn't know you knew her. You don't mean to say you've not seen her perform? Great entertainer; no one to touch her. Great lady."

Hilary looked at him sharply. How well did he know her?

"You know her then?"

"Not personally unfortunately, much as I should like to, but I don't miss any of her performances if I can help it."

The lights dimmed, the band crescendoed, and Iffey stepped into the spotlight, a mass of sequins, feathers and yards of wafting white tulle.

Hilary had difficulty in expressing his amazement silently.

"Fantastic — fantastic!" The producer joined enthusiastically in the applause that greeted her. "What a performer! Such style."

"Saint Louis woman, with her diamond rings . . ." Iffey and her voice filled every corner of the restaurant. There was nothing other than this enormous phenomenon of personality and voice. None of the usual bustle and clatter of diners and crockery. Forks were stayed on their journey to mouths, coffee remained unstirred and undrunk, brandy glasses rested, cradled and still; there was no conversation, no movement. Iffey was overwhelmingly in charge. Hilary realised, with a sense of shock, that Iffey was a star.

At the end of the performance, the whole restaurant broke into a roar of applause, something Hilary had never heard before for a cabaret performance.

"Isn't she wonderful?" The producer was pink with excitement. "Wouldn't mind meeting her old boy if you could arrange it."

Hilary winced and felt an instant desire to refuse. Why should this nasty and unattractive little man be given the chance of an entry to Iffey's bed? But she made her way over in any case, approaching their table a little later, without the feathers, without the sequins, but majestically draped in peacock-blue Indian silk, which seemed to flow from the long scarf knotted round her head, down to her ankles and the matching silk shoes studded with diamanté. Hilary noticed with irritated pique that several men greeted her as she passed, with kisses, caresses and an intimacy of approach that made his hackles rise.

The producer was both impressed and delighted when she gave her sensual attention to his praise, and Hilary realised that his own prestige had been greatly enhanced through being a friend of this remarkable celebrity. No one could fail to be impressed, and his feelings switched to childish pride at basking in the éclat that Iffey precipitated, while at the same time being testily irascible to find himself one of a crowd.

After shedding the producer, he drove her home, and found that her studio, the derelict shell he had seen when she first bought it, had been miraculously transformed into a cathedral-like edifice. This, in turn, changed itself into a palace when she switched on the lights. He found himself transfixed, in the same way he had been transfixed as a child at his first pantomime. It had been a long time since so many of his everyday assumptions had been shattered in such quick succession.

"My God," he said. "This place has changed a bit since I saw it last. How on earth have you managed to get all this luxury fitted up?"

"I'm rich and successful, like you are; didn't you know?"

He glanced at her, unsure whether the dig was intended. Her expression gave nothing away, and he looked round at the transformation of the bleak barn-like structure he remembered seeing when she first showed it to him. "But how do you get people to do it? I can't get a bloody plumber when I want one."

"You don't use the right sort of persuasion, obviously."

"Obviously not. Has Rosie seen this place lately?"

"No, she seemed to think it might give the children pneumonia. I think she found it too depressing to contemplate. Judging by your surprise, I gather she told you as much?"

"Well, yes, she did feel a little sorry for you living in such sad circumstances."

They both laughed as Iffey opened up the huge studio stove and drew the deep, soft sofa nearer to the heat.

"It helps to know the right people," she said.

"It helps even more to know them intimately I believe."

"This is absolutely true."

There was more laughter, then a sudden glow of intense intimacy apparent between them. Hilary was toppled off balance.

"I was tremendously impressed with your act," he said. "You're a star."

Keep it on a mundane level for God's sake. Didn't want to make a fool of himself. It would never occur to her that he had suddenly reverted to the awkward, infatuated youth of sixteen years ago. She was, after all, a professional; she would hardly look to him for recreation.

"So are you a star," she said, wondering just why she should feel sexually aroused by one who had, over the years, become a dear, if rather pompous old friend, far, far removed from any idea of bed. The fact that she should feel sexually aroused at all was fairly startling and extremely rare these days. A drink was the answer, give them something to do with their hands and thoughts.

She poured him his usual of sixteen years ago and took a brandy for herself in an electric silence.

"Shall we talk flippancies?" she said, settling herself on the sofa beside him, "or shall we say what's uppermost in both our minds, or should I say our libidos?"

Was this her usual approach? he wondered. Did she, in fact, say this to all the boys? Had she recognised his urge — even noticed his erection perhaps? He had to restrain himself from looking down. Was she bored to death to realise that he was just another male after the same old thing? He was frozen in an absurd embarrassment.

"Come on old darling," she said at last. "We can't really put this off, can we? For some extraordinary reason you have induced me to remember our childhood passion and I just can't wait to get into bed with you, whatever the consequences or the morals or the madness of such an act. I expect we'll both be thoroughly disillusioned and will swear never to try out anything so silly again, but I don't think we can avoid it at this moment."

He had forgotten that a kiss could be more than a titillating first step. It was an experience in its own right: a giving and a taking that was deep and emotional. He supposed they moved from sofa to fur-covered divan, but could not remember doing so, only that they were suddenly, inexplicably there, and he was wrestling with the anxiety of how to extricate himself from cuff links and trousers without the basic humiliation and embarrassment that this inevitably brought about. There was scarcely time to worry; Iffey's expertise turned the whole operation into a smooth caress, with her hands gliding over all parts of him, which left no time at all for anything but the most erotic thoughts. With a final sinuous raising of her arms, she released a

78

fastening at her own neck and the entire shimmer of peacock blue cascaded down to the floor to lie, like some collapsed marquee, at her feet. It was high drama and a fitting preliminary to the ecstasy that ensued that night in between Iffey's exquisite green linen sheets. They both experienced an even greater degree of satisfaction and delight than they had enjoyed all those years ago.

"It's a miracle," Iffey murmured a long, long time after, "I would never have thought it possible."

"To think that I had forgotten anything could be so satisfying, so exhilarating and so completely wonderful," Hilary said, lost again in the voluptuousness of Iffey's enveloping flesh. "My life begins from this moment."

They both put off the thoughts of impossible consequences until later.

9 *Later: 1948*

Later was actually postponed for several days. The affair was so shockingly unexpected to both of them that each needed time to get their breath back.

"Well?" Rosemary asked the next day. "Tell me about it. I do hope she wasn't upset that I didn't come. Did she understand that it's really too late for me? She knows I don't like to leave the boys late at night, doesn't she? I mean she did understand that didn't she? Did you explain properly why I didn't go? I do hope she wasn't upset."

"She wasn't upset Rosie."

"Well go on — what was she *like*?"

"She was quite marvellous. I was bowled over." And how true that was. He felt a little sick.

"*Really*? Of course that voice would be fantastic whatever she sang, but I don't know if I could bear to hear her wasting it like that."

"She wasn't wasting it."

"You know what I mean."

"Yes, I know what you mean, but from anybody's point of view, Iffey is a star."

"Of course she's a star, but is she appreciated in a place like that?"

"She would be appreciated anywhere by everybody. Her audience went mad."

"Did they really? Oh good, I'm so glad for her. People are usually so bad-mannered in restaurants, talking and clattering plates all the time. So degrading for any performer. But to be a success at anything is a good thing, even if it isn't the ultimate. Was she pleased that you were there?"

"I think she was."

"I'm sure she was, so now you must go again and take people along. I think you ought to make an effort to see more of her because I'm sure she must be lonely in that great big mausoleum of a place she's chosen to live in."

"I think you should go and see it Rosie."

"Yes I must, only I always ask her here instead because I think it gives her a chance to enjoy a bit of homely comfort and warmth for an hour or so. I hope you went back and had a drink with her so that you could show that you really appreciated her."

"I did that."

"We must make a special effort, I can't bear the thought that she might think we are too bound up in ourselves and our family to bother with her. Or she might even think that she can't approach us so easily as she used to because you're such a success. She might think that we haven't time for her now that we are so comfortable and so happy."

"Iffey is comfortable and happy too."

"Yes of course, but you can't really compare her life with ours can you? We are so lucky, and poor Iffey has to struggle all the time."

Hilary thought there was no sense in carrying the conversation further. It had at least taken his mind away from the real dilemma.

He spent a further four days being restless and on edge. His performances on stage began to suffer because of a lack of concentration. On the morning of the fifth day when the sun shone invigoratingly in between the branches of the still leafless trees, he walked quickly through the grounds of Holland Park. He was almost happy because of the brilliance of the day and the crispness of the air; it almost swept away the agitated craving that had bothered him since the encounter. Almost, but not quite. It was more that the song of the first thrush and the sight of crocuses suppressed, for a short space of time, his overwhelming lust for Iffey. It had returned full strength by the time he reached her front door.

Iffey had done a lot of pacing during the four days; up and down in the studio, in the sort of state that was totally alien to her. She usually found difficult situations a challenge and enjoyed tackling and dealing with them. This was different, mainly, she decided, because in this instance she did not feel in control of her own emotions.

The ring of the doorbell froze her in her tracks. It was the cleaner's day, but this was much too early. Why speculate? She knew it was Hilary didn't she?

There was scarcely time for a greeting, let alone any niceties of social conversation. It was all much too urgent, no time at all for words.

"Darling, is this the most sensible . . . ?" Iffey started to say, but the kiss magnetised and silenced her into a fused unity with this inexperienced young lover of all those years ago and the dear, boring old husband of her best friend for the last sixteen years. Nothing existed outside the kiss and themselves for an untimed interval.

"I love this man I love this man I love this man . . . ," Iffey found herself reiterating over and over, because of the intoxication and frenzy of the last few days.

She became uncomfortably conscious of physical deterioration over sixteen years.

"But I'm not as good as I was," she told him. "More rolls here and there and the bosoms several inches lower."

"Don't lie to me; I find everything perfect. I'm not interested in immaturity."

In between paroxysms of physical pleasure, snatches of amazement flitted in and out of Iffey's thoughts in moments of unequivocal truth, at the phenomenon of anyone being able to find such delight in her misshapen grossness. She had always before decided that her particular sexual attraction must invariably start as a desire for a perverted sex experience. It upset her to place Hilary in this category. She could not at this time face up to the involvement being stereotyped.

It was an hour or so later that Iffey remembered the cleaner. "You must either make yourself look respectable," she said, "or remove yourself to my bedroom and hide in the wardrobe. I can't possibly forgo the weekly cleaning session or upset my cleaning lady."

"But isn't she used to this sort of thing?"

"Of course not, I don't arrange anything on a Wednesday which is her day. And now I think of it, you can't hide in the wardrobe either because she always discovers things to tidy away into that."

"Would it matter?"

Iffey retrieved his clothes from various parts of the studio and threw them at him. She felt light-headed and drunk with satisfaction and happiness; overflowing with goodwill and pleasure, with a childish desire to prattle about nothing, because she was so in love with Hilary and life and sex.

"Of course it would matter for Mrs Delaney to find a man hiding in my wardrobe because she would be shocked and would probably leave, which would be a disaster since she is invaluable to me, and people like that are hard to find these days and, anyway, she is not only someone who makes my life much easier, but also a friend whose susceptibilities I respect and would not willingly upset."

There was a long drawn-out pause while they both pondered on the significance of that remark.

How embarrassing, Iffey thought, coming down to earth, that I haven't the courage to voice what a Freudian slip that statement was. How did one start any sort of discussion on a subject where you could tolerate no solution? Even to talk of a solution would be unbearably painful.

Hilary told himself that this whole episode was just an unfortunate transgression that he could not excuse, and yet seemed unable to prevent. As long as Rosie was caused no distress, it must be considered as one of those appalling, unforgivable misdeeds that ninety-nine percent of the population commit every now and then. No excuse; no possible justification; just plainly and simply wrong, which you admit to with a smirk, and add that you're not perfect. But then no one's perfect, you say. Admit to the sin, confess it, and you are free to sin again. How often had he berated the Catholic religion for this very inconsistency? Just protect Rosie from distress, that's all.

Iffey said at last in some confusion, "Smoked salmon it is then — with the champagne."

"I'll have to ring Rosie, she'll have prepared lunch."

Iffey passed him the telephone stonily, but he got to his feet, putting on his jacket and looking for his coat. "No, I'll do it from a call-box I think."

"Oh shit," said Iffey. "If we have to go through all that jazz you'd better go home straight away." The delirium obviously wasn't going to last.

He met Mrs Delaney on the doorstep who stared at him in vague recognition.

"Isn't that — isn't that that actor that was on at the Odeon last week?" Mrs Delaney asked Iffey as she put on her overall and sorted through dusters and polish in the cupboard. "What's his name — Harry, Harry something."

"Hilary Donovan," Iffey supplied. "Yes that's him. He's a very old friend of mine, I knew him before the war." Why did she have to make sure that Mrs Delaney should not suspect that she and Hilary had just made love? The thing was absurd.

"That was a lovely film," Mrs Delaney said. "Jim and me we went on Saturday and enjoyed it ever so much. Fancy you knowing him like that. I thought he was ever so good didn't you?"

"He's a very good actor, yes."

"Oh yes, better than that Stewart Granger any day. I don't think he ever ought to have left that Jean Simmons you know. Hollywood gets them all in the end. Shall I give the bathroom a good clean-out this week? I haven't done it for a month or so, not properly I mean, not given the whole place a good scrub, so I expect it needs it."

A good scrub, yes, that was what was needed. Iffey felt she should welcome the down-to-earth weekly gossip which could serve to take her mind off other things, but today it was quite unendurable.

"I have to go out Mrs Delaney," she said, "and I'm not sure when I'll be back, so I'll leave your money on the kitchen table. I think it would be lovely if you could do the bathroom and next week we could concentrate on my bedroom perhaps."

Just walk a little to clear her mind. The day was so full of spring, it must surely lend her some of its exhilaration. This was, after all, just another challenge.

He came again two days later, and Iffey felt exasperated and anxious. "You can't keep just dropping in like this Hilary, I'm expecting someone."

"I'm sorry. I'll ring to make an appointment next time, if you can fit me in sometime."

. "Don't be silly, but you know what my days are like, and I have to practise as well." Such stupid excuses.

"I'm sorry if I waste your time. Perhaps I don't come up to scratch."

"You're a fool. Don't you realise you've revolutionised my sex life?"

"I can hardly believe that, with all the experience you've had, I can't think I'm the one that's made all the difference."

"Well you are. I'd forgotten that the experience was enjoyable."

"Oh come now, you must get something out of it."

Iffey's laugh began to surface. There was humour lurking somewhere. Life was just carrying on in the usual way it always did.

"Of course I do — a fitted kitchen and a fairly luxurious lifestyle among other things."

He was not amused. "If I was rich enough I'd buy them all off. I wish to God you'd stop it Iffey. It's degrading. Can't you do with less and put up with what I can supply you with?"

"You don't understand, do you? Do you really think I'd accept anything from you?"

"I can't see why not."

She pulled away from him angrily. "I'm trying to say that I don't think we can carry on like this."

"Why not?"

"I should have thought it was obvious."

He sank down on to a chair and put his head in his hands. "Of course it's entirely up to you. If you think you can't go on . . . ."

"Up to me? Why is it up to me?"

"Because I'm not strong enough to stop it. I seem to have lost all control of my actions. I just know I want you and need you and I couldn't possibly give you up of my own free will. You see Rosie and I . . . ."

"I don't want to know."

"All right, but there are some things . . . I need you Iffey, to keep my sanity."

"What nonsense, you're the sanest, most balanced person I know."

"I'm glad I give that impression." He pulled her down beside him. "And you? Can you say that you can just toss me aside?"

"I presume you wish to state that this thing is bigger than both of us." She was not resisting his hands at all — she was even helping him with the fastenings on her bra. "Oh God Hilary, this is so ridiculous."

"That's not the word I would have used."

"I mean this lack of control, it's immoral. We should be able — we should — I mean — we've got to talk seriously . . . ."

But they didn't progress further than the first few sentences before the grand passion took them over yet again, carrying them well out of reach of any sort of serious talk and lasting into the afternoon. Afterwards, everything seemed so peaceful and so without anxiety that the idea of long and earnest discussion was out of place and quite impossible. Just prolong the euphoria, that was the important thing.

For Iffey, being in love or infatuated or whatever one cared to term it, for the first time, chased all discernment from her mind. She walked on air in the time-honoured way, and had little leisure to think how the rest of the world was getting along. She sang her songs with more depth and feeling, even though Hilary never came to hear her, and she behaved more sympathetically and with greater patience towards her paying clients who were also cut down to the very few and the very rich.

I am loved, she kept saying to herself, for the very first time I love and I am loved. How can this never have happened before? Even when Rosemary came to visit her with the two boys, her security in her own individual world was scarcely threatened at all. There was no outside reality.

"I am amazed Iffey. Hilary told me that I would be surprised at the transformation, but this I cannot believe. Is it really that same wreck that you bought? How wonderfully clever you are — but it must have cost the earth. I never realised how successful you were with your singing. Forgive me Iffey, how obtuse I was not to realise how well you're doing. You are so brilliant to have succeeded in the way you have." She gave Iffey a hug. "You know how much I admire you, don't you? You really are a miracle woman."

"It's like a film set," Timothy said. "You should have a cage of pumas at the back."

"I've got birds," Iffey said. "And a few goldfish in the fountain."

Timothy smiled rather sheepishly. He thought Iffey's excesses were very silly and embarrassing and he was resentful that Iffey did not like him. This was something he found difficult to understand and did not know how to deal with. "That's a bit ordinary though," he said, because he knew she was making fun of him and he wanted to be rude to her.

"Touché," Iffey agreed. "I'll send off for the pumas."

Jonathan looked hard at her to see if she was joking, and then relapsed into the sulk he had sunk into on being forced to accompany Rosemary and Timothy on this boring visit.

Iffey found them boards for Ludo, draughts and Monopoly and they retired in furious silence, while Iffey turned to face her lover's wife. Only she could not help feeling that it was Rosie who was facing her husband's lover.

"You like it?" she asked.

"I love it Iffey. I am so happy for you. I was stupid to be worried about you. Hilary always said you were more than able to look after yourself, and of course you are. And you're happy too aren't you? I can see it in your face, you are positively glowing, it just shines through. I'm not going to worry about you any more."

"I'm ecstatic."

And if I tell you why, then all our lives, as from this moment, will smash into a million irreparable pieces.

"It's all something to do with the end of the war isn't it?" Rosie said. "Though things are difficult still, there always seems to be hope just round the corner don't you think? I know Hilary feels it too, things are going so well for him at the moment, it's quite changed his whole character. Just after the war he was sometimes quite grumpy and depressed, but lately he seems to have emerged right out of that period. At the moment he appears to be walking on air, and he's so sweet to me and the boys, oh it's wonderful, really it is. And now I can see that you've been infected by the same bug. Life is good, isn't it?"

"It certainly is."

Hilary and I are obviously infected by the same bug, Rosie darling, but you? What bug affects you? The fact that Hilary is walking on air and being sweet to the boys? That his character seems to have been changed from a grumpy, depressed, middle-aged depressive into a cheerful, caring husband? This is what is making you happy, my dear Rosie.

What a bizarre situation. Everything in the garden is lovely as long as one remains a sinner and continues in the paths of evil. But if one repents and confesses one's sins — then what? If the sinners cease sinning in an orgy of self-righteous repentance towards the injured party, then these two sinners would sink into a decline, and because of that, the sun would also go in for the holy innocent. How perverse.

10   *Moving On: 1949*

Rosemary often wondered why childhood seemed to be a whole lifetime when the years after twenty sped by at such an alarming rate. Did everyone feel like this? Or was it only her?

She was still finding life satisfactory and was still grateful to fate for having provided her with such good fortune. There was much to do, so that there was never time to stand and stare. She organised her life and her family with secure confidence and great pleasure. It was so rewarding, because Hilary really did appreciate her efficiency and noticed the things she did for him. That was very satisfying.

It wasn't always easy, especially when he was depressed and anxious — though there seemed little enough for him to be depressed about. So she was proud of the fact that they seemed as close today as when they were first married, and there were few couples who could say that these days; especially among stage people. She enjoyed a certain gratification when others told her how envious they were of her happiness.

She remembered Iffey's fury when she had announced her intention of giving up the stage.

"You are mad, Rosie. Why give up your own personality and your own career to make yourself a slave to someone else?"

Rosie rounded on her angrily. "I do it because I *want* to do it," she shouted. "Acting was a lovely way to earn a living, yes, but bringing up the children and looking after Hilary is ten times better. Can't you see that? Much more worth while, much more important and far less likely to have me suffering a nervous breakdown from stage fright, anxiety and starvation when I'm out of a job."

"If you're so keen to serve humanity," Iffey said sourly, "I should have thought it was better to train as a nurse or become a teacher or a social worker or something."

"Nuts," said Rosemary, which was about the strongest expletive she ever used. "I am lucky enough to be able to look after — and nurse and educate if necessary — the people I know and love. Where could you find a more satisfying job than that?"

Iffey hugged her. "What a miserably reactionary female I have as a friend," she said. "I really believe you are a hopeless case, but I shall never cease trying to reform you, and just hope that you will grow out of it in time."

"Never!" Rosie picked up the sweater she was knitting for Hilary. "Wives and mothers are the backbone of England. Why should I have to feel apologetic for enjoying that role?"

"Hooray," said Iffey. "That sentiment gives us an excuse to open a bottle of champagne, so that we can drink a toast to Rosemary Donovan, Housewife of the year and Mother of the century."

Even now that the boys were growing up, life was still full and just as hectic for Rosie. She now had two households to keep up and two gardens to look after, and had pushed her horizons outward slightly to take in charity committees, bridge parties and serious entertaining.

Hilary and she did not see quite as much of each other as they used to. He was often away filming, sometimes for long periods, and even when he was doing a play in London, he was out a great deal of the time. Always having to have lunch with directors or producers or leading ladies; a pity that his work sometimes got in the way of their togetherness — but unavoidable, and something that a wife of a successful man had to adjust to. It was all part of the job of sustaining a loving relationship.

Was she really less of a person, a second-class citizen because of her way of life? Iffey sometimes made her feel so, and yet who was she to talk? A cabaret singer with expensive tastes, living a selfish sort of life by herself, for herself. But as soon as the thought was out, Rosemary collapsed inwardly with shame at her lack of charity and switched her thinking to other things.

She thought instead, and with a twinge of anxiety, of the friends who sometimes asked her if she was not afraid Hilary would fall for one of the glamorous young actresses he was often seen around with. It was true that she sometimes wondered. He was often out for unspecified times at unspecified places.

"You know what Mavis Enderby said to me the other day?" She was helping Iffey with her garden. Iffey enjoyed what she termed 'keeping in touch with the soil', which actually meant pruning the roses but finding it impossible to pick up the pruned branches.

"I don't know anyone with a name as absurd as Mavis Enderby, still less what she said. These Schneezweg thorns are the end, I'm being cut to ribbons."

"You remember, she's playing slaves and servants with the Royal Shakespeare. Well she said wasn't I afraid Hilary might fall for one of the glamorous young actresses he's always seen around with."

Iffey's laugh shocked a nearby blackbird into instant flight. "The little bitch! And what an idiot, Hilary isn't interested in youth."

"She said it in fun of course."

89

"Balderdash! He had probably scorned her advances. You don't worry do you?"

"No, of course I don't worry. I mean, I *suppose* he might have been inveigled into bed by some sex-starved little starlet with hopes of bettering her career — but I can't really believe it, can you?"

"Frankly, no I can't. Would you mind?"

"Oh I don't think so — it wouldn't mean anything after all, because he's so sensible, and he does so love his home comforts. He'd never risk losing all that over some silly affair would he?"

"I should hardly think so. He's not the type to take risks like that."

"Exactly. But anyway, I'm not his keeper, so I'm not going to watch his every movement. He doesn't watch mine. For all he knows, I could be up to all sorts of things if I wanted to." She contemplated for a moment the possibilities that were open to her: plenty of effusive admirers, mostly very young men or dirty old ones. The very idea of her being attracted by any of them was ludicrous, though it was pleasant enough to flirt with them occasionally, just as Hilary would flirt with his admirers. "Mind you, I don't really know what I would feel if I did find out about something; I'm not sure how much I would mind. I might behave completely out of character, one never can tell."

Iffey studied a branch intensely before snipping it off and thowing it on the ground. "The rate these things grow," she said.

"Anyway," Rosie said. "He's not particularly sexy these days, though everybody thinks he must be because he's so attractive to women. They positively drool over him." She laughed at the idea. "We suit each other very well in that way; we can both take it or leave it anytime. The perfectly matched pair in fact. Dear Iffey, you should have taken up marriage-broking and opened up a bureau; you'd have made a fortune."

She continued to laugh as she piled the rose prunings on to the rubbish heap.

Hilary found that the spring that year was a far more exhilarating season than he had previously thought it to be. It seemed brighter, fresher and altogether much more invigorating. For the first time in his life, he actually noticed that it was spring, and said as much to Rosemary.

"I've never seen the blossom looking so beautiful," he said. "There's so much colour everywhere."

Rosemary looked at him with slight anxiety. He was playing in a West End production and anything that rippled the customary calm of every day could possibly blow up into an incident which might have an effect on his performance that night. Undue enthusiasm might make it more difficult to play tragedy. Now if he had been in a farce, excess jollity would not matter at all. She decided silently to be ready with camomile tea and the Debussy records at four o'clock just in case.

The balanced rhythm of Hilary's life was certainly quite disturbed, but he found the disturbance salutary in the extreme.

Just as though I'd shed twenty years or so, he thought to himself. I feel I am capable of taking on the world single-handed. Ridiculous what clandestine sex can do for the ego. I had forgotten what the pleasure of giving complete physical satisfaction to someone could do to me, or, for that matter, how total sexual satisfaction gives such a sense of well being.

His thoughts froze, as they were wont to do recently, in doubtful unease. What excuse was there for the evasion of the primary issue that loomed up behind all this euphoric well-being? Casual affairs were one thing, and might possibly be excused on the grounds of certain circumstances. Unimportant slips from the norm. But Iffey was no casual mistake; the affair was no longer something to be overlooked or ignored on the pretext of having no relevance to real life. Iffey was life itself. And Rosemary? Where did Rosemary come in if Iffey was life itself?

He shifted uneasily from one foot to the other and decided that a sharp, solitary walk with the dog was a temporary answer.

"You going out?" Rosemary saw him take the lead from the hall. "Anywhere special? Could you possibly pick up the fish for tonight? The fishmonger told me he would have some Dover sole today, and he's keeping some for me specially. A real treat I thought, to celebrate our anniversary."

Hilary felt momentary guilt that he had forgotten, but then remembered. "Our anniversary's not till June."

"Not the *wedding* anniversary, darling, the day we met." She laughed. "And you don't have to feel guilty about forgetting that one. You know how absurd I am about anniversaries."

There was a quick sense of relief and then rage overtook him, together with a feeling of being caught out. And it wasn't as if he was intending to see Iffey. Not definitely anyway; could possibly have dropped in on the way home, but just as possibly not. She could have had someone there and he disliked getting no reply to his ring, it always left him with an unsettled feeling of irritation, having to control his desire to peer through the windows to see if she was really out or only entertaining someone else. Not that he ever would take such a degrading and reprehensible step as peering through windows. Even to let the idea cross his mind was unjustifiable, so he probably would decide against going there.

"I'm not going anywhere special," he said. "How much fish?"

"What the fishmonger can spare — he knows it's just for us two. The boys can go out and buy fish and chips, they always consider that such a treat. Oh and we need some cream as well, I want to do dauphinois for us — but no — on second thoughts, I think I'll come with you. It's such a lovely day, there's nothing I should like more than a walk with my favourite husband. Do you mind?"

"Mind? I should be honoured to have the good fortune to be accompanied by my favourite wife." And it was true too, he told himself. The momentary feeling of anger was outrageous. He even felt a sense of relief that the other insoluble problem would be postponed further into the future. He became very jolly, issuing encouraging chirps and whistles to the dog, who waited, shivering with controlled anticipation before exploding into boisterous and vociferous hysteria. "Good dog then! Who's for walks? Come on then! There's a good fellow." The barking was shrill and deafening and obliterated any guilt or uncertainty that might have been lingering in his mind.

Rosemary came down the stairs in sensible shoes and a Jaeger cashmere scarf.

"For God's sake stop that din. Shut up!" she shouted. "Get *down* Charlie." She hit out sharply at the leaping dog and both it and Hilary deflated visibly. "I'll get the fish on the way home, I just want to wallow in all this sunshine and blossom and smell all the smells of spring." She fastened the lead on to the dog's collar and slid her arm through Hilary's. "We haven't done this for ages. You remember all those walks we took before the war? Pushing the pram when the children were small? And when I was pregnant and had that awful desire to walk tremendous distances. Do you remember?"

Hilary put his arm round her shoulders. "I most certainly do."

"Idyllic wasn't it?"

"Still is."

Of course it was, as long as one kept the blinkers on and only looked at the immediate surroundings.

"Sentimental old fool."

They laughed, and the sentiment seeped out into the platitudinous spring day with its suburban cherry blossom spilling showers of confetti on them as they passed.

"We are so lucky that we still like each other." Rosemary wanted to prolong the nostalgic bliss. "I know I go on about this, but I want you to know how much I appreciate it."

Time to change the subject. Too much was too much. Hilary gave her shoulder a quick squeeze and then disentangled his arm to place himself between her and the road.

"Is it next week you're seeing Tim's teacher? Pity it's a Wednesday, I should have liked to have a talk with him."

Rosemary felt the distancing and was nettled that she had pushed the moment too far. So silly when she knew outward displays of affection embarrassed him. She jerked Charlie's lead to check his efforts to drag her more quickly to the Park.

"I'll make a special appointment for you." A short pause tended to exacerbate the sensation of a warm moment frozen. Quick change was essential. "Have you seen Iffey lately? Her new show got rave reviews. I rang her up and she seems on top of the world as usual."

She would have known if he had seen her officially. He would have told her. "Called in on Iffey today," he would say every so often, but he had not done so recently. Was she probing? He had spent an afternoon there the day before yesterday. Did she suspect?

"I saw the write-ups," he said. "But I haven't seen the new show yet. Seen one seen them all."

"But I'm sure she likes you to go. She forgives me because she knows I don't like the atmosphere nor the songs. Given me up as a bad job, but a visit from you does her ego and her publicity good; you ought to go one night."

"I'll drop in on her this week — at home, not at the night club. I think she'd prefer that, and she doesn't need any ego or publicity boost that I could give her."

"I'm not so sure. I don't think she's nearly so secure and confident as she would have us believe. She must be lonely, living there by herself."

Hilary's exasperation was barely hidden. "You are much too naïve, darling. Iffey has a stream of men friends who don't leave her alone for five minutes."

"Oh boyfriends and hangers-on no doubt, but they are all so superficial aren't they? I mean she has no one man she can call her regular companion has she?" Hilary was silent and Rosie continued. "And I can't really imagine, you know, that they're any *more* than hangers-on who want to cash in on her success. Between you and me, being the size she is, I can't believe they want to go to bed with her, can you? Unless they are slightly perverted that is. Much as I love Iffey, she must look quite revolting with no clothes on. I just can't imagine it, can you?"

She gave a quick, apologetic burst of laughter, and was jerked to a standstill by Charlie lifting his leg against a may tree in full, vulgar bloom.

Hilary waited for her, facing forwards. "Women don't have to look like Rita Hayworth to be sexually attractive," he said.

"Of course I know that." Rosemary and Charlie joined him and they continued to walk through the smells and sounds and the warmth of the season. "If that were the case ninety-nine percent of us would go unsatisfied and alone. But there are limits I would have thought. I would also have thought that anyone who found Iffey overpoweringly sexually attractive must be a tiny bit kinky. The sex act is such a ludicrous manoeuvre really when you come to think of it, that any slight deviation could make it laughable or disgusting. When two beautiful bodies get together, then it's wonderful, but when misshapen members of the human race get themselves into preposterously obscene postures and predicaments, I just can't

94

help getting a shudder of revulsion. I suppose I'm too squeamish for my own good."

"Yes, I think you are."

She sensed his irritation and wondered if he was attracted by fat ladies. He had, after all, had an affair with Iffey before she, Rosie, had met him. Obviously she had offended him. "Sorry, it's just me being silly. But I still wish Iffey would find someone who really cared for her, sex or no sex."

Hilary suddenly wanted to make a public declaration of how magnificent Iffey was; he wanted to shout out "Iffey is beautiful, exciting, lovely, passionate, exhilarating, and I am profoundly in love with her". But instead he said "I'm sure she will find someone if she hasn't already".

And they went back home via the shops to buy the Dover sole and the cream for their idyllic anniversary supper with candles and champagne.

11   *Misconceptions*

Iffey surveyed her position in the early 1950s with a hint of unease. Forty-odd years had come and gone with the new excitement of falling in love and of being loved in return; thus it had not carried with it the usual anxieties or even despair of one having reached the possible halfway mark coupled with the inevitable — from now on, one can only go down. But now that forty-four hove in sight, fifty did not seem that far off. This fact brought with it a certain dissatisfaction with life.

Nothing to do with personal circumstances like money, which was plentiful, or success which continued, but something altogether more dire. Could it be boredom that was beginning to show its face? Iffey had never suffered this disability. "Never been bored in my life thank God," she had boasted often enough. "Perhaps I should say thank Mother because she was the one who passed it on. It's a sort of childish enthusiasm we both had; might call it arrested development I suppose."

Depression began to build up round her like a sand dune. Age encroaching with disinterested inevitability. Any attraction that plump ladies might have in their youth would obviously deteriorate with age into an unsavoury, repulsive joke. This in itself was a valid reason for the unease, but there was also the uncomfortable possibility that the disquiet could be the result of an unacknowledged but rankling sense of unrighteousness. This last idea she usually stifled under layers of logic, good sense and devil-may-care reasoning.

Do I, she wondered finally when the effort of obscuring the issue destroyed her sleep for a long drawn-out period of time, include the out-dated and much misinterpreted word Morality in my particular vocabulary? And if I do, then how do I myself interpret it?

She sat up in the draped and padded comfort of her king-sized bed and took an exercise-book and a gold-plated ball-point from the locked drawer in the bedside table. Three-quarters of the book was already filled with recorded incidents, dates, telephone numbers and addresses waiting to be transferred and filed, books to be read, poems to be remembered, and separately, on the left-hand pages, there were notes and jottings of anecdotes and conversations overheard, and, in purple ink from the gold-plated pen, were her own thoughts and deliberations.

She turned to a new clean page and wrote 'Morality' large, in flowing, cursive handwriting. It was a way of bringing the whole thing to the surface once and for all.

Depends what you mean by the word, she wrote. It is, after all a very subjective and emotive appellation. How can I, a successful and contented prostitute, the daughter of another, discuss the same morality that Rosie might envisage? There is no common ground. I was relieved when Sydney Weekes was killed; I had no hint of regret. Would I not have killed him myself if I had had a gun or a knife handy? Would I have been immoral only if I had the means for killing him ready before he actually threatened me? Someone did the dirty work for me so that I could be free and delighted instead of guilty and imprisoned.

I am far more immoral to eat the sheep or chicken I could not myself kill and disembowel. More immoral to acquiesce by my silence or even encourage by my support the killing of millions in a war. I could be vegetarian, but I am not. I could be a pacifist but

I am not. I could avoid sleeping with my friend's husband, but I do not. I like eating lamb. I like eating chicken and beef and fish, I love wearing furs, and I love my friend's husband. I don't hunt, I don't bait bears, I don't throw Christians to the lions but I sleep with my friend's husband.

If we lived in a different community where polygamy was permitted, we should be able to discuss the situation and be the better for it, but as it is, our customs insist that we all play a game in which we must only tell each other part of the truth because the whole truth, whatever that truth may be, usually upsets someone or other. The rules also make it imperative that we cannot allow ourselves to be found out. And so we suffer the stress of anxiety mixed with excitement mixed with fear while we play the game. It is a dangerous game. As dangerous as crossing the road, as giving birth, as eating the wrong food, as crowding together with other human beings who might give us flu or measles or polio. I love my friend and I love my friend's husband.

She paused as she poured herself more coffee. Black-brown liquid in the exquisite French bone-china *boule*. How was it possible to get such satisfaction from material objects? That, in itself, was immoral; pure sensual pleasure.

Deceit, where it betrays trust, is also immoral. No excuse Iffey; you are immoral and damned, and should be destroyed forthwith. Swept off the face of the earth and condemned to hellfire.

Doubly damned, she wrote with the self-indulgence of a confessor, because I can't really feel the remorse I should. There is obviously no hope for me, a miserable sinner doomed to destruction.

She put down her pen and remained dissatisfied. Guilt or boredom? Either was equally reprehensible. The difference between loving and being in love might also be relevant to her present ambivalent mood. When in love one forgives the lover everything. Faults become quirks or lovable forgivable traits from which one will soon wean the loved one. Life is rosy because of the delight in having and loving someone who is equally loving and thinking of you at all times.

Wake up with love uppermost in the mind — sun through the curtains (always sunny of course) — what's today? Oh Hilary, Hilary, I shall see Hilary. And is he thinking of me now? Is he waking to thoughts of me? Is he thinking of that fabulous two hours we spent yesterday? Is he remembering that fantastic peak that exploded on both of us at about eleven-thirty last night? That was being in love.

She lay back on her pillows and tried to remember when it was like that. Seemed a long time ago. The good moments were still there — as good as ever, but they were in isolation surrounded by an everydayness that decreased their pleasure. Hilary, I love you, she thought, but the magic has faded and I am not going to be taken for granted; never have been, never will be, and there's the difference. When in love, it's a pleasure to be taken for granted. Means you're as close and as intimate as anyone could be. Means you can relax because you love each other so well that each can be sure of the other.

But now, five years later, faults were faults and were a cause for dissatisfaction, irritation and — could it be — boredom? I may love you, lover, but I also love myself. The balance has to be adjusted so that it is equally weighted on either side.

On her forty-fourth birthday Iffey asked Hilary to supper at the studio after their various performances.

"You warned Rosie you were going to be late?"

"Said I was coming to your show."

"But you didn't."

"As you weren't doing the midnight one it was difficult to get away in time."

Iffey studied the champagne in her glass. It would not have been at all difficult for him to get away on time. "Why don't you ever come to hear me?"

"But I did."

"Once."

He laughed at her gently, holding her hand. "Do you really want me to come?"

Iffey drained her glass and contained her resentment. That he should have to ask such a question was monstrous.

"You look more than usually splendid tonight," he said. "And I am greatly honoured to be invited to a special supper."

"I thought we should make an occasion of it," Iffey said. He surely couldn't have forgotten this year again, could he? Each previous year she had made sure that she could help him remember the date by mentioning it once or twice in the weeks that led up to it, but this year she had decided to make the test. Not remind him at all. He had had five years in which to remember. Quite enough hints. Quite enough celebrations of his own birthday whenever it came round. Surreptitious celebrations after the event had been fêted in his own home. Stolen intimate moments with precious presents chosen for their undetectability or for storage in her flat. Presents he might give her could, on the other hand, be not only perfectly detectable but large, expensive and chosen with insight into what might give her the most pleasure.

Only they never were. A bottle of champagne and a bunch of flowers with unfailing regularity followed the reminders, and usually on the wrong day. Why the hell did it matter? So she poured more champagne and said nothing. There were oysters, quail's eggs and mangoes and the brandy was old and expensive. But Iffey was determined to push the matter further.

"You don't enjoy my singing?"

Hilary was jolted out of a relaxed daze of champagne and brandy. "What? What do you mean? Why do you say that?"

Iffey leaned back among cushions, seemingly at ease and lazily mocking. Actually, taut and bristling with anticipated conflict. "Because you never mention the subject. Perhaps you are disinterested in what I do; perhaps you don't like the songs I sing; perhaps you can't stand my voice and don't like to say so."

I don't tell Rosie because it would upset her. We all deceive each other. We are all immoral.

Guilt was probably uppermost in Hilary's mind, though irritation ran it a close second. Most unfair to be accused in this way. It was surely obvious that she did not look on this kind of singing as anything other than a money-making device. It would have been tactless to infer that one took it seriously.

"Darling Iffey, how can you say that? I could bask delightedly for hours in the joy of hearing you sing."

"So why don't you?"

He went down on his knees, hands clasped, "Please darling, I implore you, sing to me. Sing to me now so that I can bask."

Good humour crept back through the tension, and the laugh

99

began to rumble through Iffey's person. He wasn't so bad really, she was making too much fuss. Just shy of talking about it; probably thought he didn't know enough about it to make intelligent comments. "All right lover, sit back and I'll sing to you."

She moved to the piano, remembering the songs they danced to in the Thirties. Pile on the agony, she thought with a smile, and played an elaborate introduction. Why did it matter what he thought? She scaled down her immense voice to a caressing intimacy and sang an unashamedly romantic medley.

Hilary basked, lying back on the sofa and deeply moved in spite of himself, by the sentimentality and the nostalgia of the songs. And yet he suddenly found himself thinking Rosie thoughts, like why does she waste her talent on this lightweight stuff? Her voice is too good for it. Did she perhaps consider he was not able to appreciate classical stuff? Was she actually singing down to him? He felt the urge to nag.

"Wonderful," he said when she finished. "But now use your proper voice and sing me Mozart."

Irritation returned sharply to Iffey. What an idiot. Her voice was her voice, whatever she sang, could he not appreciate that?

"Mozart be buggered," she said. "I'll sing something much more relevant." Banging out the chords with vigour, she sat up straight and angry on the piano stool. "Happy birthday to me, happy birthday to me, happy birthday dear Iffey, happy birthday to me."

"Oh God. I see, that's what's the matter. Darling Iffey, I am abject, and most desperately sorry. Of course! And you got this lovely little supper for me and I didn't have the grace to remember. I'm so very very sorry. Please forgive me. What can I do to make up for it? I'm sorry, sorry. No wonder you were sharp with me. Tell me what I can do."

"Take me to dinner at the Ritz and book the most exclusive suite for the night," she said. "I should like that very much indeed."

"You know I can't."

"Yes, I know you can't. We're both too well-known. Rosemary would read it in the *News of the World*. We must keep up appearances at all costs. So stay the night here with me tonight — all night, no sloping off at midnight."

Make impossible demands, why not? He made impossible demands on her, expecting her to be there, waiting for him, whenever he found a time that didn't upset his arrangements with his wife.

There was quite a long silence as the air between them electrified.

"You are not being fair."

"Of course I'm not being fair. I'm voicing desperate desires and things that can never be. Which I know quite well can never be. Just hoping for the small miracle that would make you show you're not like all the rest, taking what you can get and giving nothing back."

The silence returned as both mulled over the possible yet impermissible continuation of those words. She heard in her head the obvious "At least they pay". He considered and swept from his mind immediately "What's the usual fee?" And neither spoke, in mortal fear of the explosive danger threatening on all sides. A false step now and the world would collapse.

"I can't stay because . . ."

"Because of Rosie," she finished for him.

"Because of Rosie."

"Then no more sex," she said. "I'm tired of the regular Wednesday or Tuesday or Monday afternoon tumble in the hay and the occasional frolic after the show as long as you can get back by midnight. I'm not prepared to be ready for it anytime *you* feel like it or when you can find the time. And anyway, I can't stand getting undressed and then dressed again in the middle of the afternoon. Makes me feel like a prostitute," she said and burst out laughing. It really was rather funny that she should be refusing sex to the one who gave her total satisfaction and presumably love and affection. What the hell did she actually want? Certainly not a husband, so why this outburst? A wholly selfish whim, and therefore wholly immoral.

"You're such a bastard," she said, sitting beside him and enfolding him within the silk pleats of her voluminous caftan-type robe and between the softness of her breasts. "If only I was certain that you weren't like all the others, then I would be ready and willing to make all the sacrifices in the world, but you've come to take me for granted as your bi-weekly or tri-weekly indulgence, like the massage or the pint in the pub. Or, in fact, the regular prostitute."

"That's absolutely untrue," Hilary tried to keep his mind off the idea that she might actually do what she threatened and avoid intimacy. It was an altogether monstrous thought not to be considered seriously. "It is, of course, entirely up to you, and I will go along with what you decide but . . ." he kissed her chin and neck and cleavage with increasing urgency.

Fury cut short the excitement that was beginning to overwhelm Iffey's sense of injustice. "Why up to *me*?" she shouted at him. "Am I so unimportant to you that you are willing to let me go out of your life without lifting a finger to stop me?" She pushed him away from her. "Am I just a pleasant interlude that can well be done without?"

"It seems that's what I am to you."

"You are so much more than that you old fool, as I have always tried to show in every permissible way that there was. Loving you, listening to you, giving you little secret things, making much of all the private moments, like anniversaries that we were able to make much of, wanting to do other things than going to bed."

"But we couldn't do other things, could we? Couldn't go anywhere in case we were recognised. What other way could I have shown my affection?"

She turned her head away from him because she felt tears welling up. There was no point in arguing. He could not give her what she wanted, and it wasn't just because of loyalty to Rosie, he never had been able to, although she had made so many excuses for him in the early days. It was just not in him to love her. And if it wasn't love, then it was impossible. Only the excuse of love, with a capital L, stopped the affair from being cheap, crude and unthinkable. Without that, there was no excuse at all. How dare he?

"It's only the sex you want, isn't it? You're not really interested in me at all are you? I'm just the favourite whore, no more."

"Don't be so absurd, how can you suggest such a thing when you know as well as I do that we have been friends as well as lovers from the very first day we met. How can you say I think of you only as a common or garden tart?"

"I didn't suggest you thought me either common or garden, my darling, but you've put your finger on it, apart from being lovers — and remember it was the tart you fell for at first — we are great friends, good pals, tremendous chums, I'm just the friendly tart or the tarty friend from next door. I thought I was more you see."

"And so you are, my beautiful, passionate, irreplaceable lover."

She held his face between her hands. "Oh yes? And if there was no sex, how many times would we meet, you and I? Once a month? Or two months? Or whenever I called on Rosie and you happened to be at home? Take the sex away and there'd be nothing left for you." She turned away and poured some more brandy for both of them. "So no more sex, my randy old goat, for the time being at any rate."

He stared into his glass with something like anger in his heart. "If you say so, if that's what you want."

"Oh Hilary, Hilary, you haven't understood, have you?"

"No, I don't understand. Though I suppose I have to accept that some people's sex urges wane sooner than others, and if that's what you feel, I'm certainly not going to force you."

Iffey quelled the laughter she felt at his idea of her sexual urges diminishing with age. Did he really think that? Or was he being malicious in an attempt to retain his own dignity? He was hurt because he could not understand her point of view. Hurt because she was being honest with him. Hurt because she had not subdued her own feelings and opinions. Hurt because she had not deceived him. Rosie was not being hurt because they both were at pains to deceive her.

"How ironic," she said, thinking of that particular supposition.

"What's ironic about my not wanting to force you into anything?" he said. "You know I have never made love to you unless you made it clear that you wanted me to. It was you, after all, who started things up again."

What a thing to say! What a bastard! Iffey was incensed.

"What a gentleman," she said, seeing the actor playing the part of the undemonstrative English gentleman. All in impeccable taste. Afraid of over-acting in case the situation should become farcical. Emotionally back-tracking for fear of producing a hammy, embarrassing performance. Mirth took over from indignation; he was for ever missing the point and acting out the character he imagined himself to be. "Oscar to Sir Hilary for the restrained performance of the year," she said, taking his hand and kissing the palm. "Very Gielgud."

He snatched his hand away angrily. "You don't have to make fun of me."

"I'm not making fun of you, I'm laughing at you because otherwise I might cry for you and for myself." And tears started to course down her cheeks. "I might well cry," she said.

He did not see the tears and got up to go, but she pulled him back. "One last time," she said. "As a birthday treat — please."

12   *Hilary Soliloquy*

It was three days later, on Sunday, that Hilary's dejection became indignation. How dare she treat him in such an offhand manner? It was she who had always professed love and affection, he had been most careful not to express any such sentiment to her. Kept it on a light tone out of loyalty to Rosemary who was, he always let it be understood, the true centre of his life. Iffey had surely understood this even though he had not specifically spelled it out; didn't want to hurt her unnecessarily. Women don't like to be reminded they are playing second fiddle.

Outraged, he strode to his local pub where Sunday morning was a time for social convergence. It was more out of habit than anything else. He was not really in the mood for being sociable, but at the same time he had felt it necessary to escape from the family. The boys were deep in arguments and dissatisfaction, and Rosie was eager to get him to cope with them while she relaxed by doing a bit of gardening. Not possible to answer children's questions, nor to sort out quarrels this morning; too much going on in his head.

It was childish, Iffey sulking because he forgot her birthday, quite ridiculous. And all this nonsense about not taking an interest in her singing. He had kept quiet because he had imagined it would be painful for her to talk about this second-best career of hers; kept quiet particularly because of that. She was being quite unreasonable.

He greeted acquaintances and smiled vaguely at those who recognised and nudged each other discreetly, but he saw no one he wanted to spend the time of day with, so took his lager outside. Silly to have come really; done better to sit in the garden and relax, except that he wouldn't have relaxed because it would have irritated him to see Rosie working in the garden. When she mowed the lawn it was an unspoken criticism because of course he should have been doing it. Not that she would ever have said anything — less still thought it. In fact, had he offered she would have been adamant that he should do no such thing. "Don't be silly darling," she would have said, "I wouldn't dream of letting you. You do quite enough work all the week, and this is your rest day. Anyway, you probably wouldn't do it right." And that wasn't a criticism either, merely a comment to make him feel better for sitting idly by.

He scowled with the absurdity of being outside the local pub and imagining what Rosemary would or would not have said *should* he have happened to offer to mow the lawn for her *had* he happened to stay at home this morning. He probably would have been with Iffey now, had things been as they were. There was a great sense of let-down and sadness. Oh well, better get used to it; wasn't the end of the world. He'd been lucky to have enjoyed the pleasure of the relationship for so long. But anger returned immediately. No, damn it, he had every right to be aggrieved. Who did she think she was, taking all she could get and then just ditching him for some petty little reason of her own imagining? It was unpardonable.

"Morning Hilary, can I top that up for you?" It was a slightly sodden fellow-actor he hadn't seen for some months.

Conventionally social behaviour sprang to the fore, pushing aside all self-indulgent peevishness. Not a bad chap, life wrecked by alcohol. "Hal*lo* Don, haven't seen you for an age. Thank you, I'm having lager." Idiot, why didn't he say he was on the point of leaving? Didn't need another drink. Didn't really want to stay on here. Certainly didn't want to embark on some long boring conversation with this man. Probably pissed anyway. For a moment the temptation to run away almost overcame him, but that was too silly, and rude into the bargain. He'd never live down that sort of behaviour.

Don Barnard was only slightly drunk. In the amicable, relaxed stage in which he spent most of his mornings, when he was fairly sure, all things being equal, that he would be able to control things today as long as he was careful. Good to meet old Hilary, hadn't seen him for years, or months anyway, can't remember when. Better than drinking alone or with virtual strangers. It would at least keep his mind off Susie. Might be able to pick up rumours of a new show to be produced so that he could get in on auditions early. Hilary might even do him a good turn and suggest him for something. Contacts were vital.

But Hilary always forgot the small scandals and gossip that Rosemary related to him every now and then. He was not interested in the personal life of his fellow actors, and certainly not those on the fringes of his acquaintance. "How's Susie?" he said, pleased that he had at least remembered the most recent wife's name.

"Ah, Susie," Don Barnard sat down heavily and drank a large part of the vodka and tonic in front of him. Unfortunate, unfortunate; but the poor man couldn't be expected to know. Anyway, talking about it might make it go away. Must get used to talking about things that bothered him. "Truth to tell, old man, she's gone the way of all flesh. Scarpered, done a bunk; kaput; no more." He gave a very theatrical laugh coupled with a stagy performance of a man lighting a cigarette with a careless abandon. Hilary recognised the gestures and winced.

"Sorry to hear that, very sorry. Last time we met I thought . . ." He tried to remember the last time they met. Had she been with him? There was no actual recollection of meeting him at all in the past ten years but of course they must have done.

"When you and Rosemary came to dinner you mean, but that was well over a year ago. Things went badly wrong after that. Quite soon after that I suppose."

Dinner with them? Had they actually had dinner with them? He didn't blame her for walking out on him. Much too good for him if he remembered rightly; pretty little thing and not a bad actress; doing quite well for herself. But dinner with them? He poked about in his mind trying to recall and failed.

"Not easy, living together," he said in an attempt to respond to something in which he had actually no interest.

"Bloody impossible I call it. But you and Rosemary — you're still together aren't you? I always thought — I mean you've made it over a long period haven't you? You're still all right aren't you?"

"Oh yes, yes, *we're* all right, quite all right. No, thank God I'm incredibly lucky that way."

"You certainly are. Rosie is an ace, an absolute ace. You picked a winner there and no mistake."

Indignation, first that he should use the shortening, Rosie, when he had no right and second that he should assume that the grounds for the happy marriage rested solely on Rosie's saintliness. Was he, Hilary, so unreasonable and difficult?

"We get along," he said rather curtly.

"So did we, so did we — or so I thought, but then wham — along comes the unexpected and your life goes out of the window." There was a short silence, then "Same again? No please, let me, can't tell you how much good it does me to get it off my chest. Hope I'm not being a bore, but I really am a bit depressed. No, really, you do the next round," and he lurched off leaving Hilary angry with himself that he had again not been quick enough to make his getaway. Couldn't very well leave now that he'd been specified as the therapeutic mentor. And he had drunk the last drink too quickly too, in an attempt to cut the interview short. Next round indeed — he wasn't going to be rushed into a next round; but then that would leave him in the man's debt having been treated to two rounds — awkward. He waited impatiently and watched the sparrows hopping in and out of the benches and tables set out in the yard. Could have been with Iffey now instead of sitting outside in this boring London pub with a boring old soak for whom he felt a certain involuntary pity and therefore could not bring himself to send him packing. Pathetic.

Barnard came back to his trapped prey. He felt mollified that he had ensnared such a worth-while audience. Hilary was no mean actor. Good to be seen drinking in his company. He looked round to see if there was anyone likely to be impressed. No one at the moment, but you never knew, anyone could be passing.

"Brought you some of my poison this time," he said genially, "as a chaser. Seem to remember you liked vodka." He sat down and raised his glass, "Down the hatch," he said and swallowed the lot.

"Bloody friends," he said a moment later after a quiet belch. "Can't trust anyone you know. Don't know how people can do it. She ran off with my best friend you know. Someone I would have trusted with my life and she bloody ran off with him. Mind you, I don't say it was all his fault, she was a bit of a bitch, must have been because they'd evidently been having an affair for months. Right under my nose. Can you beat that? Someone you trust absolutely having it off with your wife right under your nose. Can you beat that?" He stared morosely at the beer mat on the table and tears began to make his eyes look more bloodshot than they already were.

Hilary was intensely embarrassed but also annoyed that this crude old soak could only blame others for the fact that his wife took comfort from someone else. Whether it was friend or foe, how could he expect to keep the respect and love of an attractive woman when she was given an opportunity to escape? Hilary downed the vodka and was perversely determined to bounce this self-pitying wretch out of his misery.

"I don't think it makes all that difference as to whether it's a friend or not," he said. "These things happen, and the fact that it was a friend probably made it more likely because of seeing a lot of each other."

"But my God, it's — it's immoral. I mean — my *best friend*!"

"Oh come off it, it's just circumstances I tell you, coupled with the way some women seem to think. Some of them appear to need change at certain periods of their lives."

Barnard looked shocked. "And men? What about men? Don't we need change?"

"Of course we do, but we're a bit more sensible about it, we can take our pleasures more lightly, a bit here and a bit there. We don't have to plunge into things the way women do." What am I saying? He thought. Do I really believe that? Do I really think random circumstances make Iffey justified in cutting me out just whenever she thinks she will? How dare she?

"My round," he said. Might as well be hung for a sheep as a lamb. He wasn't driving after all and he suddenly felt he wanted to spit out his rage against Iffey in the face of this stupid man who imagined he was the only one to be hard done by.

He felt a little drunk as he returned with the drinks, and why not? He could sleep it off this afternoon. "These things happen," he said. "Happened to me."

"What — Rosemary?"

"No, not Rosemary." What a fool the man was. Ought to know Rosie would never do a thing like that. Rosie would never leave him or push him out; make him feel small, rejected. Rosie wouldn't do that. Never. "No no no. But I had a girl once. Great girl she was. A prostitute actually."

"Oh a prostitute, that's different. You don't expect anything else from a prostitute surely?"

"A prostitute by profession, but we had something else. She was in love with me or so she said. Kept on saying so in fact. Quite convinced me that she really cared."

"But you can't trust them. You can never trust them, it's only the money they care about."

Hilary gave up imagining that he was talking to anyone but still felt the need to spill it all out. The drunken idiot beside him was merely the prompter who didn't have an idea what the play was all about anyhow. "Bloody unfair it was," he said. "Blamed the whole thing on me too. I told her; I said you started the whole thing off all that time ago. Made me believe you wanted it so badly. Made me believe you needed my love-making. Would never have dreamed of going to bed with her if she hadn't led me on in the first place."

"They always do. Lead you on and then give you the brush-off."

"I didn't imagine at first she would agree to it, so I never tried it on until she made it clear she wanted it, and then she made so much of enjoying it and gave me the impression I was the only one for her." He drained his glass and felt out of control. "Gave her what she needed, she was always telling me so, and then to say *I* was taking advantage of *her*! It's preposterous."

"They're all the same. Bloody women."

Hilary got up from the bench and felt humiliated and unsavoury. How could he even be talking to anyone so boorish and moronic? It was not a relief to have blurted it out in this way. Barnard had not been brought to his senses by realising that he was not the only rejected lover in the world, he had merely had his opinion of the baseness of the female sex confirmed. Hilary was shamed to realise that this unpleasant slob now classed Iffey, his beautiful Iffey, as one of the disparaged type of women he blamed for his present maudlin depression. It was odious.

"You are quite wrong," said Hilary, swaying where he stood. "There are women and women, just as there are men and men. And thank God, every one of us is different."

He felt suddenly very wise and infinitely superior to the worm with whom he had recently been consorting. "So I will bid you good afternoon," he added and made his way out into the street and towards home.

Moving away from the ignominy of the confrontation with Barnard, Hilary's spirits began to rise with each breath of air he breathed in. He was quite a little drunk, but no longer morbid.

Rosemary looked up from reading the *Sunday Times* under the lime tree in the garden.

"You're so late," she said. "I was beginning to get anxious, and also hungry, so I had my lunch, I hope you don't mind, it's only chicken salad. Oh goodness, you're drunk aren't you? Whatever's the matter?"

"I met that revolting man Barnard, Don Barnard. He got me drunk."

"I can't see why you should get drunk just because you met Barnard. In fact I would have thought it might have the opposite effect on you, seeing what drink has done to him. Poor man, he's not really revolting, just a little sad I would say. I hear Susie's left him. Can't say I blame her, but it really is rather sad."

"Gone off with his best friend; Barnard thinks it's all very immoral."

"Well, if the best friend is nicer to her and doesn't drink too much, I would think she deserves a little happiness. What a lot of unhappiness there is in the world. Are you going to have some lunch or are you going to sink into a drunken stupor?"

Hilary collapsed into a reclining garden chair. "A spot of stupor would be very pleasant," he sighed.

Rosemary arranged the foot rest and the cushions and covered him with a light rug. "I'll put a thermos of black coffee beside you," she said. "I'm going to have tea with Iffey."

13 *Conceptions: 1952*

Iffey sat at her piano practising with a certain vicious intensity. The cliché that she had cut off her nose to spite her face kept flashing through her thoughts like a night mosquito that evaded obliteration. This voluntary extinction of one of the presumably fundamental parts of her life closely approximated a death wish. A desire to rid herself of inessentials and get back to the bareness of self.

So was Hilary not an essential?

She thundered out a Bach two-part invention with a force that was never intended by the composer. Of course he was not an essential. The self was the only essential; the surroundings merely props which supported the central pivot, and the pivot had to stand on its own to be completely adequate. If she could not exist without the unreality of being loved for what she was rather than what she provided for the lover, then she was not in herself a reality.

And anyway, was not this emptiness she had experienced over the past week merely a blatant sexual lust rather than some deep emotional void? Just another appetite like her appetite for those disgustingly childish rose and violet chocolate creams?

She felt suddenly and physically very sick at the thought of rose and violet chocolate creams, and found herself, inexplicably, leaning over the lavatory and losing the few mouthfuls of breakfast she had persuaded herself to eat some fifteen minutes earlier. Could emotional upheaval really have this effect? The same thing had happened on the previous morning. She refused to believe that she was truly so disturbed by the demotion of Hilary and herself to the indignity of being Just Good Friends.

Unrelieved by the expulsion of her breakfast, Iffey sat gloomily on the lavatory in an attempt to sort out a better explanation. Gastric flu? Food poisoning? Stomach cancer? Unlikely, though always a possibility; so it had to be psychosomatic. She pondered on all these unpleasant prospects for a further moment or two before the obvious became astoundingly clear. She rushed to her diary and studied dates. Ten days late! How utterly absurd!

She rang the doctor and made an appointment for a pregnancy test and then sat back to consider the astounding revelation. So this was how Mary felt when Gabriel flew in through the window with his startling news. Because this was just as unlikely, quite as much of a miracle. Perhaps no immaculate conception here, but just as unbelievable. Three — she cogitated — no four possible fathers, each as unlikely as the other, no one with more claim than the other. Multiple rather than immaculate, this conception, and Hilary the most desirable but least likely of the lot, she decided. She discarded any idea of his being the father with resolute certainty; this baby was hers, if Hilary had been the father it would have been theirs and would have to be shared.

"Rosie," she said rather hysterically on the phone, "you have to come over here immediately. I have something quite ultra-phenomenal to discuss with you."

Rosemary felt a spasm of anxiety go through her. She recognised a note of panic in Iffey's voice and was startled at anything so unusual.

"Of course darling, I can come straight away. Are you all right? You sound a bit strange."

"I feel a bit strange as it happens. Very strange indeed, I'll tell you all when you come."

"Ten minutes?"

"Wonderful, I'll put the coffee on."

Iffey put the phone down, was sick again when she smelt the coffee and got the tea-pot out instead.

Rosemary flew out of the house and down the road towards Iffey's studio, filled now with a genuine unease as to what could be the matter. On the doorstep they kissed each other and Rosie looked at Iffey anxiously. "Whatever's the matter? You look ghastly. What's *wrong* Iffey? Are you ill? Don't say you're ill. Have you seen the doctor? What is it?"

"Don't panic you fool — nothing's wrong, really it isn't. It's all incredibly right as it happens. But come and sit down because you might faint when I tell you."

"*What* Iffey, WHAT? For God's sake tell me what's wrong."

Iffey pushed her into a chair. "Nothing's wrong, I keep telling you, but — well — I think I'm pregnant."

Rosemary gave a fairly loud shriek which startled all the birds in the aviary into a pandemonium of flying feathers and squawks.

"*Pregnant?* But Iffey you can't be. I mean not at your age. And who's the father? Oh dear, you poor thing, no wonder you are in a state, but of course you can have an abortion. There shouldn't be any difficulty, because of your age. I mean it's dangerous isn't it? Oh poor Iffey, I *am* so sorry."

Iffey bellowed with laughter. "God Rosie, I might have guessed. For heaven's sake calm down and incidentally I'm not that old. You make me sound like a nonagenarian at least. People do have babies in their forties and I'm going to be one of them. I'm absolutely delighted, I wouldn't dream of having an abortion. And I don't know who the father is. Could be any one of four."

"You shouldn't joke about this sort of thing, Iffey. How can you say it could be one of four? You must have some idea. Are you really so promiscuous?" Rosie was shocked and disbelieving. Of course she must know who the father was. She wouldn't be sleeping with *four* different men at the same time. Must just be bluffing it out because she didn't want to get the father into trouble. But how stupid she was. "The father has got to take his share of responsibility after all. You can't take on the responsibility yourself."

"I can darling, and I'm going to. I'm over the moon about it."

Rosemary was intensely shocked but couldn't bring herself to argue with Iffey. That would do no good. She would probably lose the baby though, because of her age, then she, Rosie, could help her over the loss. What a disaster. Poor, poor Iffey, forever getting into trouble. This was really the last straw.

Iffey was slightly nonplussed by Rosie's agitated reaction. She found it difficult to believe that the whole world would not be in the same state of exhilarated ebullience in which she herself was basking. There crossed her mind the slight tremor of anxiety that

Hilary might inadvertently have let slip something about their affair, but the thought was despatched immediately in the belief that God or Fate could not be so inconsiderate at this precise moment as to wreck her present exultant joy. This momentous happening was, after all, exactly what the doctor ordered; it was exactly what was needed to get her out of the unsatisfactory rut she seemed to be in at the moment, and into the exhilaration of the unknown quantity which would constitute a new, and therefore stimulating period in her life. Praise be!

The intensity of the effort with which Iffey tried to contain her own excitement in the face of Rosie's reaction gave her the character of a taut, overblown balloon waiting to be released. There was great disappointment that Rosie could not share her pleasure. But had she really expected it? For a moment, the idea that she and Hilary could perhaps indulge in an orgy of ecstatic delight over it flashed through her mind, and as quickly flashed out of it in an explosion of amusement at its flagrant absurdity. This exultation could not be shared. It was a personal, lonely thing.

"Oh Rosie," she said, full of pity that her friend could not share in her pleasure.

"Oh Iffey," said Rosie, full of pity for her unfortunate friend.

"I'm *so worried* about her," Rosie said to Hilary later. "It would be much more sensible for her to have an abortion, even though I don't approve of them. But can you imagine? How on earth is she going to cope with a baby when she lives the sort of life she does? And at her age too. What sort of existence can the poor little wretch expect? One shouldn't bring children into the world if they are bound to suffer, it just isn't fair. I wonder if she'd let us adopt it; that might be a solution. But you know what Iffey's like, obstinate as a mule."

Hilary had not recovered his composure from the shock he had experienced on hearing the news, and could do no more at the moment than utter low murmurs which could have denoted assent, disapproval or any other reaction anyone cared to infer. He immediately assumed that the child was his, but then equally quickly decided that there was no reason why it should be. That decision brought on a sense of fury and jealousy that there might be several other candidates for the role. Really too bad and pretty disgraceful. How could she have been so careless? If it was carelessness. Perhaps the whole thing was intentional. This thought brought with it the shocking idea that she might have decided to have his child so that there would be a lever to force their affair into the open. God — would she do that?

"What can we do Hilary?" Rosemary was now on the verge of an outburst of crying. He heard the waver in her voice and saw the tears forming themselves. It was outrageous of Iffey to put them in this position.

"I'll go and see her," he said. "See if I can make her see sense. Find out what plans she has, what the financial situation is like. See if she knows what she's letting herself in for if she carries it through."

"Yes, yes, do that; that would be wonderful. She respects you and will perhaps listen to reason. You are always so good to her; she ought to appreciate the fact. You're a wonderfully caring person."

She hugged him, confident that he would surely be able to do something sensible. The weight of responsibility diminished comfortably whenever Hilary took charge of something.

"You don't have to worry," Iffey told Hilary later. "It isn't yours, I promise you that."

"How do you know? How can you be so certain?"

She looked at him squarely. "Because I know it's someone else's."

"I won't be so insensitive as to ask whose."

"You wouldn't be any the wiser if I told you."

"If you actually know."

"If I actually know."

So she wasn't going to blackmail him into taking responsibility. Of course she wasn't. Unpardonable of him to imagine that she might. But equally damnable of her to have another man's child while professing to be in love with him. If she was so certain whose it was, then it must have been a predetermined action.

"I didn't know you had decided on this. Why didn't you tell me? Rather drastic, isn't it? And extremely selfish I would have thought. How on earth are you going to look after a child?" He was stiff with displeasure and indignation.

Iffey's fury seethed up inside her, but she fought it back. If he was so dense, then she would not give him the satisfaction of undignified denial.

"I told you," she said. "When I finally realised that there was really nothing about me that you were interested in other than what we got up to in bed, then I had to think of other things that might make life more complete." She marvelled at the ease with which explanations made themselves known to her as she spoke. Of course it was true, except the idea that she had had a hand in it. When you really needed something, strange how often fate takes a hand. Her anger diminished as she speculated again who the father might be. "This baby is mine, and mine only," she said. "I am perfectly able to have it on my own, support it on my own and bring it up to be every bit as good as anyone else's baby. I have more love in me than most people in this world, so it will never lack that commodity."

"Iffey you are being absurd. You have no idea what it means to bring a child into the world, nor how to look after it. Love is not enough."

"Bugger off, Hilary darling, do. You're being a terrible bore, very insulting and extremely silly."

"Poor little Rosie is worried to death about you. You just don't think of the distress you cause everybody do you?"

The preposterous idea that Rosie's piddling little worries about *her* could be set against the quite stupendous *bouleversement* in which she, herself, was immersed — that it should even be mentioned was inappropriate and unseemly.

She held open the door for him. "I expect I shall forgive you someday," she said. "But I refuse at this moment to take any more of your nonsense. Don't call me I'll call you."

They parted in furious and agitated dislike and there was no contact for several weeks, during which time Iffey received confirmation of the pregnancy, booked herself a midwife having refused the services of a doctor, and made arrangements with a stockbroker client to gamble with some of her considerable fortune on the Stock Exchange. Being Iffey, her luck held, and she made a great deal of extra money.

"That should tide me over," she told her bank manager, "until such time as I can earn my living again." She smiled at him, and felt that he would not deny her much, should she ever be in need.

Then Rosemary phoned again: "Oh Iffey, I'm terribly sorry I haven't been in touch for so long. I feel an absolute beast, but I've had such a time. Hilary has been really unwell and terribly bad-tempered with it. You can't imagine what it's been like — so unlike him. I think he's worried about you, you know. But I haven't even asked — how thoughtless — how *are* you? Are you all right? I've been thinking about you so much."

"I'm being sick as a dog and can't stand coffee or cigarettes, otherwise I'm fine, how about you?"

There was quite a considerable silence at the other end of the phone.

"Hallo? Rosie? Are you still there?"

"Yes, yes, I'm still here — but — well . . . ."

"What? What on earth's the matter with you?"

"Well — you're not going to believe this Iffey."

"Try me."

"I'm pregnant."

Rosemary did not join in Iffey's laughter. "But Iffey, it's not funny; after all this time, it was the very last thing I expected. I can't imagine how it happened. The absolutely ludicrous and unbelievable coincidence of it happening to both of us at the same time may seem funny to you, but personally, I couldn't be less amused. I mean *both* of us, it's a bit much isn't it?"

"It's wonderful, that's what it is, I am absolutely delighted and so should you be. What does Hilary think?"

"I haven't told him yet."

"Haven't *told* him? Why not?"

"Well he's been in such a bad mood that the time didn't seem right. I thought I'd wait until he felt better. And perhaps when I felt better, if I ever do."

"You idiot. Tell him straight away. It'll do him a power of good, you see if it doesn't."

"Do you think so? I thought he might drop dead from shock."

Iffey started laughing again. "God," she said, "it's so incredibly funny, and if he doesn't see the joke he deserves to drop dead."

Rosie thought what an insensitive old beast she is; can't feel anything for the upset this is going to cause in both our lives; can't visualise the hell she will probably be putting her poor little infant through; has no sympathy for my feelings at all; thinks the whole thing is a great big joke. Oh well, this was Iffey; she had tended to treat her own life as one long joke. Obviously her way of dealing with disasters.

"We're going down to Maidenhead as usual on Friday," she said, more to get them off dangerous, quarrelsome ground than anything else, "and Hilary will be joining us after the Saturday night show, why don't you come down for the weekend? I'll tell Hilary tonight." She paused fractionally, thinking about it, and realising how much she needed Iffey's support where possible confrontations were concerned. "And the boys, of course we'll have to tell the boys. Whatever will they think?"

"They will realise with shock horror," said Iffey, "that their parents do actually *do* it. Which will probably fill them with acute embarrassment."

"I'm afraid it will, how awkward." Much more than awkward; made *her* feel embarrassed and at a disadvantage, with the certainty that her children's opinion of her would be compromised; something else for Iffey to laugh at so don't admit to it.

"How splendid," Iffey said, "to think of our little darlings growing up together and being friends. Though they'll probably hate each other's guts. But never mind, lovey, I think a weekend on the banks of the Thames would be extremely good for pregnant ladies. We should have a celebration of some sort. What about a pregnancy party with all your jolly friends?"

"But it's not a celebration as far as I'm concerned, it's a disaster."

"Then you should have a party to cheer yourself up. Now off you go and tell Hilary. He's going to be beside himself with joy, and he'll take more care of you than ever. He'll just love doing that, you see if he doesn't."

Putting down the telephone, Iffey lay back in her chair and continued to laugh at the absurdity of the situation. Oh yes, this was definitely the beginning of an intoxicating period of her life.

At sixteen and fourteen, Timothy and Jonathan Donovan could

perhaps be considered to be stereotypes. Iffey thought they were, not particularly nice stereotypes either, she considered; bad-tempered, rude and arrogant, she thought, though they could lay on the good manners and charm whenever they thought it expedient to do so.

"They do what you expect them to do," she told Rosie. "Beautifully dependable." And then she would laugh and Rosie was never sure if the remark was as complimentary as it seemed.

"You mean they're thoroughly boring little public school boys?" she had said at the time rather sharply. It was true that they were usually silent in Iffey's presence which seemed to make obvious their disapproval of her. She embarrassed them both by being black and oversize and because of her effusive approach. Their friends giggled at her behind her back and the whole thing was pretty painful.

It had been easier to accept her when they were younger because she had occasionally and unexpectedly joined in their games and played riotously in a way that Rosie had never been able to do. But when you got older, and friends sniggered at her eccentricity and her vastness, it was difficult not to be mortified. "What a whopper!" one of their friends said when he came with them to a first night of Hilary's during the holidays. She could be so overpowering somehow. When you wanted to show off a bit about your father's success and there was Iffey stealing all the thunder by making too much noise and being too effusive. It was a bit sickening really.

Hilary and Rosemary were both the sort of parents you could be pleased with when they came to speech days, because Hilary was so well known that most of the chaps were quite in awe, and Rosemary was really so pretty and well dressed and had such a fantastic figure that showing them round was a pretty super thing to do. Quite a lot of the chaps had ghastly parents who didn't know how to dress or how to behave but with Hilary and Rosemary you just didn't have to worry at all. They knew exactly how to behave and it was very gratifying.

So the news of the coming baby was really a tremendous shock. Tim felt angry about the whole thing which he found difficult to explain and therefore had to keep the feeling hidden behind the enthusiastic response he felt was expected of him.

"Oh great," he had grinned when Rosemary told them that morning. "Can't sort of take it in somehow. I mean we've been like this for so long haven't we? Can't really believe it at all."

Rosemary had put a brave face on the disaster for their benefit; even raised a smile. "It *is* odd to imagine having another member of the family, isn't it? I can't really believe it myself," she said, and then cursed herself for possibly having given the impression that her sex life was abandoned and irresponsible. But the real predicament was that she had a sex life at all wasn't it?

Jonathan was rigid with agitation and embarrassment. To him it was a distressingly bizarre situation to which he could not adapt; and how on earth to tell the chaps at school? He could well imagine the ribald laughter that would greet any such announcement.

"What do you make of it?" he asked Tim when they were alone. "Can't say I like the idea really."

Tim shrugged. "Difficult to adjust after all this time, but if that's what they want. Can't imagine why Mum should need a baby at her time of life, but women are supposed to get a bit funny at her age. She likes having someone to look after, doesn't she? And Pa's very self-sufficient and so are we."

"You think they planned it?"

"Must have done, they wouldn't risk making mistakes at their age would they?" He laughed. "Can't imagine them doing it can you?"

Jonathan felt the blush creeping up his neck and turned away. "No," he said over-loudly.

Hilary was at first stunned by the announcement. He was quite unprepared for a second shock to the system and found there was a jumble of emotions with which he had to deal. Was there not a suspicion of retaliation in his gratified reaction? Anything you can do — a certain poetic justice? But equally and immediately the realisation of the absurdity of the situation; two possible slip-ups producing two irredeemable results. The coincidence of the whole affair made everything unreal and ridiculous. But it was stupid to feel responsible or in any way guilty. Iffey's pregnancy was nothing to do with him. It was just not feasible, after all these years, to consider that a possibility. But the idea that Rosie might perhaps have a daughter, gave him a remote, and sentimental flicker of pleasure.

The weekend, in the Donovans' rich, riverside evidence of Hilary's success story, was, in the end, a very carefree, riotous event. Rosemary had taken Iffey's advice, and tried to cheer the sensation of doom by arranging an elaborate party. Took her mind off depression; and the nausea she felt on preparing it all induced a martyr-like satisfaction.

Though Iffey could never feel completely at home among the cream walls, the pink alabaster lamps with their watered silk shades and the general air of pastel-shaded refinement, she and Hilary were able to suppress their recent hostility in the good wine, Rosie's outstanding cooking and the general air, among the guests at least, of celebration.

It turned into a rather theatrical gathering of family and friends. There was a lot of intense laughter and play-acting and rather hysterical jollity. Wrong, thought Iffey. Much too superficial a ceremony to honour the profundity of pregnancy; too shallow a celebration for the start of a new and fundamental period of her life. Rosie, on the other hand, did not let such misgivings surface. It was very pleasing to be surrounded by a crowd of celebrating friends whom she had gone to a great deal of trouble to please. It was a party, and parties were fun; everyone enjoyed them.

There was certainly no doubt that it was a celebration; for Iffey, a new start, and for Rosie, the beginning of a realisation that the new baby would be a fresh cause to which she could dedicate her now almost-neglected benefactory talents. Her family had grown rather self-sufficient lately, even Hilary. A new baby would need her in order to live; she would see that it had the best.

14 Birth

As soon as Caesar Simeon Daly landed, squalling, in the middle of Iffey's bed, and after his immediate needs had been attended to and Iffey felt him, squirming about among the slackened folds of her deflated body, she knew that her life had moved on to a new plane. She knew that she was no longer a single individual, but had, in that miracle moment, become a divided personality with two minds, two bodies and two responsibilities.

She held the minute handful of damp human being to her monumental breast that was heaving with laughter. "So my little king," she said, "this is your mother on whom you depend. Take a good look, little maggot, because you and I have to share and share alike from now on. I'll make sacrifices for you now, as long as you agree to do the same for me when you're old enough." She held him high in the air with both hands and laughed at him. "Behold the King!" she said.

The midwife was scandalised. "Really Mrs Daly," she said, holding out a towel to wrap him in. "You won't keep him that long if you are going to be so careless of his well-being. He will catch his death of cold unless we wrap him up." She encased him in folds of warm towelling and bore him to his bath with expressions of disapproval.

Rosemary hugged Iffey, it was impossible not to feel moved at a time like this. "Oh Iffey, he's beautiful. Quite wonderful. I only hope mine will be half as good, I wish you could be with me for that." Couldn't tell her that she dreaded the whole ghastly business, that she felt Iffey's theatrical demonstration of delight was much too superficial, but at the same time, and for no good reason that she could think of, she knew that Iffey's presence at a time like that would give undisputed comfort and strength. Must be a throw-back from when she was six years old and Iffey had provided the only comfort and strength in her life. Odd how childhood experiences linger in the subconscious mind.

"If you *will* insist on going to a nursing home," Iffey grumbled. "All so formal and medical, when the right thing is to be surrounded with friends. You should have arranged to have it at home with all the family round you — not a whole lot of doctors and students."

"Hilary could never have stood it, and of course Tim and Jonathan would have had to be sent away to stay with someone, how could I have had it at home?"

"Send the boys away? What nonsense is this? They should be present at the birth, along with the father."

Rosemary laughed at her. "What an idea! They would all die of shock and embarrassment. The boys scarcely know where babies come from, and Hilary likes to forget it."

"Silly, stupid buggers," roared Iffey, which further upset the nurse so that her mouth tightened into a thin line, and she found herself handling the infant with a degree of roughness which was really meant for his mother.

"You never told me," Iffey said to Rosemary, "you never told me what a rip-roaring, fantastic experience this whole business was. How could you have kept me ignorant of this mind-blowing, triumphant, phenomenon of giving birth?"

"I didn't want to frighten you with tales of horror."

"Tales of horror? Tales of horror? What can you mean? It was stupendous, superb, the experience of a lifetime! What bliss!"

"But the pain Iffey, the pain. You made enough noise to drown the voice of God and swore with sufficient abandon to induce a state of shock in the nurse. You don't surely insist that the event was all joy?"

"But of course it was all joy, pain merely goes to consummate the exhilaration. And anyway, the birth, the actual moment of birth is so ecstatic that the memory of pain dissolves into it. God, what an experience!" She lay back among the pillows in delighted satisfaction.

"You're impossible Iffey," Rosemary said. "You know damn well it's horrific. Thank God I was put out for the last bit of it each time, and of course it *is* mollified when you wake up all clean and tidy and rested to find you've got a new little treasure. Can't think why you didn't have any gas and air or anything, not that it did me a blind bit of good of course. I shall insist on being completely unconscious for this one. Perhaps I can persuade the doctor to give me a caesarean."

The mountain under the bedclothes heaved with laughter. "I may be impossible, but you're a fool, Rosie. Of course you remember it as horrific if you get put out at the worst moment. It's the birth, Rosie, the actual birth that's the culminating moment which makes everything else fall into place; you've missed out on that."

"I'm sure I'm going to have a girl this time," Rosemary said, changing the subject rather firmly.

"So let's marry them off straight away," Iffey said, "they're bound to be ideal for each other. They do it in India after all. I think we should start an arranged marriage cult over here, it would do everyone the world of good.

Sally Donovan arrived discreetly and in an orderly fashion at the London Clinic a few weeks later, and the combined lives of Caesar and Sally set off on apparently parallel lines that were in reality widely divergent. Almost as divergent as the views of Rosie and Iffey on upbringing.

During the first year of Caesar's life, he occupied practically every waking thought in his mother's mind and many of the sleeping ones as well. She could not bear to hear him cry, and was ever impatient for him to wake so that she could talk to him; so there were very few moments when he was not in her arms, or on her back, in a shawl tied round her.

"Back to my roots," said Iffey, "with my child attached to my person in the time-honoured way. Best possible method of cementing the mother-child relationship."

"You're being ridiculous," said Rosie. "If you're going to go native, you might just as well go and hoe the garden with him on your back and plant rice or something."

"I had thought of that," Iffey said. "The rocking movement brought about by hoeing is said to be wonderfully soothing for a child. But then I'm doing a lot of piano-playing and singing to him, which I hope will have a similar effect."

Rosie was never able to decide how serious she was. "You'll ruin that boy Iffey," she said. "Giving in to him all the time. You're making yourself his slave, he's got to realise sometime that life doesn't always do what one wants it to. You're making him into a tyrant."

Iffey fitted her son into the crook of neck and shoulder and ran scales up and down the piano with her free hand. "His name is Caesar," she said. "Of course he'll be a tyrant, but he'll probably conquer Gaul as well."

"He's certainly conquered you, my dear," said Rosie, wondering if Iffey remembered she and Hilary had once had a dog called Caesar which had died having fits. Bad omen, mustn't mention it. "He rules you with a rod of iron, the little fiend."

"He's my boundless joy and I wish to savour every minute of him," Iffey said comfortably. "I resent each moment that he is out of my sight."

Rosemary shook her head. "But Iffey it's not good for him to be so cosseted and so indulged, you're laying in a store of trouble for you both."

"It's a serious case of love. There is absolutely nothing I can do about it," said Iffey; and Sally slept serenely in her pram, perfectly content until her mother deemed the next feed to be due.

"Of course," Rosemary concurred, "Sally is a tranquil baby I have to confess; I am so lucky. She sleeps right through the night, and doesn't cry when she's awake."

"You call this luck? I call it misfortune, darling. If Caesar slept all night and all day, then when could I pick him up and play with him? Think of all those precious moments I would miss. And one never gets them again now does one? Think of that Rosie. What beats me," she added, realigning the shrieking Caesar and putting him back on the breast, "is that this creature is actually a separate entity, and not still just a part of me."

"He'll be a sick entity," Rosie observed, "if you go on stuffing milk into him like that. He's had more than enough already."

Iffey laughed. "He may not need the milk, but he obviously needs me and my tit, otherwise he wouldn't cry like this, would you my prince?"

"Don't be absurd, Iffey, he's crying because he has a stomach-ache through being overfed. You'll ruin his digestion."

She wanted to add that Iffey had extra reason for not overfeeding him because of the possible inherited overweight tendencies, but of course she refrained. She would have to influence Iffey tactfully later on to help her guard against obesity in the poor child.

"Anyway," Iffey said, "I consider my son and me as a team, or a duo if you like, ranged against the outside world. He is a part of me that I protect and nurture, like a plant growing out of me which I can show off to the world with justifiable pride. Something that I can bring up to make its mark in a way that I failed to do. He's my second chance, Rosie."

Rosie was shocked by the whole idea. Naturally, Iffey would

want Caesar to have the success she herself had not achieved, she understood that, but how could Iffey look on the thing so selfishly?

"That's rather a dangerous idea, Iffey dear. Personally, I feel afraid that I might influence Sally in any way, really. I just like to guide my children by example, and let them grow up as individuals. I am so afraid of being an influence that might cause them to fail or to suffer. I would never forgive myself if I was responsible for pushing any child of mine into disaster or unhappiness."

"Oh Rosie," Iffey smiled at her friend's opting out of responsibility. "You're sometimes so negative when you actually have so much you could offer."

Rosie was deeply hurt by the remark, and not a little irritated; but she did realise that Iffey would never be able to restrain her overpowering and overbearing self; would never be able to realise what dangerous power she exerted over people.

"But it's good that we complement each other in this way," Iffey said, "in the same way that our babies do. They are obviously made for each other don't you think? Shall we arrange the marriage day this week or next?"

Thus the two babies fitted perfectly into their respective households. Caesar thrived in the tempestuous and noisy atmosphere of Iffey's aura. Music was his background, and he was cuddled, cosseted and fed whenever he cried, which was often in the first two years. He was difficult, aggressive and obstinate, and sometimes had screaming matches with his mother when she finally became exasperated. His skin was the colour of an autumn beech leaf, his hair chestnut and his eyes aquamarine and Iffey had never before seen anything so beautiful.

"Don't you think he's beautiful Rosie? I know I shouldn't say it, but don't you really think he is?"

Rosemary genuinely agreed with her; he was beautiful, there was no doubt about that, and he was also extremely forward in every possible way. Her small twinges of jealousy at such a paragon were mollified by the knowledge that he was also unbearably precocious. Her Sally was not only the pinnacle of pink and white prettiness, with white-blonde hair, but her behaviour was exemplary.

Iffey was mortified by her lack of tact at praising her own to the parent of poor little pale shrimp Sally, who was so obviously insipid and characterless. She sought rather desperately for a way to make up for her thoughtlessness. Impossible to add "So is Sally" because that would show up her train of thought, and anyway, it was manifestly untrue, Rosie would see through such a ploy. She snatched up Sally and hugged her. "You sweet little angel," she said, "do you approve of your fiancé? Do you think he will make a suitable match for such an elegant young lady as you?"

Because of course she was a sweet child; just no real match for Caesar, that was all.

PART THREE

Pivotal Period

15 Siblings: 1960

"Mummy says we're really just like brother and sister, like twins really. She always says to her friends they're just like twins."

"But we're not in the least like twins. I think she's pretty silly to say things like that because we're not, not in the least. Twins look exactly alike and we don't look anything alike, thank goodness."

"Twins don't have to look alike, we've got twins in our class who don't look anything alike." Sally, as ever, was stung by Caesar's insults to her mother and herself. "And I think you've got a silly name, so does Mummy because she had a dog once called Caesar only he died and he wasn't even old."

"Well I shan't die when I'm not old."

"You don't know you won't."

"Yes I do."

"How do you know?"

"Because I'm particularly clever, Iffey said so, and she says I'm going to be great and famous when I grow up so I can't die until I'm old can I stupid. And Caesar's a very special name because it's the Latin name for king so that I'm probably going to be a king when I grow up." He paused for a moment. "The Greek name for king is Christ so I might even turn into Jesus."

Sally subsided in the face of such cleverness. Her mother was always saying he was clever, and saying it in a way which showed she wished Sally was equally clever, which of course she wasn't. Anger made her face red; it wasn't fair.

"You can't talk Greek," she said finally. "I bet you can't talk Greek, you're pretending."

"No I'm not. I know lots of foreign languages. I know French."

"Well say some, say some French."

"*Merde tais-toi.* That means bother you shut up."

131

Sally started to cry and ran into the house from the garden. "Mummy Caesar's being horrible to me and he's telling me to shut up. Why does he have to be here? Can't we send him home?"

"Don't be silly darling," Rosemary looked up tearfully from chopping onions for spaghetti bolognese, the only thing she could induce Caesar to eat. "You know Iffey has to work all day Thursday and all day Tuesday, and the au pair has her class until six o'clock in the evening. He stays with us till then."

"Why are you crying, Mummy? Is it because you hate Caesar too?"

"Of course I don't hate Caesar, what a silly thing to say."

"Is it because you hate cooking spaghetti for him then? Or because you hate eating it? I hate it, you know I do, so I don't see why we have to have it just for Caesar, Mummy why do we have to have it just for Caesar? It isn't fair, we always have to do things because of Caesar and we never do things because of me."

"But I'm always doing special treats for you Sally, you know I am. And peeling onions makes everyone cry."

"Let me try," Caesar came in from the garden. "Can I peel one and see if it makes me cry. I bet it doesn't because I hardly ever cry."

"Put your nose over that and sniff," Rosemary said, holding out the chopped onions feeling more than a little irritated, very unreasonably she told herself, that her word should be doubted by this annoying infant who made her daughter cry.

Caesar inhaled deeply for several minutes before turning away with his hands to his eyes. "Ow — it hurts. It stings — ow."

Sally crowed with delight. "So? Who's crying now then? See Mr Cleverdick? What a cry baby then."

Caesar turned furiously, snatched up a handful of the chopped onions and rubbed them under Sally's nose. "I'm not crying you silly pig. My eyes are watering, that's all."

Sally set up a shriek of angry pain as the onion began to burn the inside of her nose, and her eyes began to smart. Rosemary became irrationally beside herself. She felt for a moment that she might hit Caesar far harder than was entirely necessary to punish him for hurting Sally. How dare he cause poor Sally such pain? How dare he?

"Stop it at once," she managed to say to both of them while meaning it for Caesar. "You do nothing but quarrel. Why ever can't you play together like normal children? You'd both better come and wash your faces and hands in the bathroom and get the smell off you."

"I like the smell," Caesar said, smelling his hands. "It's an exciting sort of smell."

Rosie felt vaguely nauseated because his words and gestures seemed to her to have sexual overtones. But that was ridiculous, and was obviously some wild fantasy of her own.

"And I like the smell of pigs too," Caesar added dreamily. "So rich."

Now that really was too much; he was just saying it to shock. "I can't agree with you there," she said firmly. "I don't think anyone could truly like the smell of pigs."

"I bet he likes the smell of ploppies," Sally said with a burst of guilty giggles. "He's so disgusting, I bet he does."

"*Ploppies?*" jeered Caesar. "*Ploppies?* Do you mean shit? Because if you do, yes I do, but only mine." He suddenly joined in the giggles. "I wouldn't like *yours*." And they both shrieked with laughter while Rosemary tried to sponge their faces as they washed their hands.

"Hold *still*," she said irritably, shaking Caesar fairly hard. "And you can both stop all that dirty talk."

The children's laughter increased hysterically so that their bodies became loose, uncontrollable bundles of convulsive jelly until Caesar stood up suddenly and tautly. "Get to the top of the bent tree before you do." And of course he did.

Rosemary at once felt guilty. Why could she not control her irritation with Caesar? It was quite unforgivable that a small boy of seven could bring her to such a pitch of outraged resentment. Was it because he was the precious, precocious little genius that he was? Surely she was not so prejudiced as that sounded. Poor wretched child couldn't help being clever and Iffey treated him like an adult, so no wonder he had a high opinion of himself. But was it fair to infer that he was a conceited brat? Was he not just being honest rather than smugly self-effacing and full of the false modesty that an adult or a more conventionally brought-up child might have? He was a child, for God's sake, and he behaved and thought as a child. Did she have to condemn him for that?

She kept the idea that she could be jealous of his gifts right out of her conscious mind, because that would have been too immoral to contemplate. She thanked God constantly that Sally was *not* like Caesar did she not? Thanked God that Sally was not a genius, nor so beautiful that strangers gasped or commented upon the fact. It was very much easier to bring up a child who was ordinarily clever, ordinarily beautiful and splendidly normal. Much, much easier. And Sally would obviously find life easier later on too. These outstanding children never lived up to their early promise and were always neurotic and impossible all through their lives. It had been proved over and over again. So praise the Lord for normality and she must make much more effort to treat this tiresome little brat with adult understanding in an attempt to make his future life less paranoid than it might otherwise be.

Must have a word with Iffey though. Talk about paranoia, Iffey was making a complete fool of herself over the boy. It was all very well to be eccentric, but Iffey carried it too far in her adoration of her son and her consequent treatment of him. No discipline, no understanding of the childishness of the boy, no common sense — not an ounce of common sense.

"Iffey, don't you think you're spoiling Caesar a bit?" Iffey had come to collect and they sat in the garden while the children, now closely united, insisted on one further game before they were parted.

"Oh God, has he been impossible?"

"No, of course he hasn't, don't be silly."

"I realise he behaves in a monstrous fashion with everyone else, Rosie I'm so sorry. He could quite well stay with the au pair . . . ."

"I'm not complaining about him, Iffey, it's just that I'm worried about you, because you are so besotted about him and I'm wondering . . ." How difficult it was to offer advice and how unwise. But something had to be said, surely something had to be said. "I'm wondering if you don't go overboard a bit — I mean it may give him the wrong impression of what life is really like — I mean if he — he's always told how clever he is — then — well . . . ."

Iffey experienced a mixture of amusement and resentment. The idea of Rosie giving *her* advice was so new and so unexpected that it threw her off-balance for a moment. Caesar must have behaved atrociously to evoke this sort of response from Rosie. "What can I say?" It was probably that odious little Sally who had incited him to devildom. "Am I really wrong to heap praise on him? I don't believe so. Don't we all need praise to blossom? Children especially. My darling Mama praised me incessantly and I have never stopped being grateful to her for doing so. I should have foundered completely in childhood if I had not had a mother who believed in me and told me so constantly."

And look what a mess she made of her child, thought Rosie. Illegitimate, neither one race nor the other, too fat, too eccentric and now a lonely woman with an illegitimate child herself in imitation of Mother. Scarcely a good advertisement for her style of upbringing.

"I think you can overdo the praise if you stint on the discipline at the same time," she said. "It's inclined to make the child confused, and they do take advantage, you know. They do play up their mothers if they know they can get away with it."

Iffey studied Rosie with interest and tolerant amusement. How trite can you get? Did Rosie not know that Caesar never played her up in the sense that Sally played up Rosie? Caesar was only odious to those who condescended to him, and Rosie continually condescended to him. "I'll beat him to within an inch of his life," she said, laughing, and Rosie turned aside in annoyance. Why could she not be serious over something that was so important? Would she never learn that certain things in life could not be laughed off? She, Rosie would have to make the extra effort to influence the boy when he was with her. She owed it to Iffey to help her and her son through life.

Sally and Caesar came through the door with their arms twined round each other. "Sally and I are in love," Caesar said. "We are thinking of getting married, so you mustn't keep telling us we are like brother and sister or twins because twins and brothers and sisters can't marry each other except in Egypt."

"I don't tell you you are brother and sister," said Iffey, "because you are not." Of course they weren't.

"No but Rosie keeps saying we are *like* brother and sister and that might make us feel we are and then we might not like each other."

"Well you didn't like each other five minutes ago," said Rosie. "And anyway, I don't *keep* telling you. I just said you should be able to get along like brother and sister instead of keeping on quarrelling like you do."

"But brothers and sisters quarrel much more than friends do so that's not a very sensible thing to say is it?" Caesar pointed out.

"Caesar, don't be rude to Rosie," said Iffey, thinking how sensible he was being.

"Couldn't we go and live in Egypt?" Sally said, but Caesar shook his head.

"That wouldn't work," he said. "Unless we were Pharaohs. It was only the Pharaohs who married their sisters."

"How on earth does he know all this?" Rosie asked. "I mean he's only seven."

"We're doing this project at school," Caesar told her, "and I wound shit paper all round John Spencer and made him into a mummy, only he couldn't breathe and so he cried and went and told his mother which was very silly of him. I wrote my story in hieroglyphics."

"Good gracious, could anyone read it?" Rosie said, feeling inelegantly spiteful.

"People who understood hieroglyphics could," said Caesar.

Iffey and Caesar walked home, hand in hand.

"You get on Rosie's wick," Iffey said. "You must be a bit more careful, because she's really very kind and such a nice person too. She's my best friend you know, always has been. I'd like you to be nice to her."

Caesar sighed. "I do try," he said. "I really do try, but she's so silly about Sally, you know. And she gets angry with me because Sally's stupid."

"Sally isn't stupid."

"But Rosie makes her stupid by talking to her as though she is. And she talks to me the same way, as though I don't understand anything, and I do."

"I know you do, it's just that most people think children of seven won't be able to understand things because they're not old enough to have learned. Rosie likes teaching people things."

136

"Does she try to teach you things?"

Iffey laughed. "Yes she does sometimes. Just today she wanted to teach me how to bring you up."

They both laughed at the idea.

"But she doesn't know, does she? You won't do what she says will you? I think you're about the best bringer-up I know. Better than all my friends' mothers."

"Do you really think so? Perhaps Rosie's right you know; I should probably be much more strict and more like a mother. You're quite a pain sometimes."

"So are you."

They swung their arms in the contented belief that they were right and other people were wrong, that they were happy, and that they loved each other more than anyone else they knew.

Why don't I ever grow up? Iffey thought. Why do I consider my seven-year-old son to be the best friend I ever had in the world, Rosie or no Rosie?

"You're nicer than any of my friends' mothers," Caesar said.

"And you are *much* nicer than any of my friends' children," Iffey replied.

16   Iffey and Caesar: 1961

Iffey found the smart of the criticism that Rosemary had made concerning Caesar's upbringing would not readily go away. It was annoying, because she was sure that the accusation was quite invalid. It was not possible to overpraise a child as long as the praise was justified. Encouragement was the spur to achievement. Every small piece of encouragement which had been handed out to her as a child she remembered, and had nurtured through her life. 'Iphegenia has a strong and pleasing voice. Her musical ability is marked.' And her own mother's comment: "My darling, you sing like an angel, you'll conquer the world with that voice one day." Not that she had conquered the world, but without that encouragement she would never have even tried. Of course she did him no harm by praising him

— even over-praising him, come to that; just as if that were possible.

What if he *were* pleased with himself? Had he not every reason to be? He was the most extraordinarily talented child she had ever come across. His teachers raved over him; he had the mind of someone twice or even three times his age, and if that was precocity, then what was wrong with precocity? Presumably Mozart was precocious, but nonetheless a genius.

And then her mind immediately collapsed in the realisation that every mother thought her own child to be a mixture between Einstein and Adonis. Only surely, in her case, it was true. How many other children had that perfection of pale olive skin, the chestnut curls, the pale blue-green eyes? Surely this was beauty that was not only in the eye of the beholder? She checked herself sharply for the clichés her thoughts kept turning out, and decided she must make more effort to suppress these beliefs both in front of Caesar, and certainly in front of the rest of the world. Rosie could be right that Caesar might grow up to expect too much from the community at large.

"Music practice time," she said, far more firmly than usual. More disciplined time-keeping perhaps; stricter timetable.

Caesar leaped up from the floor with obvious delight. "Oh yes, let's do that duet from *The Marriage of Figaro* like we did the other day, I've learned the words now. I'll be Cherubino and you be the Countess."

He was obviously a genius.

"I'm going to get someone else to teach you music," Iffey said. "As well as me I mean, because I think it would be good for you to hear other people's opinions and to get outside ideas."

"I'd like to sing in a church choir," Caesar said. "My friend sings in one and he gets two and six for weddings. And he wears a red dressing-gown and a collar like Sir Walter Raleigh's."

Perhaps he *was* still a child.

The transformation of the precocious stripling into a choir boy began almost at once. Iffey did her best to suppress her pleasure in watching the new development, but found it difficult.

"He looks so adorable," she told Rosie. "I realise I'm a bore, but when you see your son in cassock and surplice for the first time, it does something to the soul. And all the other boys seem to be so big. When Caesar kneels down beside them in the choir stalls, he disappears from view, there's just a gap. And you know when they go out in procession and they bow to the altar as they pass it? Well he bowed to *us* — the audience! I shall have to go to church every Sunday now just to watch."

"This is what I mean," Rosie said. "No sane mother would take up religion just so that she could see her son in the choir. You make too much of everything Iffey; make him feel as though he's somehow more important than anyone else. I don't stay at Sally's dancing class every week because all that attention wouldn't be good for her. It's not because I don't want to." Or is it? she thought. Wouldn't I be bored watching her every week? Am I really denying myself a special pleasure for the sake of ensuring that she grows into a nice normal human being? Or is it that I just hate to see her failing to keep up with the other children?

"All right, so I'm self-indulgent," Iffey agreed, "but, as I've said so many times before, I can't bear the thought that there should be a moment of his life that I might miss. Once that moment's gone it's gone for ever. That's what I keep thinking of. Maybe I shan't even remember it in a few years, but at least I'm making the most of all the parts of my life I enjoy."

Rosemary marvelled at the enthusiasm for life that Iffey possessed. One could say it was childish and superficial, but at the same time it was courageous to tackle life's complexities with the zest and vigour she invariably showed. Never a thought for her difficulties concerning coping with the child without a husband to help and support. Splendid in many ways, but also rather irresponsible.

How, thought Iffey, could she bear not to go to Sally's dancing class? And how could she be so unmindful of the child's feelings as not to give her the encouragement she so badly needed? No wonder Sally was such a sad little thing. So very pale and uninteresting; it was only when she came to stay the night and she and Caesar were in the bath together that Iffey remembered that her son was a different colour to most of his friends. It struck her forcibly then and gave her quite a shock and a sense of pity for the pale pink shrimp sitting there beside him.

"We did the *Messiah* at St Paul's with a whole lot of other choirs," Caesar told Sally, winding up his clockwork submarine.

"Who's Miss Sigher?"

"It's not a who stupid, it's an it. A horatorio actually and you know I was really sweating after the Hallelujah Chorus."

"Why?"

Caesar stopped winding and looked at her. No use talking about this sort of thing to someone like her, this was private mother talk, and he smiled up at Iffey who sat beside the bath, her mountainous form draped in a soft pink bath towel ready to dry and cuddle him when he got out. For a second he saw Rosie's spare angular shape there instead and thought how dreadful to be cuddled by a bag of bones like that.

"Do you get tingles in your spine when you sing special songs?" he asked Iffey.

"All the time, and it always makes me sweat too, just with the excitement of it all."

"The Hallelujah Chorus is like shouting for joy isn't it?"

"Exactly." You extraordinarily perceptive child.

Sally felt unwanted. "Why are you so fat?" she asked Iffey and brought the conversation back to normal levels. Both Caesar and Iffey felt as though they had been plunged in cold water.

"Why is your mother so bony?" said Caesar full of fury without knowing why.

Sally thought for a moment, wondering whether Iffey would actually burst if you put a pin into her. "She isn't bony."

Caesar propelled himself from the bath into the soft folds of both towel and Iffey in an effort to compensate for any hurt she might feel, wanting to cry for her, while Sally stiffened with distaste at the thought of being enveloped in all that squidgy, disgusting fat. She left the bath primly, wrapped herself in another towel and stalked from the bathroom.

As fast as Caesar excelled, so Sally plodded, at her own pace, slightly behind other children of her age.

"It isn't as though she can't keep up," Rosemary told Hilary. "It almost seems as though she won't. When she wants to do something, then she just goes ahead and does it better than the others. Poor darling, she usually seems so morose, I can't get her to enthuse over anything. Except you," she added as an afterthought. "All she seems to want to do is follow in your footsteps, and she doesn't believe anything she might learn at school could have any possible bearing on that ambition."

"She could be right."

"Oh Hilary, stop being so tiresome. She won't get anywhere with this sulky sort of antagonism she affects."

"I think you're being over-anxious. Sally's all right."

Rosie suddenly felt angry at Hilary's refusal to admit to even a small hiccup in the success story of their life. Of course everything was lovely and satisfactory and without worries, but perhaps Sally needed something more than they were giving. Perhaps their own happy complacency was not the right soil in which Sally could flourish. Rosie suddenly felt that she actually knew better, but how to say it? As it happened, there was no time to say anything, because at that precise moment Hilary took both her hands in his and said with a smile, "I've got a surprise for you Lady Donovan; they're making me a bloody knight."

So other thoughts and worries slipped out of everybody's minds for a considerable time to come, and Sally's attitudes and shortcomings were swamped in the general excitements and rejoicings. Even Caesar was impressed.

"Will you be a hon?" he asked Sally.

"What's a hon?"

"Well if you don't know what it is you can't be one."

"I don't see why not, if Daddy's a sir and Mummy's a lady I could quite well be a hon without knowing about it."

"No you couldn't. They know they're sirs and ladies. You'd have had a letter from the Queen if she'd made you a hon."

"We're all going to Buckingham Palace so that the Queen can put a sword on Daddy's shoulder and say Rise Sir Hilary so she might make me a hon then."

Caesar felt wildly and uncomfortably jealous. "I shall be a Sir when I grow up," he said. "Or I might marry a princess."

"Don't be silly."

He realised that Sally had the upper hand and that nothing he could say or do could make him her equal at the moment. His searing anger got the better of him and he smacked her sharply in the face before running out of their house and back to his own, where he hid under the shelf in the shed at the bottom of the garden and wept out his despair at the unfairness of life.

Later he discussed the situation with Iffey. "Can't you get the Queen to make you a lady?"

"It would take more than a queen to make me a lady, darling boy."

"But why? You're cleverer and nicer than Rosie."

"But it's Hilary who's being made a knight; Rosie becomes a lady because of him."

"I think that's silly, to make her a lady because he is a famous actor; that's very silly. Will he get some armour and a horse and a lance?"

"Afraid not. It's too expensive these days."

"I shall be a knight when I grow up and you can be my lady."

"That I should really like."

And how true that is, she thought. How much more satisfactory it would be to her own ego for success to be heaped upon Caesar rather than upon her. For this would be no virtuous selflessness on her part, but rather a self-satisfied pride in the well-deserved recognition of the perfection of her own un-doubted masterpiece. She basked for a moment in the smugness of self-congratulation before plunging headlong into the uncomfortable certainty that what Rosie had said was most probably true. By creating a being as exceptional as Caesar, she was possibly laying him open to endless difficulties in his adult life.

17   *The Middle Years: 1970*

In spite of realising the truth of the situation, Iffey was never, in the following decade, able to act upon it. It was probably because Caesar progressed, inevitably, from strength to strength. As a boy soprano and as a piano virtuoso he became the child prodigy that she had predicted. It was certainly an over-the-top success story. She worried about the possibility that she doted upon his success as much as upon him. What a sobering and upsetting thought. Was it possible to differentiate the child from the success? Would she have been so besotted had he had Sally's temperament and Sally's lack of — well, you might call it lack of personality? Was all this adoration and love genuine and unadulterated? In fact *what* was this all-enveloping emotion that appeared to overwhelm her? Should it be controlled or suppressed or tempered because of its possible harmful effect upon Caesar?

Rosie still thought so, though she decided not to interfere further.

"It's useless to say anything more," she told Hilary. "I've been on at her for years now, in a very guarded and undercover sort of way, but she never really listens because she feels heaping praise is the way to get the best out of people. It's obviously because of her own deprived childhood, she's trying to make it different for Caesar, you can't blame her I suppose, but it seems so sad that she's well on the way to making that boy the most objectionable creature. Don't you agree darling?"

Hilary had not given the matter a great deal of thought. It was true that he found Caesar a pretty objectionable adolescent, but whether it was Iffey's fault or the random distribution of genes at conception — a slight quickening of the heart beat at the word — he had not considered to any depth. He looked up at Rosie over his glasses and the script he was reading. "Yes, I suppose — well no, I don't think one should blame it on Iffey."

"Oh I don't mean blame it all on her, of course it isn't entirely her fault, but I just think she makes it worse with all that rather odious mother love she pours out all the time. Of course I do realise it's because she's had such a bleak sort of life herself with no one else she can love or care for. But I'm sure she's heading for trouble, for herself as much as for him. He's bound to break free pretty soon. I would think she'd have a nervous breakdown when he gets his first girlfriend. Such a shame really because that will lead to conflict and it will break her heart if he takes off with someone she doesn't like."

Hilary found himself becoming irritated. Why did she consistently misjudge Iffey's character after all these years? At first one could put it down to genuine compassion, but now there seemed to be something almost frenetic about her insistence on what might be called the misfortunes of Iffey.

He mused for a moment but then returned to his script. "Best not to interfere," he said, and regretted suddenly and quite without warning the absence of the exciting sexual warmth of the days Iffey and he had shared together. Long past now, but he had never ceased to want them back. "After all," he added, "you and I were pretty upset when Tim and Jon started to bring their first attempts back home. I don't see why Iffey's reactions should be so different."

Rosemary sighed. Hilary was sometimes rather obtuse; could he really not see the difference? "That's just what I mean — don't you see? Of course we were worried and upset, like any other parent would have been. But with Iffey and Caesar it will be quite different. If Caesar ever tries to rebel, Iffey will be devastated, I'm sure of it."

Hilary read the same words of the script for the fourth time and found he was not taking them in; he became suddenly furious. "I just cannot understand why you should consider yourself Iffey's keeper. She is one of the most intelligent, most successful, most well-organised women I have ever had the good fortune to meet, far more able than you or I to run her own life. Can you not see that?" And he wrenched himself from the chair and strode from the room in dark rage.

Rosie found herself trembling. Stupid, *stupid* to upset him like this when he was in rehearsal. She knew quite well that he did not want to be bothered with other people's troubles at any time and yet she was always doing it; upsetting him for no reason. He was quite right, why *should* she take on Iffey's troubles as though they were her own? What did it matter if Iffey made a mess of her life? The tears started to form from exasperation of her own idiocy. She seemed unable to avoid irritating Hilary these days. So stupid.

It had been the same with the boys; almost as though she had driven them away on purpose because she could not restrain her criticism. Though Hilary had probably been more upset than she by the long hair and the dreadful record playing and the crowds of unsuitable friends, she was the one who had nagged and shouted at them in the effort to keep them from disturbing him.

"What does he think he looks like?" Hilary had exploded once, on returning home after a three-month film location stint to find Timothy with hair down to his shoulders. "My God, he looks like a girl. Why haven't you had it cut, Rosie?"

"But it wasn't me who had to have it cut, Hilary, it was him. I tried to suggest it, but you can't force him. I'm sure they'll insist on it once he gets back to school."

"*They'll* insist? But what sort of parents does that make us? They'll presumably imagine we condone it."

Rosie raged silently against Timothy for Hilary's anger with her. She knocked furiously on his locked door. "Tim? Tim? Turn down that wretched noise and open the door at once."

The response was insolently slow. Tim's face appeared round the half-open door. "What do you want?"

"Open the *door*." She pushed her way inside and shut the door quickly behind her, so that Hilary should not hear the din. "Turn the gramophone *off*."

Hoots of laughter from both the boys greeted the statement.

"*Gramophone?* What does she mean Jon boy?"

Jonathan was less bold than his brother, but anxious to please. His laugh was nervously mocking, and Tim had to continue the attack on his own. "You mean record-player Mumsie?"

Rosie wrenched the stylus from the record. "You know perfectly well what I mean Timothy. And now that your father is back, the din is to be confined to your own room and not let loose all over the house. He is incidentally shocked by the length of your hair, so I would suggest you go straight out now and get it cut. Here is some money. Now go, at once."

"Look Mum," Tim adopted an air of exasperated impatience, "I *have* to get it cut before I go back, the powers that be insist. Can't you *please* leave me in peace during the hols? I need to relax and not have you jumping down my throat all the time." He put the money in his pocket and placed the stylus back on the record. Jonathan giggled.

Rosie was incensed. Hilary was perfectly right, they would respect the school's authority, but not their parents'.

"How can you be so un*feeling*?" she said, her voice insecure with anger. "When you know how this whole hippy, slipshod attitude upsets your father and makes both of us extremely unhappy."

She had tried so hard to impress upon them all their lives the importance of putting the feelings of others before their own; tried with all three children in fact; think of others, she had kept saying to them, not just of yourselves. Tried to show them by example, always putting their comfort and pleasure before her own, and enjoying so doing. Explaining the expression 'do as you would be done by'; how often she had emphasised that maxim when she read *The Water Babies* to them. It should have worked, it really should.

And now, a decade or so later, exactly the same sort of scene was being reenacted with Sally. It was really quite ridiculous, Rosie wondered how she had always managed to make herself the culprit in these situations. If only she had been able to sail through life devoid of any feelings of responsibility — as Iffey always seemed to be able to do. And now Hilary calling Iffey intelligent, successful and well organised, when really she was not; not in any conventional sense anyway. When had Hilary ever called *her* successful and well organised? Even intelligent? Did he actually think Iffey was more intelligent than she was? *Was* she more intelligent? It was quite a sobering thought, and one she had not considered before. Anyway, she thought, I have a great deal more common sense than Iffey has, and that's really what matters. Iffey was able to bludgeon her way through the many disasters of her life — but well organised? Intelligent? Hilary was occasionally quite undiscerning. His outbursts had become rather more frequent lately and she never failed to react badly. It was this distressing feeling that it was somehow always her fault.

She went in search of Sally in an attempt to blot out bleak thoughts of Tim's unsatisfactory marriage and the suspicion that Jonathan was involved in the drugs scene. A general feeling of uselessness always ensued when she allowed herself to dwell upon the problems of Tim and Jonathan.

Sally was curled into an untidy heap among cushions in her bedroom. The door was open. If it had not been, Rosie would not, these days, have taken the liberty of invading her daughter's privacy. It was so important not to seem to be prying, she had learned that from the boys. No way was she going to make the same mistake with Sally. Bob Dylan blared out his ballad loudly from the record-player, not that Rosie recognised either the song or the singer as anything other than a miserable dirge with communist overtones.

"Could you tone it down a fraction darling? Daddy's trying to cope with a script."

Sally glowered. "Hilary is never disturbed by music when he's learning his words," she said, realising that Rosie was using that as an opening gambit to a possible lecture on the merits of doing some school work. So her O level results had been abysmal, so what did that prove? That she was not going to be a success in life? What had O levels to do with acting? And she'd got English anyway; with flying colours too. That was all she had meant to get in any case; the others were a waste of time. Try to get that across to Rosie though — that was also a complete waste of time. She kept her eyes fixed on the page of her book and waited, biting fiercely at her nails.

"Do stop chewing at those nails darling." What a disastrous way to start a conversation. Rosie smiled to mask the criticism and knew the mask would appear humiliatingly apologetic. What a fool; why couldn't she storm in and swipe the offending hand from Sally's mouth? At least that would be a sharp, clean statement of fact. Sally ignored her, so she crossed the room and twitched the curtains straight.

"Any plans for today?" Did that sound nosy? For God's sake stop *apologising*. She stared out of the window miserably and saw Hilary sitting on the terrace, learning his words. What was she doing here in this silent prison where she counted for nothing and her presence was not even noticed? Where her daughter and her sons despised her and her husband preferred the more intelligent, better organised, more successful Iffey.

Jealous of Iffey? What nonsense was this? So ridiculous that it raised a smile. Where she had everything and Iffey had nothing, there was nothing to be jealous of. Though Caesar might be brilliantly successful, with his seemingly remarkable musical talent and nine outstanding O levels before he was sixteen, but disaster lay in store for them when he finally grew up, of that Rosie was certain. Iffey would have to be supported then, there was no doubt of that. She, Rosie, would be needed then all right. But now? Now appeared to be a very grey period.

Hilary, on a sudden impulse, got up from the garden seat and walked quickly through the house and into the street. There was an explosive sensation of total dissatisfaction milling around in

147

the region of his solar plexus. Was he suddenly going to lose his ability to pick up the words almost instantaneously? To struggle for over an hour on one small piece of script was preposterous.

It took less than fifteen minutes to reach Iffey's studio, and he heard her voice ringing out over the trees and shrubs and pavements some time before he arrived at the door. However long had it been? he wondered, and in any case, why was he here?

Iffey opened the door. "Well, well, look who's here. To what do I owe the honour? But how nice darling, how very nice. A drink in the winter garden? A gin? A vodka? A martini?"

The birds fluttered and chirped and sang in the central aviary and water splashed in the courtyard fountain. From an upstairs room in the main house Caesar could be heard practising Bach; the sound filtered down into the courtyard and merged with the water splutter. All very idyllic.

"Idyllic is the word," Hilary said, "though I could add glamorous, sophisticated and immensely cosy."

They sat in wicker chairs and looked at each other.

"It's changed so little over the years," Hilary said. "How have you managed to keep it idyllic over such a long time? Our house doesn't seem to have retained any of the attractions it had when we first moved in. I become daily more bored, dissatisfied and bad-tempered."

"You're just looking at the old haunt with a nostalgic eye. Looking back at a situation is both glamorous and cosy, but living in the same situation might become just as boring to you after a while."

"It was a magical episode wasn't it?"

"Of course, but life is full of magical episodes; they follow one after the other I find."

"I don't find that."

"God, Hilary, all the success you've had — you're just about the top of the tree. How can you say you don't appreciate it?"

"I do appreciate it, but material success is strange, the excitement goes after a bit. You get to take it for granted."

"The tedium of too much security in fact, thank God I've never been lumbered with that affliction."

"But you're still doing well?" He wanted an answer to a question he would never dream of asking.

"Yes, yes, extremely well I'm glad to say; more engagements than I can handle and recordings too; and I have a zealous young accountant who plays games in the Stock Exchange and wins."

Hilary felt jealousy sear straight through him and was amazed and not a little humiliated. "Still on the game then?" His dignity fell away from him as the anger and disappointment took over. He found he wanted to cause her pain. Iffey's belly laugh further incensed him. "You may think it funny, but I find it demeaning and unworthy of you. I would have thought you were too old to be able to make anything but a low and vulgar living out of it."

"You old fool." Iffey was still heaving with laughter. "But I can't help liking you for still being jealous."

"Jealous? Are you mad? Why should I be jealous?"

"Why indeed?" Iffey regarded him with deep affection. She had forgotten how appealing his idiotic intensity could be. And here it was still showing itself all these years after he should have grown out of it. "Darling old idiot," she said, "do you really think I could be making a good living as a whore of some sixty summers, not to mention the winters? When will you get it into your thick head that I'm a star and have been for many years? I've made a great deal of money and my dear young accountant, with whom I have been to bed on several occasions I have to admit, makes a great deal of money also from his percentage of my not inconsiderable wealth."

No need to expand on the role played by Laurence, the accountant, now. She had never been absolutely certain of her own sentiments where Laurence was concerned, nor what the relationship had actually meant to her. There was no doubt, when it started some ten years ago, that the flattering adulation of a twenty-five-year-old for an overweight freak of fifty had been extremely pleasurable.

Steeped as she had been, at that time, in the intense mother-hood phase, Laurence's adoration had come as a morale-boosting surprise. But did she just feel the affection one would experience for a devoted pet dog? And was it any the worse for being just that? To call it yet another mother-son relationship was slightly more shocking she supposed. It finally ceased when she helped him to choose a wife and became godmother to his first baby.

And here was Hilary being just as babyish in some respects.

"I do go to bed with one or two now and then," she said to this charmingly retarded old man who would never really have insight into a woman's point of view, "because I occasionally feel the need, and the need is not financial I can assure you."

Hilary relaxed a fraction. "You still feel the need then?"

"Of course I still feel the need. I haven't died or anything, I'm still capable of wanting love, affection and sex — not that I've ever found anything completely satisfactory since you and me, nothing approaching that in fact."

"Nothing could ever approach that."

"I only said I hadn't found anything yet, but I suppose I must concede that time is running out, can't pick and choose quite as I used to."

"I don't know why. You're just as beautiful as you were. I wouldn't want to pick anyone else."

"Carry on my darling. I lap it up these days, can't get enough flattery to satisfy my immense ego."

"I mean it though."

"Of course you do, but time does wither, you know, I'm rather more of a Leonardo grotesque these days. You have to be pretty kinky to appreciate me. But I do believe you are older and wiser than you were seventeen years ago. I don't think you'd ever forget my birthday now, would you?"

"I swear I never would. I still need you, Iffey, more now than ever. My life is dismally empty."

Iffey regarded him silently and with continued amusement. Was it coincidence that she had been experiencing quite a strong sexual urge these past few months? A feeling she had put down to the fact that Caesar had started to need her less. A feeling she had deemed to herself evidence of distress at the thought of being abandoned in the near future as not being of any real further use to her practically adult son. She saw the emptiness approaching and was steeling herself against it. There had been a slight anxiety about the need to fill the void.

The recent increase in her sexual appetite had, she was convinced, been her bodily functions stepping smartly into the breach. And now, here was the opportunity marching in to back it up. She laughed again at the aptitude with which fate always seemed to step conveniently forward with the means whenever it was necessary. It must happen to others she supposed, but perhaps they did not always recognise the opportunities as they presented themselves, or found them too unlikely to believe.

"I should so much like to lie beside you in my bed," she said. "Not necessarily to do anything more than to feel you there, and to remember a little how it was, and to chat together in the comfort and pleasure of linen sheets, with soft music and the sun slanting through the trees outside and champagne and cherries. Wouldn't that be very pleasant?"

"There is nothing in the world I could imagine to be a better idea."

There was very little chatting, a great deal of laughter and the momentous realisation that time passing had actually enhanced the extraordinary phenomenon of their love-making.

18   Breakout: 1971

It was a mystery to everyone how Sally ever got into drama school at all without having any of the right qualifications. It wasn't RADA, but then Sally insisted she never applied there because she considered it too stuffy. She did question herself now and then as to whether that excuse was true, and thought probably she did not like the idea of going to the place where Hilary had been before her. There were bound to be comparisons. It was going to be bad enough anyway if anyone found out who her father was. Added to which, she thought it imperative to distance herself from London and the family, so had applied to places like Manchester and Glasgow and Leeds. She entered her name on the various forms she filled in as Sally Frances, which was her second name anyway.

The secrecy with which she made the applications was total. Rosemary knew nothing about it and worried, though Hilary thought it best to leave her alone until she found her feet.

"But Hilary she's never going to find her feet at this rate, dropping out of school like this before she's finished anything properly, and this dreadful non-communication. It's not only hurtful to us but it alienates her from everyone. I suppose it's somehow my fault, I've never been much good at communicating with her, you've always been much better. Can't you try to get through to her? When she was actually talking to us, she always seemed to be set on acting, but how can she hope to get into that profession without a training? And with her inability to communicate I should have thought that was the last thing she ought to aim for."

Hilary considered how best to answer Rosemary rather than how he might deal with Sally. "Give her a year or so," he said. "She seems very immature at the moment. Perhaps she could get abroad for a bit, she could visit some of our friends in France. Make a change for her."

"But none of our friends want to be saddled with a silent, sulky girl for an indefinite period just because we can't cope."

"That's being a bit too critical, surely?"

Rosemary made a gesture of impatience. Why could he not see how impossible Sally was? Was it just an obstinate failure to admit? Or did he really see nothing wrong with her? "Perhaps you could persuade her to see a psychotherapist. I'm sure she could be helped if we could only get her to go."

"I don't think she needs psychotherapy — at least, I don't think she would be helped in that way. Once she gets really interested in something or someone she'll be all right."

It was at that precise moment that Sally came into the room holding a letter and looking unusually triumphant. "It seems I'm not so stupid after all," she said. "Leeds have accepted me."

"Accepted you? But I didn't know —"

"No good telling you before, was it? Because you'd have got all edgy and anxious and just think what I'd have felt like then if they'd refused. And anyway it's no use doing something unless you do it on your own. No use if you have to be helped with everything because then it isn't you who's doing it."

Sally was probably as startled as Hilary and Rosemary by the fact that she had succeeded. Her conviction that will-power and determination can get you the things you want in the end was given a decided boost just at a time when she had begun to doubt the concept. She thought that this was probably one of the best moments in her life. Made up for all the hate and distress she had experienced on hearing of yet another of Caesar's masterstrokes, and yet it was not, oddly enough, in any retaliatory sense that she rushed to tell him the news that same morning. Not at all the same feeling of vicious satisfaction she had felt in throwing down the letter of acceptance before Hilary and Rosemary.

Instead, there was exhilaration in her step as she approached the studio. It was doubly pleasing, too, to find Caesar there alone. Iffey would have over-reacted, and that would have taken away a portion of her own pleasure in an attempt to keep the balance. As it was, the satisfaction and pleasure could not have been more complete. When she told him, they came together in a long, affectionate hug, which was for Sally only a very occasional experience. She felt her frustration and her tension melting away just because of the warmth and comfort of being in someone's arms. How absurd, she thought; I'm just being self-indulgent, I don't really need physical contact. But she found to her chagrin that she was crying.

"Why am I *crying?*" she said crossly, fighting free of him. "I never cry: far too humiliating. It can be quite easily controlled. Usually." She wiped her eyes on her sleeve and sat down on the floor to recover.

"But you should cry," Caesar said. "At every possible opportunity. I've told you so often. As soon as I was old enough to cry whenever I wanted to, I did, and it does me the world of good."

"You and Iffey are just absurd emotional extraverts. All very embarrassing and silly."

"You may be right. But Sally I'm so *glad* for you about this. Really the best news I've had for ages. The beginning of so many things for you isn't it?"

"Is it? Is it really? I can never be sure. It's so much what I've wanted for so long that I'm not sure how to cope with it now I've got it. Suppose it fails, suppose I fail."

"You won't fail."

"I always have, so far."

"But that's because you've been doing what Hilary and Rosie thought was right for you, now you're doing something for yourself."

How was it, Sally thought, that she felt at ease when she was with Caesar? There was always this lack of tension — except when they quarrelled, and even then the tension was not really threatening, more exhilarating really. "I have to admit," she said, "you always manage to make me feel I'm doing the right thing. Thank you for that."

"So mind you ask me whenever you take a step into the unknown."

"You don't ask me."

"Oh but I do. In my mind I do. I say to myself now would Sally be pleased with me if I did this, I always say that."

"You're such a liar."

"It's true, I swear it's true. You're my other half."

"Rubbish, Iffey's your other half — if not your other three-quarters."

"Well you are my other quarter, then. Will you settle for that? I'm afraid I must insist that you are at least a part of me for the rest of my life."

"You talk nonsense. If the drama school is a beginning for me, is Cambridge a beginning for you?"

He pulled her over beside him on the floor and put his arm round her. "Oh me, I'm different. I never had to fight for things, they always just dropped into my lap or Iffey put them there. I suppose birth was my beginning. Being adult is far more difficult."

"But you're still being ridiculously successful, scholarships to Cambridge that'll give you a professorship or whatever else you want, and your music, you've got your music too. I mean you can just do anything, anything at all with your life. You only have to choose, that's all."

"That's exactly it. I just have to choose. I think probably that Cambridge may be an end rather than a beginning. I think it has to be, otherwise I'm going to be doomed to mediocrity for the rest of my life."

"That sounds a very silly remark, but I suppose it makes sense to somebody. How can you be doomed to mediocrity when your whole childhood has had star quality from start to finish?"

"End of childhood, start of Life with a capital L. But you didn't have this absurd childhood that I did, did you? I have to be careful that my childhood is not going to be the whole of my life. I had a child's belief at that time that I could achieve anything, and so I did. You were much more adult and serious because you considered the problems that lay ahead, and started to realise your own limitations long before I tumbled to the fact that I had any."

"I did?" Sally decided he was being his usual pseudo-intellectual self, about to propound deep philosophy and great thoughts which she did not have to consider because she would not, in the end, follow them. He would probably now start quoting, which was always boring. She turned her back on him. "Boring," she said.

"Just because I shifted the interest to me instead of you, you old cow. But I suppose it *is* your day, so how did Rosie and Hilary take it?"

"Oh I don't know, I didn't give them the chance to react with more than immediate shock. Just announced it and fled. Couldn't stand the idea of their applauding and then pontificating and demanding why I hadn't told them before."

"You could possibly let them applaud, couldn't you? They do mean well, after all, and they're very nice people."

"That's what makes them so deadly. And they're not so nice really. Mum's stupid and Pa's pompous, I have to fight free of them, keep them at a distance, otherwise they'd eat me up, like Iffey eats you up."

"I'm not going to argue with you, not today. You know I don't agree with you. Iffey and I are a team, always have been."

"Team nothing, you're besotted with her and she rides roughshod, whatever you say to the contrary."

It was difficult not to fight with her. The idea of grasping her by the neck and shaking her flashed vividly through his mind; it would be very satisfying. "You do invite first-degree murder you know."

"It's an art form; I work hard to perfect it." She got up and moved away from him, standing finally in front of the aviary. "Caged, like these birds," she said.

"Stop being so obvious, or I'll come back with the obvious

answer: they're perfectly content because they don't know anything else."

"Anyway, you were the one who said I failed because I was doing what the parents wanted instead of what I wanted."

"I didn't say you had failed."

"Yes you did, just now you did."

"No I didn't." Caesar was transported back into childhood and those endless arguments that all ended in tears because he could always outshine her in words, only to be defeated by the crying at the end of it. "Yes you did. No I didn't. Yes you did. Can't we ever talk?"

She smiled then, and came back to him on the floor. "All right, I'll stop being aggressive, because for a fleeting moment I feel almost as good as you are. So are you content with your life just because you haven't known anything else?"

"Who said I was content?"

"Well what have you got to be discontented about? Anything you do succeeds, doesn't it? You're obviously going to go from strength to strength without raising a finger, and with a doting mother cushioning your every step. It's obscene."

"No aggression, remember. And Iffey supports, she doesn't cushion."

"Oh cushion smushion — why do you have to champion Mummy all the time? Are you in love with her or something? She certainly is with you."

"Depends what you mean by being in love. I suppose we are to all intents and purposes."

"But that's revolting. I suppose you go to bed with her too?" Sally's cheeks flamed with the revulsion she felt at voicing such thoughts. Had they been there all the time? Hidden away? She scarcely knew.

Caesar laughed. "Often," he said, "though probably not in the way you mean. We don't indulge in sexual practices as such, though I suppose we could; I think she's fantastically attractive and I love her to death."

Sally froze. "You are disgusting," she said. "I did sometimes suspect there was something unnatural about you two."

"This is the most disjointed conversation I think I've ever had," Caesar said, putting his hands to his head. "We start off celebrating your great news and within half an hour we're bickering about the pros and cons of incest."

"Don't be stupid, there are no pros for incest."

"You mean the big taboo that keeps us to the straight and narrow? But that, after all, was only introduced to avoid interbreeding when communities were small, doesn't really apply now."

"So you don't think there's anything wrong with it?"

"I didn't say that. Depends on the circumstances. As long as rape and subjugation don't enter into it, I can't see much wrong with it where consenting adults are concerned."

Sally's eyes widened as she looked at him. "You can't mean it — so you *do* do it."

Caesar's irritation exploded. "For God's sake Sally, have I said so? Have I not just said exactly the opposite? I love my mother, yes. I think she's fantastically sexy and sympathetic and over the top in every way. Do we have to be sexually involved because of that? I have sexual fantasies along with everyone else in the world, and some of them are incestuous, along with hundreds of others' fantasies, but they are in no way connected with reality. They are fantasies, understood?"

"We always end up quarrelling."

"Just like husband and wife or brother and sister." Caesar became quite certain at that moment that Sally was his sister. The bond he felt then, and had always felt in a strange, unexplained way, was overwhelming. Iffey had never even hinted that Hilary might be his father in spite of his endless questions, and Caesar certainly felt no filial leanings in that direction, but Sally? He had a love for Sally which he liked to imagine was more than a mere amicable friendship. It was a pleasant, sentimental thought in any case.

"Do you think we are brother and sister?" he said.

Sally stared at him, laughing. "What do you *mean*, brother and sister?"

"I think Hilary might be my father."

Sally still laughed. "You're mad," she said. "Whatever makes you think that? What total rubbish you talk. Your mother had hundreds of affairs didn't she?"

"Hundreds."

"Well then — why should you imagine first, that poor old Dad could have been one of them, and second, why pick on him out of the hundreds as a possible father? Dad's such an old stick and insanely devoted to Mum. He'd never have done a thing like that, it's unthinkable." She continued to laugh at the absurdity of the idea.

So don't disillusion her, Caesar decided.

They lay back among the floor cushions, arms entwined. Sally sensed, with intense embarrassment, the attraction that suddenly surged between them, and sat up sharply.

"So I'm beginning and you're finishing. Wonder where we'll be a few years hence," she said.

Caesar felt the excitement recede slowly. "At the top of our various trees I shouldn't wonder."

"Nice thought, but I don't mind betting you're still at the top of yours while I'm failing to get a foothold at the bottom."

"I promise here and now to give you a leg up if you'll do the same for me should the positions be reversed."

"Bargain?"

"Bargain. And here's my hand on't."

He pulled her over as they shook hands, and they kissed and giggled and hugged in a welter of Iffey's oriental cushions and rugs.

19   *Ends and Beginnings: 1974*

Caesar had been thrown by the Cambridge experience from the first few days. He had never before thought there would be problems in standing alone, but confronted as he was with a large number of Etonians and other public-school men who, as a block, seemed to consider him dross, brought hidden fears to the surface. His colour was not a trendy colour, his looks were disparaged as being camp, his dress as conceited freakishness. On home ground and at school he welcomed the overt notoriety that eccentricity brought with it, felt above it in fact; but here, he sensed a cold indifference and a marked disdain.

The old fears of rejection built up in him and the ploy of putting forward outlandish behaviour, to invite repudiation before it was offered, was not working as it used to. Was it possible that he felt at a disadvantage among all these individual success pinnacles? Each at the top of his own particular tree after many years of striving, they had a right to be pleased with themselves. Had he? Pure Mathematics had been a kind of second nature to him at all times, never a chore, because he had been so far ahead of everyone else. Here, he found a kind of solemn striving, quite alien to anything he had met before. His fellow undergraduates filled him with gloom; there seemed to be nobody with whom he had any sort of accord, and the idea of spending three years in solitary confinement appalled him.

He had accepted the choral scholarship offered and settled to read for the Mathematics Tripos, which meant a certain amount of time to be put aside for services and choir practice. It had seemed an ideal combination of study, though he had toyed with the idea of reading Celestial Mathematics just because of the glamour of the name alone. "Imagine," he had said to Iffey as they discussed the fun of being able to tell others of the choice. "You could adopt such a God-fearing face when you let slip I was reading Celestial Maths. They would immediately think I was doing a course of heavenly accounting so as to get a good job when I die. Specially if it was combined with joining a heavenly choir as well."

The combination of mathematics and chapel duties he considered to be the best option in the end; enough time spent singing to counteract the absorption that took him over when working on his main subject. But without human contact he began to equate life with death. Pressed obscenely to join societies at the Freshers' Squash — the geniality and jollity of the schoolboy designation filled him with foreboding — at the start of term, he drew back from the heartiness and felt primly superior to these rowdy oafs, so keen to amalgamate, intermingle and fuse with their fellows. But was it truly superiority? Or was it fear of showing up badly in whatever group he chose? Because here at Cambridge it would seem that he was not going to shine. He was no star here. So what possible reason was there for him to gang up with others to play games of politics or theatricals or chess or glee clubs? These were merely childish fear gangs that magnetised men and women together protectively, to avoid the loneliness, to prove one's worth, to present a united front to the enemy. But childish things should now surely be put away?

Life, for Caesar, changed so drastically and shockingly in those first few days, that he was frozen with the intensity of the spasm that had appeared without warning and downed his defences. No good to cry for help. That would not be expected; he would not expect it of himself. The fear rose in his throat; how to extricate himself from the situation which was presumably of his own making?

He phoned Iffey a week later. There should be no apparent urgency.

"Hi darling."

"Caesar, you fiend, why didn't you phone me before now? You knew quite well I'd want to know how it is for you. Tell me all."

"It's great, you've no idea; amazing really, so ritualistic somehow." Ritual slaughter. "Quite another world, I mean all these bedmakers — bedders they call them, isn't that revolting? — and the dinners and high tables and grace before eating." And droves of awful young men and awful young women all striving to live together in this mock-up of real life that was in no way real. "My room looks fantastic with that bedcover and the cushions, and I've put my pictures up. Quite like home." Nothing at all like home. He wanted to cry. "You must come up soon and see it all and we'll have Chelsea buns. They're special here. I'll give you tea in my rooms — room actually. I've only got a bed-sit at the moment but I'm seeing about changing it for a set with a study as well." Others seemed to have been better informed about getting hold of the best rooms. Even other freshmen had managed to get better rooms than he had. And he wouldn't be able to change them for some time; just another thing he'd messed up. "All very exciting," he said. "It's going to be great, I can tell you."

"I'm so glad. I'd been worrying about you, not having heard, I kept having feelings that you hated it and believed it was all a ghastly mistake. I even thought of coming up because I felt it so strongly that you weren't happy. Very pleased it's all right darling boyo. Can't tell you how relieved. Just let me know when you'd like me to visit and I'll be there in a flash as you well know."

"Angel, thanks. Better leave it till I get settled in and find out what's what." Time to compose himself to act a part because Iffey would see through anything that wasn't a first-rate performance, and she so much wanted him to enjoy himself at Cambridge; it had been a goal for her, something she had aimed at for him ever since he could remember. Such a baby she was sometimes in always wanting the best for him; wanting him to have everything just that little bit better than anyone else; being petulant and trying to hide it when any of his friends seemed to be trespassing slightly on his success field. Any one of them who might be, perhaps a little taller, better looking, better dressed, attracting more attention. Oh Iffey, your pride and love, that had in turn cushioned, spurred, exasperated and filled him with joy long ago, now filled him with tears because of the idea that he was in some way letting her down. It was his duty to be happy, so happy she would think he was.

He remembered other crisis times he had coped with in the past: first day at school and the almost superhuman effort not to cry as he was led, by a kind but silly teacher, to a table full of jigsaws. They were baby jigsaws which he had outgrown years ago. But if he had protested at such humiliation, he would have cried, and that would have made Iffey cry too as she backed out of the room, leaving him with all these silly noisy children and the silly smiling teacher. Iffey had asked him to try not to mind staying at school without her too much, because if she saw he minded, she would mind too. Sitting there in his ugly Cambridge room which stared out at a high wall, he was back at the small table in the light-filled, noise-filled classroom that smelt of polish, piecing together the giant-sized parts of the baby puzzle, which were made more huge through the tears in his eyes.

Nightmare! Nightmare! Like the crockledile in the Punch and Judy, like clowns, like the ear-splitting terror of low-flying jets, like dogs, like knives, like the nightmares themselves, where huge white shapes danced and drooled all over him, all terrifying things that had sent him hurtling into Iffey's all-enfolding largeness to be restored. They came back to him now as he sat alone in the stark fear of being alone and unloved. Like the mornings of piano exams or the whole week before the dentist appointment or the horror of measles or being sick — things with which he had not been able to cope. The dread of being plunged into another such appalling situation paralysed him into a hopeless stupor that blotted out his being.

The feeling never quite left him all the time he was at University, even though there were compensations which gathered momentum throughout the three years. The pureness of mathematics, for instance; pleasure that came from being surrounded by the glories of old stone buildings and tolling bells, and English history; exhilaration which exploded through him when he walked by the river among the spring blossom and the daffodils; and the singing of anthems in the chapel. There were experiences that enhanced the joy of living and would remain with him always. It was just humanity that was missing.

Always the troublesome plague of conventional thinking nagging away in the background: have you made any good friends yet? Who do you go around with? What are your special interests? Got a girlfriend? Why not? And was it because he found it impossible to answer the conventional questions without embarrassment, or did he actually feel the lack of communion with his fellow beings? More likely that he resented the idea that others should consider him a social failure; should believe that his solitariness was not of his own choosing, but rather thrust upon him by the contemptuous mob. This was really the trouble, wasn't it? People might think . . . .

He started drinking at one of the Townies' pubs. Yobbos he could deal with and impress; he'd done it before at primary school, before joining the élite of the grammar school. He'd flattered the frightened bullies whose only protection was violent attack, by putting himself in their charge and treating them to discourses on the psychology of their separate characters. He did the same thing now, and discovered the wide boys of Cambridge were amused by the audacity of such a weirdo, and became gradually becalmed by his flow of unintelligible words. He found himself able to entertain them with an ability to send them up by impersonating the more oafish behaviour and speech of some of them, to the delight of the rest. Before long as individuals, they began to fear this trick, so that he became a power within, an accepted stranger in their midst who was at the same time a protected protégé. It worked every time, and had protected him before from the disapprobation of the more orthodox.

"You're our mate Ceeze, don't let them Gownies get you down. We'll beat the shit out of them. You only got to say the word Ceeze."

Simple words that eased many of his anxieties. Even though now he was not frightened by the thought of physical violence from the University élite in the same way that he had been frightened of infant school bullies or the grammar-school rugger gang. But now, as then, with the town boys' acceptance of him, he was king again, if only of a small underworld.

He began to find balance in their midst; these were real, down-to-earth people, were they not? He checked himself — what the hell did *real* mean? Was the absorbed intellectual any less real than the uneducated simpleton? Inverted snobbery inferred that the simpler someone was, the more worthwhile, didn't it? The pub-crawler found security in bawdy jokes and legless behaviour, the scholar in knowing his subject, so keep the balance, find the security and forget this habit of either patronising or fearing what you weren't. And here he was, making use of those he might have patronised — or been afraid of; hiding among those who coped with their insecurity with aggression, making use of their violence because he was too afraid to show his own. Pretty despicable, but he might be able to give something in return for the protection they offered now. Might be able to give them a bit of confidence in themselves too; you never knew. The more he was with them, the more he liked them. How could he ever have been afraid of them he wondered. They were as insecure as he was.

He impressed them with his ability to play and sing a parody of any singer or band they suggested.

"Hey boy, you're the man you know, and I got the drums and Sid here on guitar's a real Joe Pass. How about a get-together? We could be as good as anybody."

"As *good* as anybody?" Caesar protested. "Look chaps, you never want to try to be as good as anybody else; unless you're going to be better, then you might as well give up before you start. Who do you want to be as good as, for God's sake? Rock music's at such a low ebb everywhere at the moment, there's no one we want to emulate; we want to go one better, get things stirred up a bit."

"But what about Led Zeppelin, Ceeze? Wouldn't mind following that lead. Even Pink Floyd and Hendrix and Clapton and that lot, what's wrong with them?"

"Old hat, boy, old hat. We got to have something new if we want to go down big; not get stuck in a groove and go on turning out the same old rubbish. Take it from me boy, we got to shock people into something new."

Ideas grew as he spoke. What about making some sort of outrageous statement with this lot? It would be a laugh and might lead somewhere; make this smug place at least sit up a bit and take notice.

And that was how it started; in the small bedroom of the drummer, and later, when other residents complained, in a garage; later still, threatened with arrest for excessive noise, in an empty warehouse. Caesar wrote some scandalously obscene words for them to yell over arrangements of basic chords and rhythms and suggested that their appearance might shock more if it were to take on a studied scruffy look. "We want to get attention fellahs, and the best way to do that is to outrage. When they notice us, then we'll give them some proper music."

The gloom began to lift, the blood began to circulate and under Caesar's leadership at the keyboard, the group flung themselves, with bawdy enthusiasm, into the creation of an aggressively new sort of noise. It shocked; it horrified; it was banned from certain places and so at once took on the guise of a rebelliously forward-looking youth trend. They called themselves Julius Caesar and the Sperms, and within a year had caused a furore in the local press and were beginning to be talked about. It was a start.

"It's a triumph," Caesar told them. "We're going to make it really big. Just you wait and see."

He had managed, by the change of name and change of appearance, to carry out the more infamous performances incognito, and thus had not, so far, been brought before the college authorities. He was elated by the success of the band; this was far more satisfactory he decided, than the fact that he gained a first both in the prelims and the finals, so a double first, thus becoming a Wrangler and being offered the chance to stay on and research for his Ph.D. Surely more encouraging to have succeeded in a new field rather than in the old, facile and much less demanding fashion. He considered that he had triumphed over his fellow graduates not through his Tripos results but rather because of overcoming his previous sense of inferiority. He had beaten them at *his* own game as well as theirs. He felt childishly jubilant. Good show chaps.

Caesar had stayed in Cambridge after the end of his final term to fulfil various engagements with the band, and until his results came through. The pride that Iffey felt when he telephoned her with these results was, without doubt, overweening. She kept repeating the word to herself: Overweening. Overweening. Overweening. Mainly, she decided because the word itself had such a splendid sound, but also to attempt to make herself come down to earth; to attempt to calm herself, not be quite so proud just in case there should be a fall somewhere in the offing.

It was impossible to rush to Rosemary and Hilary with the news because Sally was struggling and had another year to go before her finals. Iffey would have to wait until they asked or saw it in the papers. She drove at once up to Cambridge and booked herself into the University Arms. She felt it was quite imperative to congratulate him in person; there was too much emotion inside her to contain it alone. Caesar held both her hands and watched her pleasure. He felt the three years of guilt and anxiety at not having been able to enjoy Cambridge as she wanted him to slip quite suddenly from him.

"Pleased with me?"

"Talk about cups running over," she said. "I feel like celebrating for ever."

The next hurdle lay a little ahead. Caesar drew breath and wondered if he should approach it now, or wait. Looking at her, it was obvious that two such large steps in both their lives should have two very distinct periods in which they might encapsulate themselves into particular memories. So they celebrated alone together that evening, and he kept her laughing and happy by recounting stories of May week balls, of punting escapades, of drunken revels and all the other conventional things that one will remember as being the University Experience. As he relived it with her, he enjoyed every moment of it ten times more than he had ever done at the time.

This, then, was the real way to enjoy a period of living: look back — even a short way — exaggerate a little, add humour and relate the whole thing to an appreciative audience. At the end of the evening, the Cambridge era had become a memorable experience that he would treasure for the rest of his life. He had not let her down after all. Hilary phoned the next day when she got back. "So he really is a genius it seems. Can I come round and congratulate you in person for producing such a clever son? Rosie would join me, but she's up seeing Sally's end-of-term production. Shame the play prevented my going too."

A *shame*? Iffey imagined her own mortification had she ever been prevented from attending any one of Caesar's milestones. How could Hilary bear not to be there? It was Rosie and the dancing class all over again. And Hilary able merely to remark on the mild annoyance it was not being able to get to his daughter's performance. Iffey was wrapped in the euphoria of her son's success; Caesar's triumph was her own. Love-making that day was just another celebration of the ending of another notable period of her life.

For Hilary though, celebration was no real part of that day. When he read the results in *The Times*, the only reaction he felt was inexplicable fury. How was it possible for this boy to go from strength to strength with such seeming ease when his own Sally had to struggle for every small step that she took? And then probably fail at the end of it all. He felt such a sense of injustice and was quite taken aback by the sensation of hate that took him over. He hated this upstart but could not really understand why; could not, or perhaps would not recognise the jealousy that had eaten away for so long. To be safe, it had to be stored away in the belief that the envy was only for the sake of Sally; but other resentments flared occasionally. Had not Caesar also deprived him of Iffey for so many years? Transplanted him in fact; from the time that he was born, Iffey's love and affection had been blatantly transferred. Had it ever returned completely?

Unable to voice to Iffey any of the unadmitted thoughts that blocked his mind, he snatched her to him with no niceties at all that day, and made passionate love to her with a hatred that was made more intense by the love which could not be expressed in any other way. It was short, fervent and furious for both of them, and they lay entwined in total silence and sleep for a long time after.

"I once read in some dreadful medical book," Iffey said at length, heaving herself up on an elbow, "that in the case of the average man or woman in the street, the sexual organs along with the sex drive start to wilt, lose their potency and gradually become completely atrophied after the age of fifty."

Hilary opened his eyes. "Nice to think we don't live in the street. Do you think we ought to write to *The Times* about it?"

"Could do, or we might submit a paper to *The Lancet*. You know I feel a fulfilled and replenished woman at this moment, eager to set out on a perfectly fresh and exciting new phase of my life."

"Can't it wait till tomorrow?" Hilary said. "I don't feel we've quite finished this phase yet."

PART FOUR

Seasonal Shift

"I really think it's the most dreadful thing to have done. After all Iffey has done for *him*, *what* must she be thinking now? Throwing away those golden opportunities like that. I just can't understand it. So utterly stupid and cruel. Poor, poor Iffey."

"She may not mind as much as you think, Rosie."

"Of course she'll mind. What mother could stand by and watch her son throw away the chances of an exceptional career as a first-class mathematician so that he can be a *pop singer*, without being desperately disappointed? I mean what sort of a career is a singer in a band? They're ten a penny nowadays, and what a terrible drug-crazed lot they are too. Iffey must be frantic with worry."

Rosie had seldom been so distracted about Iffey's proneness to disaster. It really was the last straw, after all the devotion with which she had brought him up, sacrificing so much in order that he might have the best of everything. And now he calmly opts out of it all; wastes his talent, wastes all the education he had received. The stupid, stupid boy.

Hilary lit a pipe very slowly in order to let her spill out her frustrations. With a rare spark of insight, he wondered if her outpourings were not really rather exultant. A kind of I told you so attitude that rejoiced in the downfall of the tyrant. But that was unkind of him. Rosie was not vindictive, just not in her character to be vindictive.

"He's only following in his mother's footsteps after all," he said. "Iffey might find it very flattering that he should want to emulate her career. It could be a highly profitable career too; hers was."

Rosemary made a gesture of impatience. "How *could* she take pleasure in the fear that he might have to struggle in the same way she had to struggle in that sordid sort of world? Especially when she had moved heaven and earth to make sure he could raise himself out of it and break into a worth-while career. I mean he could do anything, get anywhere with his brains and a degree like that; politics, big business, the Bank — anything at all."

Hilary wondered suddenly if she would have preferred *him* to have made it in one of those professions himself. "It certainly seems a waste of a good brain," he said. "But seeing that his musical talent was also so strong, I suppose he should be allowed to follow the profession he would most enjoy. I can't see Caesar ever being happy in a ten-to-five office job."

Rosemary made a snorting sound of pure fury. "That's just it," she said. "Only thinks of himself, *he* wouldn't be happy — what about her? And anyway, what use is musical talent to the average pop singer of today? I warned Iffey he would become impossibly selfish if she treated him like a little god when he was young, but she would never listen."

Hilary felt some of Rosie's rage rise up inside him, but his anger was not directed towards Caesar nor towards the over-indulgent Iffey. He got up and absented himself swiftly before he could allow the fury to escape.

"It all sounds tremendously exciting," Iffey said to Caesar as he developed the whole idea. "Can I be of any help? I mean my agent would be only too glad, though of course I'm pretty old hat these days, I might be more of a drag than a help."

Caesar bounced on to her lap and hugged as much of her as he could circumscribe. "Of course you'd be an impossible drag you out-of-date old harridan. Can't even call myself Daly in case some of your bad influence rubs off on me; I may be Julius Caesar at the moment, but later, after I've got this lot really going, I shall break through with my new image and go solo as Caesar Simeon. Like it?"

"I think it's dire, but never mind, what's my part in the affair?"

"Money," Caesar said. "I need a backer. I've found a manager and the record companies are interested but nervous because we're a bit rude."

Iffey made a swift calculation, sorting through her own list of patrons, past and present. "I could possibly persuade one of my friends," she said.

"Of course you could, darling, you could persuade God, and we're doing our first demo disc any minute now. We can't fail, I'm sure of it."

"Well if you do fail, at least you've got quite a good degree to fall back on, you could easily become something in the city or a professor or something."

"I'm not going to fail you fat old fool, you know perfectly well I won't fail, don't you? You know also that I would never succeed at being something in the city nor could I stand being a don, so I can't let myself fail can I? Don't think my darling," he added, suddenly serious, "that I don't realise that Cambridge and the MA and all that rubbish were absolutely right for me. I'm so glad you made me do it; it was essential because I had to find other ways of succeeding there that didn't really involve brain power and reasoning ability and being precociously clever. When I do succeed, finally, it will be you, plus a small percentage of the Cambridge experience that have done it. Thank you, dear Mother for making everything possible."

"If you carry on like this I shall become embarrassingly sentimental and probably start crying. I'm very pleased with the whole idea." Was she though? Her thoughts clogged for a second or two. But of course she was; the achievement of the task in hand was the thing that made her so proud and happy. What he did with the achievement was merely the setting of a new goal. "Just wanted to be sure," she said, "that you had all the opportunities you were capable of pointed out to you, so that you could choose. Between you and me, I was pretty certain that the one thing you'd really excel at would be the same sort of thing that I seem to be good at. Can't help being flattered you want to try, not, of course that you'll ever be as good as me. And what do you mean, 'made you do it'?"

"You did, you know you did," he laughed. "All that overt encouragement to do better than anyone else, all that praise, all that love, all that pressure. I couldn't let you down at the end of it could I?"

"You could have."

"But I didn't did I?"

"Of course you didn't. Now get off me and get me a drink or I shall start to drown in maudlin schmaltz."

"O.k. my yiddishe momma, I do agree that we can't go on meeting like this. As soon as I'm rich I'll buy myself a flat and put you in a home. All right?"

"Just as long as it's a nice home."

"Depends how rich I get."

Iffey felt uplifted, satisfied, justified and quite humbly grateful for having such a son. She really could not have wished for anything better.

It was ten days later that Rosie felt sufficiently controlled to consider visiting Iffey to offer her sympathy about Caesar. "I must really go round and talk to Iffey about it," she told Hilary. She had felt far too upset at first to be able to give Iffey any sort of comfort. "I don't know even now if I'll be able to stop myself criticising that wretched boy, and then she will feel obliged to stick up for him. She should just let her feelings about him go for once, instead of bottling up her natural anger."

She had got herself all ready to go, when Sally's telephone call put paid to the idea for another period of time.

"Hi Mum. Thought you'd like to know, I got married yesterday." A short, embarrassed laugh. "Thought you might like to congratulate us; might even like to meet your new son-in-law. Here, have a word with him." There was scuffling and giggles and a male voice. "Hi Mum, this is Andy. Heard so much about you, hope we can meet soon." Sally's voice again. "We got a free weekend coming up; thought we might come over and see you, o.k.?"

Rosie felt the heat rising from the soles of her feet right up through her body and sweat prickled out of her scalp. "My God — Sally — what? I mean what — ? Er . . . Hilary, here Hilary, it's Sally." She handed the phone to Hilary and sat down very quickly thinking how can I be having a menopausal flush now, at this late age? She heard Hilary's responses from a distance.

"This is a bit sudden isn't it? . . . Well yes, I expect I'll be overjoyed when I know a bit more about it. . . . But what can you expect when you jump it on us like this? . . . Yes that would be a good idea, in fact essential I would think . . . next weekend would seem to be all right. I'll have a matinée of course but otherwise . . . yes, Maidenhead as usual . . . we'll look forward to meeting him . . . bless you."

"*Bless* her? That's the last thing she could expect. What in God's name does she think she's doing? I mean why get *married*? Without a word and I'm sure without a thought either. She's never even mentioned anyone called Andy has she? Who is he?

She didn't even give him a second name. It's monstrous, the whole thing is monstrous."

Hilary also sat down in a hard chair facing her; unable to support, unable to comfort, unable to sift his own emotions and thoughts into any kind of order. Sally could be right to do it like this, he supposed. It might be better for her not to be swayed by their advice and suggestions. Even if they had not disapproved loudly or verbally, she was so ultra-sensitive that she would have picked up any real or imagined disapproval. Best for her to make up her own mind regardless; parents can be far too possessive. Like Iffey for instance. He checked himself angrily; that was not his thought, it was Rosie's. But whatever the upbringing, it seems the offspring disappoint and cause one pain. Check again — that was a Rosie thought as well; it was just the idea that Sally might be piling up trouble for herself that made it painful wasn't it? And she had been such a loser so far; just the dread that she'd done it again. The anxiety that she couldn't win and that you were powerless to stop the suffering. The desire to weep on Iffey's shoulder was too strong to resist.

"They'll be coming to Maidenhead on Saturday. There's no reason to suppose that the man's an ogre. He may be the best thing that's happened to Sally yet. No good making up our minds before we meet him."

"We can only hope for the best, I agree, but knowing Sally as we do, I can't imagine that I'll sleep much till then. I wish to goodness I could be as calm as you. I am useless at putting things out of my mind and concentrating on something else."

"It's all the stage training." He felt a little guilty that he found the exercise relatively easy. "I think I'd better go and walk it out of my system for a while. Why don't you go and talk it over with Iffey? I'm sure she would be able to offer comfort." Rosie probably needed Iffey's comfort more than he did at this moment. His guilt was slightly assuaged at the idea of making the sacrifice.

"No no — not now. How could I go and pour out my troubles to her now when she needs far more comfort than I do? I can't possibly go to her now, I'd be useless to her, feeling like I do."

Well, at least he'd offered; or had he just been making sure that Rosie would not call on Iffey unexpectedly while he was there? He suppressed the thought before it had time to take hold and made for the front door. "I shall have something to eat at the pub," he said. "So you don't have to worry about preparing any food or anything. But please don't sit there and worry yourself into a state. Ring Tim or something, go over and see them." Why could he not do the comforting himself? He felt miserably inadequate and more than ever in need of Iffey's strength.

Iffey's reaction was amusement, of course. Did he not know that it would be? In spite of the irritation he felt at having the whole thing treated far too lightly, he supposed it gave him a chance to question his own ability to dismiss Rosie's tragic reaction and push the problem to the back of his mind. Was this what he sought from Iffey? A sense of balance?

Huffily, he argued back. "You always treat everything as a great big joke, don't you? Can't you for once consider something seriously? Can't you see that we might be worried about Sally doing herself irreparable harm?"

"Of course I can see it you old fool," Iffey felt far more annoyance than sympathy. "So what do you expect me to do about it? Fling my arms round you and kiss away your tears?" Like Rosie would, they both thought, with varying degrees of malice. Iffey felt the more culpable, and relented. "Not that I won't do that," she said, "because you know how much I pick up on any old excuse to kiss you, but you do put such a doleful interpretation on everything. It may be absolutely the right thing that she is doing."

"That's what I told Rosie."

"And just want me to confirm?"

He reacted irritably to her assumption that he had to refer his thoughts to her for confirmation. "I suppose I shouldn't be bothering you with my troubles just now when you have plenty of your own where Caesar's concerned."

Iffey sat down heavily. "Oh God," she said. "I've been expecting this sort of reaction from Rosie all the week, and have been bracing myself to stand up to it without sounding like the brave little woman, biting her lip and fighting off despair. But I didn't expect it from you, not after a lifetime of being your mistress and lover and best beloved. Do you still not understand what I'm about?" And all this without his knowing about her financial backing for the scheme. He would have a fit if he ever

176

guessed that. What an old fogey the man was. A pity she could not call on him to come up with the money; he could perfectly well afford it. The irony of the situation made her laugh out loud.

Hilary turned his back and stared angrily out at the plane trees beyond the window. "I understand that you are often unnecessarily offensive and that you labour under the false impression that your bloody son can do no wrong."

She quelled the fury. Of course he was jealous of Caesar; she couldn't possibly blame him for that, and of course he was worried silly over that unfortunate daughter of his. She, Iffey, was an unsympathetic, self-centred swine and must make immediate amends.

"Darling man, I'm sorry. It's just that I am delighted about Caesar's decision to try out something new — even if he does make a balls-up of the whole thing. Of course he can do lots of wrong things, and I'm sure I'm mad and very irritating to have such faith in him; but if I didn't, then I'd be as unhappy as you are about Sally, over his every decision, wouldn't I? Even if Sally does make a mess of her life, there's nothing you can do now to stop it, is there? All you *can* do is stand by and pick up the pieces."

Absurd, corny sentiments, she thought to herself, totally unprepared and off the top of my head. Do I really think all those wise and wonderful things about Caesar? Of course I don't, I just think I'm very clever to have spawned such a miracle boy, which should make me humble and sympathetic towards those who haven't had the same good fortune as me.

"Dear, sweet Hilary, light of my life," she said. "Why don't we forget our bloody sons and daughters for the rest of the day?"

So they did.

21   *Success and Failure: 1976*

It was a golden period for Sally; the only one she had ever known, as it happened. It could perhaps be said that the average person looks back on childhood as being a kind of sun-drenched nostalgia trip, though there are exceptions to this rule. Sally was one of the exceptions. Any memory she had of her childhood were memories of disasters, failures and frustration. It could have been that she was never able to count her blessings because she did not recognise them. She had always found it difficult to appreciate a beautiful day because of the fear that it might rain tomorrow.

How was it, she wondered, that Andy had managed to convince her that tomorrow was probably going to be just as good as today — perhaps even better? The whole thing was a miracle. Even the weekend at Maidenhead was bearable, almost amusing. Andy had sailed through it with spirited enthusiasm which Sally found quite wonderful; he could deal with any situation. The family even *liked* him, and this somehow became a triumph for her because it meant that, against their better judgement — because she saw the disapproval in both their faces as soon as she set foot in the house — they couldn't help liking him. So she could take it that they actually approved her choice.

"Of course they'll approve of me," Andy had said when he suggested the visit. "I'll make myself irresistible to them."

"They may quite like you, but they'll never forgive us for getting married without telling them or anything." Sally was still breathless at this time with the enormity of the step she had taken. Well, Andy had taken it really; just swept away all her arguments and made them sound silly and childish and not worth considering. And of course he was right. She had to stand up to people if she ever was going to succeed. She was far too negative about everything. If only she could believe in herself a little more. He had said it so often, that the idea was beginning to sink in. He had started to convince her where no one else had been able to. She was immersed in grateful love.

He had insisted on the marriage bit. "I think we need binding," he said. "If we just move in together, then you are not going to get out of this disbelieving attitude. Thinking all the time that it's not going to last, and probably saying it too. And that's just the sort of thing that would endanger the whole relationship from the start. I want to make you certain of things, and I think getting married is the first step. *I* am absolutely certain that we are right for each other, and marriage will make you absolutely certain too. We'll get married and *then* we'll go and see the family."

Sally demurred, wanting him to convince her. "Do we have to? They'll ruin everything by being against it and I shall only get furious. We're so happy now, can't we just leave it for a bit and perhaps tell them much later. There's no real need to tell them yet is there?"

"Of course there's a need. If you keep running away you'll have them at your heels for the rest of your life. If you face up to them and show them that you are perfectly able to make your own decisions, then they won't be a threat any longer."

It was all part of the exhilarating dream she was having where responsibilities were deftly and painlessly removed, and she was being carried through life, shoulder high, by someone with whom she was deeply in love. It was a height from which she could not ever imagine herself descending. She could not, nor did she want to see tomorrow. And the way he swept all before him in his approach to Rosie and Hilary was pure genius, she decided.

"Wonderful of you to let me come, Lady Donovan. Sally insisted you'd want me to."

"But of course we would want you to come." Rosie held out her hand to him. Poor boy, he must be feeling embarrassed and frightened. She smiled at him and covered their clasped hands with her other one. "How nice to meet you."

Hilary stared at him without speaking, trying to fathom what had attracted Sally. Very good-looking, certainly, but a bit ordinary. Must have a strength of character somewhere there to be able to influence her sufficiently to take the step she had. He struggled with himself trying to decide whether to be glad or sorry to note the obvious transformation of his daughter. The look she had now reminded him of fleeting memories of her childhood; those rare times when she had momentarily seemed to forget her anxieties enough to be able to laugh at one of his corny jokes, or to enjoy bathing in rough seas, or to fling herself into his arms on arriving back from boarding school for the holidays. He had quite forgotten those looks until he noticed the warmth and sparkle with which she now regarded this Andy creature. Did he really merit it? Sounded suspiciously smooth to him. Couldn't ever imagine Sally insisting he should come and meet them. Much more like her to try to keep him away and at a distance. But she could have changed in more ways than one he supposed.

Andy turned to him, full of self-effacing humility. "Hallo sir, very honoured to meet you. If it wasn't platitudinous to say that I'm full of envious admiration regarding your career, then I'd say I'm full of envious admiration regarding your career."

They all laughed, Sally a little too hysterically, and Hilary resisting the tendency to respond favourably to the flattery.

"You're in the same line of business are you?"

"Oh yes, you didn't know? Sally and I met at Leeds. I'm third year so nearly through."

Hilary immediately had the distinct impression that Andy had married Sally in the hope that father-in-law Sir Hilary Donovan might be an asset to his career. He checked himself; this was just prejudice and an absurd assumption. But the instinctive dislike grew: that would have to be subdued as well.

Sally said very little the whole weekend, intent on letting Andy show off his own qualities. There was nothing she could say that could prove his worth better than he did himself. And anyway, the family would never believe her. She felt that he succeeded magnificently. The only uneasy moment was when Iffey and Caesar came down in the afternoon. She was suspicious that Rosie had asked them so that they could view him as a kind of exhibit A.

"Well? What's he *like*?" Iffey took the whispered opportunity when Rosie opened the door to them.

"Charming, charming. Good-looking and self-assured, and Sally seems over the moon."

Caesar walked away from them through the hall and into the sitting-room. "Sally baby," he said. "How could you do this to me when you knew I was only waiting for you to grow up? You bastard," he said amiably to Andy, shaking him by the hand. "Very many congratulations for landing the girl I love."

Andy felt displaced and displeased, because he could think of nothing clever or witty enough to say. There was a smiling freeze-up between the two men as they circled each other warily. But Iffey flowed into the room at that moment and engulfed everyone.

"Sally darling, I just can't believe this news, but how wonderful for you both." She kissed first Sally and then Andy and produced a parcel wrapped in pink tissue paper. "Just a little something for the home darling."

It was a very large Chinese embroidered wall-hanging, and Rosie gasped as Sally unfolded it. "But Iffey it's magnificent, must be worth a fortune." In her mind, she cast about as to how best to get Sally to leave it at home so that she could look after it for her. She imagined it bundled into a crammed drawer in sleazy digs.

Sally thought how inappropriate a present it was for someone who hadn't even got a home together yet. Typical of Iffey to give some priceless thing that only she could appreciate or have room to display. But it might fetch good money.

"Thank you very much," she said, but Andy went into rhapsodies, holding it up, studying the embroidery. "But it's *won*derful," he said. "Quite fantastic. And you must be Iffey, whose records I've collected since I was so high. I'm so very pleased to meet you in the flesh."

Iffey's laugh boomed out. "Flesh is a very rude word to use in my presence laddie," she said. "But I'll forgive you since you obviously appreciate a beautiful object when you see one." A smart one this, she thought. Much, much too smart for Sally. She glanced at Hilary and saw him thinking the same sort of thing in a refined, gentlemanly way. Poor old Sally, in the soup again.

Sally and Andy split up eighteen months or so later, just about the same time as Caesar met Lavender Corby.

Hilary and Rosemary had no idea of the split, as they had lost touch with Sally soon after she had qualified and moved into the Manchester area to join Andy. He had become involved with a small company who made puppets and produced shows for schools. "So worth while," he had told Sally. "It's great to be doing something that actually does some good in the world instead of just becoming another of the superficial drones of society, perpetuating the useless fringe."

"Why don't I come with you?" Sally had suggested, questioning briefly in her mind at the time just why puppets should be more worth while than actors. Primarily however, she was paralysed with the fear of his leaving her. "I don't have to finish this course for all the good it's doing me; I shall probably fail the finals anyway."

He had been at his most persuasive and earnest. "Darling no — I wouldn't dream of letting you. Spoil your chances just to be with me? Unthinkable sweetheart. I'll dash back here whenever I get the chance, and you can come to Manchester at weekends, and it's only another year, remember, before you can join me for good."

But the interims between work had been unsatisfactory, seldom coinciding and therefore often non-existent, and by the time her final year came to its protracted and leisurely close, Sally had long lost interest in what she was or was not achieving, in the tense anxiety of waiting to snatch back her transitory happiness. She sped to Manchester as soon as she was released. There must be some work for her, she had written endless applications and given Andy's address for replies. Just as long as they could move in together again all would be well.

But Andy had by then taken up lodgings with the six members of the puppet company. "Such a great opportunity," he told Sally. "We got this warehouse place for next to nothing and it means we can live in the shop as it were. So important to be on the spot all the time so that office and workshop and digs are all together. Just isn't really room for anyone outside the group darling. I couldn't bring in an extra body, it wouldn't be fair on the others. You do see don't you? And anyway it's pretty uncomfortable and very temporary because as soon as we are ready with the production we shall be off on tour. Much better if you can get some place for us to be when I get back. Will you do that for us?"

Sally stared round bleakly at the rest of the company who stood around awkwardly with strained smiles, and she saw that they all shared something which she did not. She saw that one of the two female members of the company did not smile, but kept her head low over the costume she was creating, and she knew immediately that Andy had moved on.

There was no fight left in her. What little she had mustered for the escape from Leeds left her as she looked at that lowered female head. The farce was played out: back to reality. And the reality was hard, consisting of loneliness, despair and social security, backed here and there by the inevitable round of waitress, cinema usherette and the occasional one night stand for a decent meal or a room warmer than her own.

The bastard! The crummy skunk! She had fumed and wept at the humiliation of not having had the sense to see through him from the beginning. Enough that she had to deal with that shame without submitting to the scorn of the family as well. So no going home until she had emerged from the abyss — if indeed that were ever possible.

Lavender Corby was largely responsible for the running of a slick and sophisticated glossy. She had reached quite a way up the ladder fairly quickly, partly through brains and a good degree, partly through knowing the right people and a great deal through having the ability to recognise a future trend before anyone else did. She recognised Caesar's potential almost before his first recording was off the press, and the article she ran on him in her magazine went a long way to clinch his early success.

She was as beautiful, as eccentric and as clever as Caesar himself, and being twelve years older had a good head start on him. Thus she was a challenge which he took up with enthusiasm, and in the heady days of his phenomenal climb to the top, she helped him to retain a modicum of balance in his life. They had produced two children together, though Caesar tended to think of them as another of Lavender's enterprises. Something done without prior consultation with anybody.

"Entirely my responsibility," she told him on announcing the news. "Thought it was a good time to do it before it's too late. It will give me more insight and thus much wider scope."

Caesar certainly felt very little responsibility before Scarlet was born. He was touring for most of that year and only managed to meet his daughter two months after she arrived. Having relegated the matter to one of Lavender's hare-brained schemes, it was only when he saw Scarlet, lying in her cot squirming, and living up to her name, that he was hit by the realisation that half of this small piece of humanity belonged to him.

"It's a sobering thought, Iffey," he said. "Whatever Lavender may say about my not being responsible is totally untrue. That hideous little object is my daughter, and I love her already. Now isn't that strange?"

"So you are human after all. Thank God for that, I was beginning to wonder if you'd caught a lethal dose of inhumanity from her mother."

She and Lavender regarded each other with hostility.

"It's not that she hasn't done a lot for you," Iffey said. "Even though you would have got there anyway, she did ease the way and incidentally gave me a good return on the money I put up, I will say that for her. We have to be grateful for small mercies, and looked at from one point of view, I suppose I must concede that Lavender could be considered a small mercy. But then I'm not really sure that it's good for you to have achieved so much with so much ease. Might have been better if you had had more of a struggle, like I did."

"Don't be so stupid you jealous old tart," he said. "I won't have a word said against Lavender. Nor of course," he added, "will I let her say a word against you, however much she tries."

"How hard does she try then?"

"Quite hard. You know, the 'tied to mother's apron strings' line, and 'you don't have to wilt in your mother's shadow, you're far better than she ever was' sort of thing."

"Bloody cheek and quite untrue."

"Of course it's untrue, light of my life. I couldn't ever hold a candle to you at any time. And by the way, I want you to come to my next concert, because it's actually going to be the swan song of Caesar and the Sperms, I'm going solo after that; got an album all lined up for Caesar Simeon, real music; all those songs I've been working on for the past year. It'll be a wow."

Iffey glowed in spite of herself. Though she basked, with great delight in Caesar's success, there was the occasional twinge of sadness that her own renown and perhaps her general usefulness were beginning to wear out. The horror round the corner of becoming a geriatric nuisance hovered menacingly. There was no way she would ever allow herself to be a burden to anyone — least of all to Caesar, so she had to make sure that she kept a firm hold on her marbles to ensure that he should never be so lumbered. The thought of it paralysed her.

So she accepted with great alacrity and only slight misgiving his suggestion that she attend the concert; it was just another of those moments in his life that she would take part in — like sitting through school concerts, Sunday church services, carol concerts, prize givings, school plays, another memory to be stored away. She refused the offer of the stately box, and milled round the auditorium with the packed collection of fans. Naturally she caused a sensation, dressed entirely in black satin, weighed down by heavy gold chains, bangles and earrings and with osprey plumes in her hair, but she overrode the startled looks, occasional jibes and unstifled laughter.

"That's my boy," she told them as they roared applause. "Don't you just love him?"

She pogo-jumped with the best of them, causing consternation among those closest to her in case they might be crushed, and she joined Caesar on the stage for a final encore. The evening was hailed as a sensation in the press the following day.

"With any luck," Iffey said, after discussing with Hilary the wisdom of such antics, "I shall die of a heart attack because of the size I am; and I would much prefer it to be earlier rather than later."

"Well you're certainly going about it the right way," said Hilary, "even though there seems to be nothing wrong with your heart at the moment."

"There's nothing wrong with any of me at the moment, it's just that I pray the heart's the thing that'll go first. Pouf, zap and that's that."

"That's what we'd all like isn't it?"

"Of course, of course. But whatever happens, I'm determined not to linger on and be a pest. God, that would be awful. Promise you won't let that happen to me darling?"

"What, you mean get in a good supply of plastic bags and whatever is the pill of the moment?"

"That's about it. Promise?"

"Old men die before old women."

"Well I'll do the same for you if I see you popping off into senility."

"Don't you dare. I wish to die in dignity with my sorrowing children round my bed."

"A, you're likely to be an incontinent, batty old geriatric so that B, your children are most unlikely to sorrow about you at all."

"In that case I'll be none the wiser, and I'm sure it won't do them any harm at all to have to put up with their senile old father for a bit; I've put up with them for long enough."

"I want to go out with all flags flying, Hilary. I couldn't bear not to."

"And you will, my darling, I'd lay a hundred to one on it."

"I wish I was so sure; already I'm deteriorating, can't hear so well, can't see so well, can't sing so well and I can't remember a bloody thing."

Hilary placed himself in front of her and waved. "Hallo!" he said loudly. "Hallo there — Iffey! Can you hear me? Can you see me? Now, think carefully, can you remember who I am?"

Iffey hugged him. Of course you had to make a joke of the whole thing, if you didn't, you ran the risk of becoming a bore even earlier than otherwise you might.

"I shall start by driving Caesar from the nest," she said, making the decision as she spoke. "He's probably staying on here because he thinks I would be lost without him, and that must cramp his style horribly."

Hilary looked at her with wonder. Did she really think the boy had her feelings at heart? Could she not see that he was using her luxurious surroundings and her good nature for his own comfort? He should have moved out years ago both for his own good and for hers. He was just taking care of number one, that was obvious.

"Only thing is," Iffey pondered, "he'll probably move in with that Lavender Corby, and I'm not sure if that's such a good thing."

"You'll have to let him decide that," Hilary said, thinking it was just the sort of thing he was very likely to do. If Mother stopped supporting him, then find someone else to do it. "You've just got to start thinking of yourself, Iffey, and what is best for you. Caesar must learn to fend for himself and not to rely on you all the time."

Iffey smiled at him. What an old fool the man was, not to realise that she would be the one to suffer, not Caesar. It was she who would have to learn to fend for herself not him. Silly old buffer.

"Why on earth are we still together, Hilary, after all these bloody years?" Looking at him, listening to him, understanding him, she found at that moment she really could not fathom the answer. It struck her as intensely amusing.

Hilary was startled by the unexpected question. "What?" he said, in order to gather his thoughts together.

"Together," Iffey said loudly. "Why are we still together? you deaf old bat. Why do we still jump in and out of bed like we do? Why do we still enjoy it? We ought to know better at our age, really we should. Seventy next birthday, it's positively obscene."

"Speak for yourself," he said. "And anyway, I'm very partial to a bit of obscenity now and then. You ought to know that by now."

"I suppose life might become a little dull without you," said Iffey. "So perhaps I'll take your advice — throw out the son and keep the lover yes?"

"Excellent decision," said Hilary.

22 Decisions

There followed this decade of sorting out, setting up and consolidating for all. It might have been a new exciting phase for Iffey, because she found every phase in her life new and exciting, but for the others it was the kind of muddled living that flies along at tremendous speed in the middle of one's life. Those years that disappear in moments, leaving very little trace behind except the feeling of where did it all go? And what have I done in all that time? For the young in this period, there was also the shock of seeing for the first time some of their contemporaries looking middle-aged, while for the old there was the ever-increasing struggle to remember what happened yesterday.

Rosemary was no longer happy with her life, though she castigated herself for being ungrateful; after all, she had so much to be grateful for. Everything she could have hoped for. She sat alone in the London house after the daily cook-housekeeper had left, and wondered why on earth they had to keep on two large establishments. Superstition really, she supposed; if ever they did sell the London house and take a small flat, then one or other of the children, and she thought only of Sally, would at once turn up and want somewhere to live. Not Tim, of course, Tim would never need any help from anyone; would probably consider it an insult to suggest it; the idea of staying with his parents would be totally alien. A smart executive did not sponge; it would have spoiled the image. Later, perhaps, he would build a granny flat for them both; separate from his own house of course.

Rosie was able to picture the extension in the large, well kept garden of their son's Elstree house: clean, bright, efficient, in antique style so that they could bring their own furniture. How ghastly. I'm being disloyal, she told herself. Tim was scrupulously fair, and would always do the right thing by his parents, but admit that he could ever need help — no, that was not in his nature. She tried, but failed, to feel pleased that she and Hilary had produced such a self-sufficient and confident son.

And Jonathan? Well, poor Jonathan was in constant need of support, but the difficulty was to know where he was in order to offer it. So sad that Tim's brilliance and self-confidence had reacted adversely on Jonathan, even though she had made a special point of treating both boys exactly the same; never praising one more than the other, never showing more affection towards either. She and Hilary had both been most careful. Extraordinary that Jonathan had allowed himself to fall in with such bad company.

But he just *might* turn up on the doorstep one day, she supposed, in the sme way that Sally just *might*. She told herself how lucky she was to have two establishments where she had the room to house her family if necessary. She kept her mind resolutely off the danger of self-pity; even though none of them seemed able to look to her for the assistance she was so willing to give, this should be a matter for satisfaction rather than regret.

She was knitting a sweater for Caesar because no one else wanted one, and she had to keep herself busy all the time. Always had been like that. It was so boring to watch television except for one or two of the more interesting programmes, and she found reading in the evenings in an empty house a little eerie unless she was in bed. There were the bridge evenings and the committee meetings — true, but the overall loneliness was frightening. My own fault, naturally, she thought grimly. I should be self-sufficient enough to enjoy being on my own. Iffey seems to be perfectly content, and she has been alone much longer than I have. I do have Hilary with me most mornings. How can I possibly complain? I see much more of him than normal wives see of their husbands. I am fortunate in the extreme. What more could I possibly want? And tears welled up and the constriction in her throat was positively painful. The real sadness was probably the children, she supposed. She made every effort to quell the guilt, or at least not think about it too much. It was very difficult for her to think about Sally at all because then she lost all control; just cried unrestrainedly.

All her life, it seemed, she had been dogged by this emotional lack of restraint. Just as though there was a great reservoir of tears stored up and always threatening to overflow. Though she prided herself on her ability to hide her real feelings when necessary, she was constantly being let down by this flood of tears so ineffectively dammed up and always ready to flow. At the back of her mind, she blamed Iffey who had been absurdly indulgent to her when she was a child. Had Iffey not positively encouraged her to cry during those first few dreadful weeks at boarding school? Just used to sit and cuddle her while she cried and cried. It was a vivid memory still. She should have been forced to control herself at that time, then perhaps she would not have to contend with this embarrassment now, in her adult life. It's surely not that I'm a weak character, she thought. I'm really quite forceful in many ways, and in control of myself. Have to be, to deal with Iffey's problems as well as my own.

But not knowing what had happened to Sally was such unendurable pain. The last card she had received said they were going abroad and would write from there, and then one or two phone calls, nothing more, nothing at all. She stopped the thoughts abruptly and studied the knitting pattern with deep concentration to take her mind away from the intolerable.

The ploy was not successful, these three lost children of hers could not be dismissed from her mind so easily. They constantly occupied her thoughts and filled her with anxiety. Tim was the one who could perhaps be called the best of the bunch, in the eyes of the world at any rate; and yet he was so obviously an unhappy, morose person, whose coldness was embarrassing. His whole family was cold, his wife, Donna, the children, strange, lifeless little creatures who never seemed to smile, living out their rich, luxurious life in an aura of disinterested, boring unapproachability. She sometimes found the profligate, drunken Jonathan and his partner of the moment, better company.

But then the continuous anxiety she felt about Jonathan's exploits was also an unbearable burden. She never knew when the police were going to turn up at the door, having found her son in the gutter. She raged inwardly against the unfairness of the whole thing. They had taken so much care to give their children the best, most secure upbringing; so how was it possible for the results to backfire in this way? And there was Iffey — she tried not to compare, but it was really impossible — with all her irresponsibility, producing a prodigy, who was still having everything all his own way.

She curbed her resentment sharply, reminding herself that there was really no comparison. Caesar might be a successful prodigy, but he was an impossible character. Wildly eccentric, constantly making a fool of himself in public; his crazy exploits continually written up in the press; immoral and selfish to a degree, just as she had always prophesied he would be.

One of the regular waves of despair flooded its way slowly through her, leaving death and destruction in its wake, and she allowed herself to cry, giving way to great sobs and moans and groans because she knew she was alone and could do as she liked. Was this then what she liked? What she chose to do when there was no one else to think of other than herself? Thank God Hilary would be back soon from the theatre. He was her rock; without him she would die.

Hilary came home to find her in a state of depression and hiding it up with some extremely bad acting. Unforgivably, he felt tense with irritation and thought how this anger would have been instantly dispelled by Iffey, who would have had food, drink and herself lying in wait for him.

"Hallo darling," Rosie made a little rush towards him and took his stick and scarf. "I have your favourite ready and waiting on a tray. Come and sit down and relax. How was it tonight? All went well?"

He could have strangled her. "Thank you darling. How very comforting to be spoilt like this."

This was real life, after all; the other was the fantasy. It wasn't as if he could discuss it with Iffey either because that would have been only just short of treason. Rosie would die of shame if she thought her shortcomings were talked about to Iffey. She thought she was the strong one on whom Iffey relied.

What would Rosie die of if she knew the whole story? Hilary only occasionally allowed that question to escape. It flashed in and out of his mind now, far too quickly to do more than register cursorily. For all her self-denigration and lack of confidence, Rosie still considered herself infinitely superior to the down-trodden, unfortunate Iffey. Almost a servant and mistress situation, Hilary thought suddenly with surprise. What an extraordinary simile! He let fly an explosion of laughter, which he realised was most inappropriate.

Rosie picked it up at once, at first hurt and suspicious that he should not have guessed her mood in spite of the brave face, and then controlled and smiling. "You're always so wonderfully cheerful," she said. "Such a tonic for me after a boring day." Did that sound too much like a complaint? Just in case, she added: "Mrs Smith and I had a real good turn out of the spare room today and amassed a great pile of jumble." Sally and Andy *might* arrive unannounced; you never knew. One had to be ready.

Hilary ate his supper off a tray and joined her in her depression.

"The time has come," Iffey said to Caesar, "when I have to admit to agreeing with Lavender Corby in one or two respects."

"Jesus!" said Caesar. "Whatever brought that on?"

"I think you're sufficiently a person to live on your own, so you ought to start looking for a flat."

Caesar grinned, "Such psychic intuition you have. It was only the thought that you wouldn't like it that stopped me bringing up the question."

Incredible how their thoughts merged. How could she have known about his anxieties of the past few weeks? The desire to move out without hurting her feelings. He had surely not given anything away?

"I realised that, fool," said Iffey. "But I'm not ready to make the move into a home yet. Don't think that. I can't wait to get this place to myself."

They both knew the distress of the split could not be brought into the open for fear of the sentimentality that might make it visibly obvious with weeping and lamentation. Everything must be kept on a buoyant level.

"Sure you won't pine, mountainous Mama?"

"Of course I'll pine. End of an era isn't it?"

"You'll never be able to find your glasses or remember appointments or decide which dress to wear."

"And you won't have any clean clothes to put on."

"Oh I shall employ slaves to do that."

"And incidentally, when I said living on your own, I did mean living on your own, not just moving in with that Corby woman."

"Not that it's any of your business who I live with or have living with me, I have no intention of sharing. Not on a regular basis anyway. If my lovers can't afford a place of their own then I shall drop them immediately."

"What about finance? Do I have to lend you vast sums?"

"Darling mother, I keep telling you, you no longer have vast sums to lend. My money is starting to roll in very nicely and Lavender pays generously for my services."

Iffey eyed him with amusement, wondering exactly what he meant.

"We complement each other very well," he said. "She's rich and clever and I'm clever and rich. And we are both good business persons. You shouldn't resent her."

"I don't resent her, and as long as you are both equally capable of taking advantage of each other, then I think the relationship is good for both of you. I just don't want her to take over my role of supporter, protector and controller of your life."

"I promise she won't. You will always be my favourite lady."

Caesar jumped up from the lunch table to dispel any embarrassment likely to be caused by sentimentality. "So I'm off to the estate agents. Want to come with me?"

"Of course not, I should only influence you and get annoyed because you won't like the places I do. But I'd like to help you make up your mind when you think you've found something."

She shut her eyes when he had gone and tried to pull herself together, and when that didn't work, she allowed herself the indulgence of a good cry so that the scene might be cleared for her to set out on the way ahead.

There was no way, Sally thought, that one ever recovered from disasters. I might learn something, she mused, sitting on her one chair in her cheap rented room in Manchester. I suppose I might forget the worst of the pain, I do sometimes become interested in other things or other people, but disaster, or loss, or sorrow remains with you for ever and tears at your heart whenever it surfaces. So many disasters in my life, they crowd out other things, like pleasure and laughter and enjoyment. Much too much disaster, it constitutes nine-tenths of my life, leaving only that small ten per cent for the business of living.

She read about Caesar's successes in the newpapers and saw him perform on television. She positively abominated the type of punk music he played. All put on, she thought to herself. Caesar would never, never enjoy that sort of cacophony. He was a musician, as far as she remembered, and this rubbish was not musicianship. Why should he be exploiting this sort of thing if it were not just in order to get his name in the papers? Would he sink so low? Presumably, she thought. What a shit.

She saw him exploding with delight and satisfaction and virility with every movement he made. He certainly knew how to pull the masses. Even Iffey she saw on television singing with her son in one of the programmes, being interviewed, being praised, being applauded. She found it sickening. I suppose it's just jealousy, she thought, but I feel I hate them both, sometimes I even wish them dead. But that's despicable, surely. Perhaps I don't hate Caesar, I only hate Iffey who's so puffed up with pride over this ridiculous son of hers. Making a spectacle of herself by joining him in his distorted shambles of what he mistakenly terms performances. It's not Caesar's fault, it's just that he's not a person in his own right, merely a puppet, created by Iffey and made to think, work and be by her efforts alone. It's that that makes me hate Caesar as well. He's just Iffey's image, nothing more. And all she wants for him is vulgar publicity; she was forever flaunting his so-called brilliance as a child, and he's still allowing her to do the same thing now. It made her puke.

On the other hand, she read of Hilary's career with pride and satisfaction. It was probably the only thing that did give her satisfaction. That and the fact that she had never relied on him for anything. Unlike Caesar, she had made her own way in life. There immediately followed a flood of despair because of the absurd analogy of Caesar's life and hers. Even though she had managed to satisfy the examiners that her dramatic talents were adequate, the colours with which she passed the test did not actually fly. There had been no paid work for her in the theatre since leaving the School and she kept herself alive by waiting, washing up, sweeping up, stacking shelves. Even that was never a success for long. Her unhappiness made her silent, surly and almost unemployable. Jobs lasted no longer than affairs; she went into them without hope and came out of them with yet more proof of her inferiority.

But then, in the way things sometimes happen, she met up with Terry Banks who reminded her of Andy, which should have been the very last thing that attracted her to him. But was I actually attracted? she asked herself. It had been so long since I felt anything for anybody, even the ones I went to bed with more than once, it was like being paralysed, just no feeling at all. Why Terry was different I have no idea. Could have been because he was obstinate and wouldn't give up even when I didn't respond. I just went through the motions in a way I'd got used to, and I remember that first day he came back to my place he actually slapped me and told me to wake up out of this cold sleep I was in and think about giving value for money.

I got furious at that because I resented being termed a slag — though in truth I was one when things got really bad. I told him to get lost there and then and said if he wasn't able to rouse me out of the disinterest I felt, then it was his fault and not mine. That made him quite mad too, so he pulled out all the stops, and for the first time since Andy I was knocked sideways and we had a fantastically wild night.

It turned out that he was pretty well off too and had just broken up with his last girlfriend with whom he'd been living since his divorce, so we sort of fell for each other in a weird sort of way, first of all because of the sex, which continued to be quite superb, and for me he was really heaven-sent because I started to eat properly and live properly and have some decent clothes and everything. And then, having someone who liked me — loved me he insisted — thought me attractive and sexy, oh it did wonders for my ego. Couldn't believe it was happening, and was on tenterhooks for ages in case it stopped.

But we really did care for each other; I was quite mad about him. Partly through a sort of gratitude I suppose because of how he had dragged me out of the gutter, but it was much more than that, we were wild about each other, I can't actually fathom why. Just one of those things. So I moved into his flat which was pretty good because he worked for television and was quite well paid. We were both still married to our exes but we didn't bother about that even when I got pregnant. The whole affair was so whirlwind and violent and we didn't get much time for anything other than work and sex.

Things went a bit wrong over the pregnancy and Ben's birth. Terry got impatient and jealous and therefore rough, but he adored Ben and the sex troubles ironed themselves out again until Emily was on the way, and then it really got rough. I suppose when there was so much violence in his love-making, one would have to expect it in his ordinary life as well. It didn't show up when I was able to take and enjoy the sex, but when babies got in the way and especially when I was feeding, then all hell broke loose. But we did have five fantastic years for which I shall be ever grateful.

I was even able to get in touch with the family again, though I never let them know where I was. Pretended I went abroad in fact; said I was touring all over the place and always on the move, but I did tell them about Terry and the kids. I telephoned them now and again without ever giving my address or number, so they couldn't check up on me or anything. Kept up the pretence I was abroad — Yugoslavia I said — which was sometimes quite difficult because they said things like 'But you sound so near', and the kids occasionally got close to giving it away. Quite a good thing, as it turned out, that I did keep in touch, because when things became impossible, I did at least have somewhere to run to.

And you know I was desperately sorry to leave the bugger, would you believe, because he'd given me more than a good time. He had somehow restored me and I'll always be grateful for that, but I was pretty certain, if I had stayed, he would have done me in, and I couldn't let that happen to the kids could I?

23   *Removals*

The flat that Caesar and Iffey had finally chosen for him was a studio extension built in the garden of a rambling old house near Clapham Common. "Disgusting district," Iffey had grumbled. "I shall never get used to trundling out here to visit you."

"That's why I chose it, silly, that and so that I can live among my black brothers who can't afford Holland Park. Got to get back to my roots, haven't I?"

"Listening to your music I would have thought you were already well on the way."

"Dearest ignoramus, I'm not into reggae, or only very superficially. You are a disgrace not to have encouraged my ethnic background you know. I could probably report you to the Council for racial bias."

"Oh fiddle, don't carp. Where was I to get ethnicity I'd like to know, when I was brought up as a daughter of the British Empire? No way was I going to throw myself on the mercy of my black ancestors. Where would that have got me? By the time you were born I'd managed to succeed in spite of being only half-white."

"Being black these days is a positive advantage in our profession. Trouble is, I'm insufficiently black, I should feel disadvantaged, yet I don't."

"Well I did when I was young, so let that salve your conscience. It made me so mad that I was more determined than ever to succeed, so it probably did me good in the end."

Caesar stopped the car. "Well this is it," he said. "Has all the mod cons I want, like seclusion and space, I think it's ideal. On its own and only just connected to the main house, so that I can play my piano and indulge in all my strange sexual practices and smoke my pot and take other hallucinatory trips to my heart's content. And also, it's really a miniature of our place isn't it? See how reluctantly I relinquish the ties?"

"All very abnormal; and incidentally, if I really thought you were deep into drugs I would probably get hysterical and go into a decline; but I suppose any normal child would have got really hooked by way of rebelling against the overpowering influence which I'm supposed to be. You ought to have rushed out and squatted in a council flat in Brixton to show that you are at last breaking free of the white middle-class stranglehold I have exerted upon you. All offspring are meant to defy their parents like that."

"Clichéd claptrap, I shall never break free of you, will I? If I did, I should probably sit in a corner and die quietly."

"Show me over then. You should have had a father, he'd have driven you out with far more force than I could, and probably beaten you to within an inch of your life, which I'm sure would have done you a tremendous amount of good." She already felt that the replica of her own studio in miniature and in Clapham was just another cosy part of their shared home. "I promise I shall never visit you unless I'm asked, nor shall I ever disapprove of whoever you have staying here for however long — unless it's Lavender Corby of course."

"Idiot; Lavender won't be able to stand this place for more than a couple of nights at a time, it's far too primitive. Two miles west of Kensington is a foreign land to her. I look on this as my temporary place of work, and the recording studio is just down the road. Perfect I call it, got the mortgage and all."

So began the new, separate existences, which were actually not far removed from the shared experience. Instead of meeting occasionally at breakfast and supper, they used the telephone to communicate, and found they discussed more things at greater length that way. The joy of having her home entirely to herself struck Iffey with a surprising sense of release which was quite unexpected. She liked the absolute certainty of the locked door and the empty house. "It's only us," she said aloud to the birds and the cat. "We only have ourselves to please, and I can talk to you out loud because there's no one here; I can talk to myself; give vent to eccentric moans and groans and shrieks, and go to the bog with the door open. I can eat when I'm hungry and not bother to go out and buy extra in case Caesar wants a meal." The pleasure of being able to act completely selfishly without thought for anyone else produced a sense of voluptuous sin that she found most refreshing. Was this merely a mental dishonesty to offset the pain of the ending of their way of life up till now? It was possible.

Caesar furnished much of his flat with extraneous pieces of furniture that Iffey had bought and crammed into her studio at various periods even when there was no more space.

"You don't need this, mother dear," a Louis Quinze bureau in the conservatory.

"But I keep old receipts in it and my secateurs and gardening gloves."

"So we'll have a big turn out, shall we?"

"Well you'll have to do it, you know I can't throw anything away."

Caesar did the sorting, which took several weeks, particularly because Iffey fought doggedly to keep everything. But in the end, when his flat had been furnished, and bills, business letters, Christmas cards, receipts and cheque stubs, some twenty years old, had finally all been burned, she looked round her still opulent surroundings with a certain surprise. "You know I had quite forgotten that painting, and this piece of brocade, where in heaven's name did I get that?" She put her arm round his neck. "I realise that you are an acquisitive monster and have denuded your poor mother of all her priceless treasures, but it *does* look rather nice, doesn't it? Positively bare of course, but the few things you have left me certainly show up to great advantage."

"Acquisitive monster nothing," he said. "You can't take it with you they tell me. And I wouldn't have taken at all kindly to sorting through all this stuff when you die, thinking all the time how you had far too much to appreciate while you were alive. It would have been horribly depressing."

The thought of her dying was allowed to surface in his mind for a very brief moment. Because it was going to happen. Possibly quite soon now. Could happen any moment, today, tomorrow, any time at all. Frenziedly he collected together newspapers and magazines and put them into a plastic bag. The grim inevitability of death relentlessly following life, and life having to carry on regardless. "I should probably have burned the lot then, or given everything away to the undeserving poor. How much better that it should have gone to the deserving rich — me." He felt suddenly very frightened and was whisked back to the memory of a dark bedroom with wind rattling the windows and making tree shadows dance crazily on the blind and of Iffey holding him tight against her to soothe the terror.

"Come on you old miser, let's celebrate with an extravagant dinner."

Lavender's flat was elegantly and sparsely furnished with everything of today, or possibly tomorrow, but certainly not yesterday. "I'm thinking of changing it all," she told Caesar. "To a wartime Forties' utility look."

"You can't," Caesar said. "This stuff is too new to be fashionable, you couldn't get anything for it."

"Don't be silly, of course I could. Most people are still trying to catch up with the todayness of this stuff after getting fed up with art deco. They'll buy it. And even if they don't, I can get the new stuff on expenses; they'll write it up in *Vogue*. Anyway, I shall probably sell the flat complete to the Americans and then I can start again from scratch."

"It's absurd to keep changing, just shows you're as superficial as your job."

"Perhaps that's why I'm so good at it."

"This," she said looking round at Iffey's belongings in Caesar's flat, "is positively morbid. Haven't you a mind of your own?"

"Your taste is for you, mine is for me."

"That's just not true is it? Your taste, such as it is, is your mother's — overpowering, like she is."

"So you can't appreciate antique furniture, so what else is new?"

"But Caesar it's dead, can't you understand that? You're surrounding yourself with the dead. You're harking back rather than starting out. Still clinging to Mummy who will also be dead before too long." And not before time, she thought to herself.

Caesar wanted to hit her but didn't. He was not absolutely sure that she was not right. Tomorrow frightened him even now. And it was because of that that he was irresistibly drawn to Lavender, someone to whom the past was done with and could therefore be rejected. He felt it was necessary at this time in his life to ally himself with an opposite outlook. Hers seemed such a brave point of view, though one he felt he could never, himself, embrace. Iffey's influence? Possibly, but he still believed that he profited from that influence, rather than being submerged by it. The fact that he did not break free was presumably because he did not wish to break free, and the reason for that . . . ? Laziness? Fear? Love? As difficult to ascertain as the reasons for not giving up heroin or gin or chocolate creams. Lavender ensured his equilibrium.

Rosemary viewed Iffey's studio with concern and raised eyebrows. "So tidy," she laughed. "Whatever have you done with everything?" A great improvement to my way of thinking, she said to herself, but whatever could have come over Iffey to make her get rid of so many things? Financial trouble? She started to contemplate ways of being able to help her out; could pretend it was a loan.

"It's my acquisitive son," Iffey said. "Turned him out of the nest and he took half of it with him. I'm just getting adjusted to the improvement of being able to see things properly again."

Rosie tutted angrily. "That's just typical of you Iffey, he makes off with dozens of your priceless treasures and you talk about the improvement."

"But Rosie, I had far too much, you were always telling me I was a hoarder."

"That's not the point. Why should you allow Caesar, who must be making thousands with his records now and could perfectly well buy his own furniture, why should you let him take all the lovely things you have collected over the years?"

Iffey shook her head. "Darling, any minute now I shall be dead, and then he'll get the lot."

"That's no reason for depriving you of your things now. We should be allowed to enjoy our possessions in our old age."

"You're such an idiot, Rosie. So blind sometimes. Can't you see how much it pleases me that Caesar likes what I like? That we can share so many things?"

Rosie preserved a hurt silence; liked what she liked indeed! More likely knew the value of it, much more likely.

"Don't sulk you silly woman," Iffey controlled her impatience with some difficulty. How was it possible for someone to be so over-protective? Just what she accuses me of where Caesar is concerned, she thought, but I am surely not as blindly silly as that?

"I'm not sulking," Rosie said sulkily. "But I'm sure Hilary would agree with me. He told me he came to see you the other day, didn't he say the same thing?"

"He didn't notice anything was different, never said a word."

"I'm sure he *did* notice but just didn't like to say so in case it upset you."

Not to realise even now how unobservant Hilary had always been. Not to have understood that blinkered, unswerving character that so typified him. It would have been amusing if it wasn't sad. To live all one's life beside someone and to have no real idea at the end of it who it was you were living with. Very sad, even if possibly more comfortable; meant you could make up someone's character, and then live your life keeping up the pretence, so that you were never disillusioned.

"It's just", Rosie continued, "that we, Hilary and me I mean, have always had this distaste for children taking their parents completely for granted and preying on their generosity. We believe children should be made to feel they are in charge of their own lives. Otherwise how can they be expected to stand on their own feet later? One thing our children have never done is to expect anything from us by right. They would never take anything for granted, much too proud."

Iffey looked at her with amazement. Naturally, one did not say 'and look where that's got Sally and Jonathan', because Rosie was one's best friend, and the reminder would be unthinkable. It was possible that the same thought had crossed Rosie's subconscious at the same moment, because she carried on in a different direction.

"Sally telephoned the other day," she said with a relaxed smile. "It's wonderful how happy she seems with this new man, Terry. Such a relief to me, as you can imagine. The two babies sound lovely; they speak to us sometimes on the phone. It's really surprising how clear it sounds, she said they were touring in Yugoslavia at the moment." There was a brief uncertainty in her voice. "It sounded just as though they were in the next room."

"Does she say anything about coming back?"

"Oh no, they are obviously doing well over there. We wanted to send her the money for a holiday over here, but of course Sally won't hear of it."

Iffey pondered on the innate pleasure that shone through Rosie's statement and compared it with her own pleasure at being able to share thoughts, love and furniture with Caesar. Was it not ultimately the same thing? Turning disadvantages into advantages; looking on faults as successes. To Rosie, Caesar was a monster because he was fleecing his mother for his own benefit, while Sally was the epitome of unselfish moral fibre, refusing to be a burden on anyone. Remarkable how perception can be so distorted, and who was to say which conception was the right one?

PART FIVE

Back to the Beginning

Sally in Manchester packs her clothes in two large suitcases. Around her are boxes, packing cases, plastic bags and a back-pack. Take as much as she can carry at least. The hire van is a fair size. But it has to be done quickly, just in case he comes back unexpectedly. She doesn't want him to suspect so that she can avoid a final scene. If he suspects he will just empty the flat, and pretty well everything is hers. How ugly it all is and how humiliating. Try not to see herself running home with her tail between her legs. If only there was some alternative, but she finally had had to admit that it would be mad to descend to social security and a home for battered wives when home meant comfort and hot baths and a safe place for the children. And a possibility of work perhaps. Might have to swallow pride and get Hilary to help. There was really no pride left in her. If only they weren't such kind, drearily understanding parents it wouldn't be so bad. She hates their magnanimity.

Fiercely, she slams newspaper round a glass jug and forces it into a bag. They could all live upstairs on the top floor and be virtually self-contained. There was plenty of room in that London house and eventually she could pay, and Rosie would love to baby-sit.

"Will we have a bodyguard in London?" Benedict was five.

"Why on earth should we have a bodyguard?"

"Because of Grandpa being a famous actor. Will I be called Sir Benedict when I live with him?"

"No of course you won't."

"Why won't I?"

"Because you have to do something important yourself to become a sir. Do you really need to take your space station tent?"

"Yes of course I do, otherwise I won't have somewhere to live. What sort of important thing?"

"What? Oh anything — be a famous actor. For God's sake put

Emily's bricks back in the box, I've done it at least six times and she keeps tipping them out."

Her mind starts to seize up with anxiety and fury. How dare that bastard put her through all this? A waver of hopelessness surges through her. It's impossible. She can't face it. All this stuff to be packed in the van and supposing, just supposing he comes back in the middle of it. He might kill her. Oh God, don't think of it. Just get out, pick up the kids and get out now. If only there was someone to help, but he'd been violent to pretty well all her friends and they're now too frightened to do anything. God what a shambles.

"Watch Emily while I start to pack up the van. Can you do that?"

"Yes of course I can. I'll hit her if she moves."

She feels like screaming. "No don't hit her because that will make her cry and that wouldn't help at all. Be very nice and kind to her, and if she wants to follow me out make her think of something else by playing with her."

"Shall I build something with her bricks?"

"Yes, that would be a good idea."

"But then I'll have to tip the bricks out again and that will be one more time you'll have to put them away."

There was a lot to be said in favour of shutting children up in a sound-proof cupboard for long periods of time. She had never wanted children anyway.

But what is she going back to? Cloying pity and sympathy and everyone falling over backwards in their attempts not to say I told you so? It was only to get away from them and their pious respectability that she'd teamed up with Andy all those years ago. He was so sure of himself and so smooth, unlike Terry who just bulldozed his way through life relentlessly. Andy had been a breath of fresh air in the staid, successful and smug sort of surroundings she'd been brought up in. The wise, wonderful Rosemary, whose life was lived for others and the pompous, self-satisfied Hilary who couldn't put a foot wrong it seemed. No wonder their children were such disasters.

She, herself, was just a mistake of course, in the same way that her own children were. It was obvious they had never wanted her, though Rosemary would have died rather than show it. But it must have been infuriating to have their perfect little plans for a perfect little marriage with the compulsory two children up-ended right at the last moment with another little stranger appearing, unexpected and unwelcome. When brother Jonathan, at thirteen, had already been proving a problem even though big brother Timothy at fifteen had obviously started on his successful career, that of becoming a paragon of the conventional businessman. No, Hilary and Rosemary couldn't possibly have wanted another added anxiety that might well have put spokes into the smooth running of their lives.

And hadn't she just lived up to that early promise too. Insisting on the stage as a career against their advice. They had both wanted her to get some sort of a degree or secretarial training, just in case. But she would have none of it. Drama school or nothing. She was going to show them, wasn't she? She was going to show them that she could be just as successful as bloody Hilary wasn't she? Stop him being so pompous and pleased with himself if he had a daughter that was as good as he was. Then he couldn't be so smug and benign and condescending could he?

So here she is, a bloody failure all round. Failed actress, failed wife and failed mother, running back to Mummy and Daddy to be comforted, and looked after. Like Hell she is. All she wants is bed and board for a short time until she finds her feet again and then she can move out. Nothing more. No bloody sympathy. They'd got to get that straight from the first.

With Emily carrying two dolls, Benedict with a bear, a lorry, a football and a hamster in a cage, and Sally with the final suitcase, plastic bag and cat basket, they emerge into the street and Sally slams the front door without bothering to lock it. Let them burgle for all they'd find there, and good luck to them if they got there before Terry. Don't look back at disaster. Into the van, tie up the kids and get out — fast.

Sally's arrival in London causes chaos and confusion in the Donovan household. However much Rosemary believes that she can adapt and enjoy the immediate presence of part of her family, she finds that age does weary and the years do condemn.

Hilary does not complain, but the small luxury of having a

study on the top floor where he could be alone to memorise scripts, to write down thoughts is temporarily denied him, and it hurts.

"I think we must give them the whole top floor," Rosemary had said, "both for the sake of their privacy and for ours. After all, it shouldn't be for ever, just until she can pull herself together and find somewhere else."

"You must be really careful, Rosie, that you don't overtire yourself. We must try to make some sort of provisions in order to ensure that the situation is not a permanent one." The idea of Rosemary being changed from a practical, ministering angel into a harassed housewife, is worrying. Iffey's warnings hang about in his mind. But this is nonsense, Rosemary is very capable and always will be. She is enjoying this new challenge, thriving on it in fact. It's written all over her face. Strange how she still enjoys the idea of being needed by the children. Himself, he likes the position of being progressively less needed as time goes on. Setting the kids up, getting them off his back had been the aim. He finds it difficult to see why Rosemary cannot be content just dealing with his own dependence on her, which he had always taken every opportunity to emphasise, rather than searching around for further responsibilities.

"You should be contemplating a life of ease at this time old woman," he says. "It's the kids' place to look after you now, not the other way round."

"You cosset me too much my darling," she says. "I'm a big strong girl, and I just love having them here."

Later, she says to Sally, "I can perfectly well entertain the children for you while you look around for somewhere permanent," and Sally is at once irritated.

"Not sure that I want to look around at the moment," she says. "I rather feel that I want to sit back for years and years and not attempt anything at all."

Hilary's heart sinks, but it would be tactless to retaliate so soon. Above all keep the atmosphere good until she has recovered from the natural distress and shock. Poor wretched girl, what a mess she's made of her life. Must really try to get something going for her. Speak to his agent tomorrow, but must do it under cover so that she won't guess. He feels, quite illogically as he keeps telling himself, completely disorientated and upset. This is a sign of age and must be suppressed. Just because he cannot always get into the lavatory exactly when he wants to, and because the noise of children crying jars on his nerves, means that *he* is at fault, not them. Sally is down, so must be boosted, not nagged about the bad manners of her children. He puts on his coat and goes out for a walk in the park. Might drop in on Iffey.

"Pa doesn't seem to be able to take the children being here," Sally says. "Sorry if I'm putting you out."

"He finds noise difficult because of his deafness," Rosie says in conspiratorial tones. She wonders why she, also, finds noise difficult, because she is not deaf — well not very. Emily is clinging to Sally's knees, screaming to be picked up. Sally is trying to wash clothes in the kitchen sink.

Rosie moves in because she can't stand the noise, nor the fact that Sally is ignoring Emily. "Emily darling, shall we go and find a biscuit?"

"Oh *please* Ma, I do try to keep her off the sweet things, you know what my teeth are like, and anyway she shouldn't be rewarded for screaming."

A small flicker of rage shoots through Rosie as she clutches the shrieking, kicking granddaughter far more firmly than tolerance allows, and bears her out of the room. Guilt-ridden concerning the state of Sally's teeth, she carries Emily past the biscuit tin and presses the repeater on the carriage clock in the drawing room. Benedict approaches immediately to listen to the chimes.

"How does it do that? Stop yelling silly cow Em so I can listen." There is an immediate silence, and they both watch the golden wheels turning and the hammer striking the previous hour. "You can see it working," Benedict says, "can I push it again?"

Rosie finds his concentration and interest show intelligence well beyond his years, and notices yet again how strikingly handsome her grandson is. Almost too good to be true; completely beautiful. And such control over silly cow Em. She feels a great desire to hug him there and then, but restrains herself in case Emily might be jealous.

Sally is annoyed with herself for not being more tactful. It is really quite strange that, far from being received with the expected sympathy and overbearing understanding that would have been hiding their underlying satisfaction that all their worst fears had been realised, she finds herself surrounded with thinly veiled resentment and irritation.

It's really a bit much to be made to feel so unwelcome. Shows how little they ever really cared. But to vent their irritation on the children, well, that's unforgivable. Horribly selfish too, with this great big house all to themselves. Of course they have no idea how the poor have to live. She should have had them up to Manchester just to show them. They have become a couple of selfish old reactionaries, always had been she supposes. Been spoilt all their lives, that's the trouble, far too much success; takes failure to teach people how to live in the real world.

She shakes the clothes angrily and takes them into the garden to hang them on the line she has rigged up between the trees. She had seen Hilary's distaste when he saw it, but of course he had said nothing at all. Do them both good to come face to face with a bit of reality for a change. At the same time, she thinks how good it is to have some space to dry, other than in a drippy, steamy bathroom. She decides she might take the opportunity to nip out now that Rosie has got the children quiet. She hears her reading to them. Rosie loves doing that, and she did say she'd keep an eye on them.

"Caesar's asked me over to see his flat," she says. "Mind if I go? I haven't seen him for years and years, and he might have some ideas about a job."

"Of course I don't mind. We shall be very happy here."

Sally looks at her mother with a mixture of feelings. Seeing her sitting there, looking beautifully poised, like some *Vogue* model for the mature woman, a sort of Charity figure with her arms round the children, Sally experiences a stab of admiration which is all set about with a scarcely admitted affection. She's a pretty nice old girl really, but unbearably aged. Sally finds herself alienated on account of being nearly two generations removed. Rosie is much more of a grandmother than a mother. Can't be expected to understand or identify with Sally's age group.

Anyway, she had always been too devoted to the old man to have much time for her own children. He has always come first in her life, so that she's turned him into an old male chauvinist pig.

Sally swings on to a bus to find her way over to Caesar's flat, with a different set of emotions surging within her. Over the years that she has been away, Caesar remained obstinately in her thoughts, and she could not resist talking about him. Almost as though she was keeping him alive for some purpose. She had obviously felt that he was an important part of her life. Something she could never actually consider doing without altogether.

Terry had been jealous when she had talked about Caesar. It was possibly bravado that made her continue.

"If you're so mad about him, why don't you go back to him then? He's got all the money, that ought to please you."

"What do you mean, go back to him? We weren't lovers you know, I don't have any claim on his money."

"I find that hard to believe; you only have to read the papers to know about that man's love life. Why should he have made an exception of you when he's had nearly every other woman in London — and man for that matter?"

"You're paranoid. We grew up together, that's all: more like brother and sister. I haven't any other interest in him, nor he in me. Couldn't even think of it."

Was that completely true? She believes it to be; it was a sort of taboo. She dreamed of making love with him, but the contemplation in reality is shocking; something she could not admit to.

So today she sits on the top of the bus and wonders, because the heartbeats are strong and the excitement of anticipation pretty stifling. Not that she approves of anything about him — apart, perhaps, from his success — but what did she actually know about him now? What she read in the papers? Of course not, that was just monstrous media imagination. All those screaming fans, those mad photographs, the crazy costumes and hairdos. He'd always been eccentric, but now — ? He had sounded just the same on the phone. Weren't all the trappings just a part of his mad old mother's creation? She had turned him into something he was not, the old harpy. She had created some sort of *enfant terrible* to bolster her own ego.

Sally suddenly feels an elated sense of freedom sitting here on top of the old red double-decker. Back in London; back to her roots; back to the beginning and ready to start again. This was not the cringing return she had envisaged before she came. No tail between *her* legs, there is something waiting for her down here. No doubt about it.

The same sense of euphoria follows her right to the front door of Caesar's flat and straight into his arms when he opens the door.

"Sally! My darling! What an age. God but I've missed you. Like Hell I've missed you darling. Couldn't do a thing without you."

All so silly, but so welcome. A homecoming. "You fool!" she shouts back at him. "You know you haven't given me a thought over the past decade. But it's good to see you even so."

He stands back and stares at her. "Can't believe it. God, Sally we're so old — thirty-five next birthday, think of that! Verging on the frightful forties, do you realise? How do you cope with that? Look, look at my hair — greying at the temples."

"But Caesar it's pink, temples and all."

"Oh yes of course, I forgot, I only had it done yesterday. But come in, come in and have some champagne to match."

It's all as it had once been only on a different plane. When she had left he had not been such a success, only on his way up. And she on her way down. The pleasure freezes as it touches on her humiliation. But the champagne will make it better, just like Mummy's kisses — except that they never did, because Sally could never admit to making mistakes when she was young. Could she now?

They plunge together into talk, nostalgia, memories, gossip, laughter and a lot of champagne and Sally escapes from the drear into the dream, because this delight cannot last of course.

"You see I failed, just like I said I'd fail. You remember our last conversation?"

"No. Should I?"

She shrugged angrily. "I would scarcely expect it. You must be steeped in your own success."

"Completely."

"You always were wrapped up in yourself."

"So were you."

"I wasn't."

"You were."

"I wasn't. What's it like to be successful?"

"Frightening, and often boring."

"A likely story. I'm the one that's frightened and bored. I'm the failure, remember."

"And revelling in it by the sound of you."

"It's all right for some; I've been rejected by two lovers and the stage. A penniless, unmarried mother. Is it any wonder I'm down?"

"With all that experience behind you, you should now have all the attributes to make you into a real wow, an undoubted, undisputed wow."

Ridiculous how he could influence her; quite ridiculous. She tried hard to retain her depression, but found it impossible, and because her smile became visible, she covered her mouth with her hands. "I'm not laughing," she said. "I'm downtrodden and hopeless, and nobody loves me." She gave a shout of laughter and wound her arms round Caesar's neck. "Oh Caesar, you make me feel great!"

Caesar's emotions became suddenly and wildly out of control; "Ah Sally. Sally, I love you to distraction. Shall we crown it by going to bed? It would be such a new experience. I do feel so like it."

"No we shan't. We are friends, not lovers, and I am just not going to become another of your shocking little affairs that the papers talk so much about."

"Oh all right, spoil sport, but let's not ever lose touch again. I always knew we were vital to each other."

"Knickers, you never did. You never appreciated me."

"Nor did you me."

"This is true. But I would if you could get me a job."

"Of course I'll get you a job. You could either be one of my secretaries or one of my backing group or both. Can you sing?"

"Well enough."

"So that's settled then."

How easy it all was. Life was beginning.

25 *Depression*

How very strange to meet Sally again. How very strange.

He sees her out of his flat and pours vodka and tonic over a glass full of ice. The sight and sound of ice, glittering, clinking, cracking and reassembling as it meets the vodka in an outsize crystal tumbler, fills him with satisfaction. The hiss of the tonic and the bubbles winking at the brim; who said that? Keats was it? Or Milton? Whoever said it, it's exhilarating and reminds him of the Gordon's gin commercial. Could be a Keats commercial: Thou wast not born for death, immortal bird — to the accompaniment of the piercing, whistling monotone of the nightingale's song. He can see the picture. But what could it advertise? Shampoo? Clean, clear, beautiful. Toothpaste? Theme for song? It would be rather nice to direct commercials; he'd often thought about it, but all those dreadful production company people in their fake trendy clothes and hairdos — these he couldn't do with at all, much too pseud.

He moves to the piano and tries out a sequence of notes. No hungry generations tread thee down, or, alternatively, come thou goddess sage and holy, come divinest melancholy. Excellent first line. Quite a girl, Sally. A great feeling of nostalgic sentiment overtakes him. Quite a girl. But what, he thinks, is this unusual interest I'm showing? A girl is a girl is a girl. Apart from Lavender, that is how he has seen them. No flicker before; rather a studied uninterest, male or female; a cool appraisal, and then an almost artificial sex reaction which could be stimulated at will. He took great pleasure in fooling the media. Lavender was different because he had to fight to get her and struggle to keep her, so that was always an interesting challenge. But Sally? What *is* it with Sally? Could it be the titillation that she might be his half-sister? Was that the appetiser that made her so attractive to him? What idiocy was this? What did that matter? So this sensation, that was a mixture of sex and responsibility, was it fraternal? Paternal? Proprietary?

And what does she think of me? he wonders. These meetings that come after years of absence are upsetting. Worse, of course when you meet ghosts of the past in the street, unexpectedly, and you can't, for a moment, place them. To be caught off-balance not actually remembering them at all because they look so different. Or perhaps because you haven't thought about them at all when they weren't there, and the whole thing shows up in your eyes in that first flashed second of non-recognition. Not that I wouldn't have recognised Sally. She was like family, and she hasn't changed in looks that much. But living away from her for so long, I think I've probably got a false memory of what she was actually like.

When I opened the door to her this time, I saw, for a fraction of a second, this rather drab lady staring at me in quite a hostile way. I suppose she was feeling defensive. Perhaps wondering if she appeared much older than the last time I saw her. Which she did. Just that unguarded second before our upbringing and good manners took over, and genuine pleasure dispelled embarrassment. I stopped wondering whether she thought I'd deteriorated, and I was just very glad she was there. Delighted really and brim full of excitement so that I just clasped her and hugged her. So spontaneous it was, this feeling of *love* I felt at that moment.

He laughs out loud at the shocking idea and stares unseeingly out of the window. Hardly bears thinking about; switch the mind, quick, to childhood and the memory of it. The meeting with Sally, he thinks, took me straight back to the time when we fought each other and raced each other and climbed trees, black, dirty, London trees at the bottom of our black, dirty London garden full of privet and lime trees and ivy and London Pride. Was it all really so magical? Probably not, but looking back on it seems like looking back on heaven from the hell of now.

A wave of depression catches up with him in the way that it does every morning at four o'clock when he wakes to the realisation that he cannot possibly cope with life any longer. Why is it always four o'clock that I wake? he thinks. Whatever time I go to bed, I always wake at four. Is it that my sleep pattern is timed to change at that precise hour? Does some actual noise at that particular time wake me up? Do I have an anxiety dream at this moment in the earth's cycle?

He rings Sally on impulse: "I'll tell you why it's frightening to be successful," he says. "It's because I wake every morning at four o'clock with that awful dead dread feeling of hopelessness. The dream I cannot remember, but know that it was presenting me with an insuperable problem, one I could never solve in a hundred years. And that sets me off into the usual maze of insuperable difficulties I have to face tomorrow. Will the next album be successful? Are the songs really as good as I thought yesterday they might be? And if it's a flop, then might it not be the beginning of a slide into oblivion? I could lose everything."

"But Caesar, you won't lose everything, can't you see? You're not like me, you can cope with life. And in any case, now that I'm back, I wouldn't ever *let* you slide into oblivion."

"You? How could you stop me, you nincompoop?"

Her laugh seems to Caesar quite the most comforting and exhilarating thing he has heard for years. How *absurd* this is. He joins in the laughter. "You mean I shall overcome this slide some day-ay-ay-ay-ay."

"Deep in my heart," she yells through giggles. "I do believe . . ." They sang the last line together, exploding with laughter.

"O.k., o.k.," Caesar finally agrees, "so I am convinced you can stop my slide into obscurity. Thank you, darling. See you extremely soon."

So in spite of the fact that he might not have enough to pay the present outstanding expenses, nor to keep up with Iffey's extravagances, all was not irretrievably lost.

Monstrous, lovable Iffey, he thinks, who is sure that she is still paying her own way through what her men left her. Iffey who leaves all her business dealings for me to deal with because she feels ex-lover Laurence no longer takes enough personal interest; who has virtually entrusted me with her entire means of livelihood, and who actually thinks she is still keeping me. Darling Iffey, why do I love you like I do? His mind immediately takes off into the song. *I don't know why I love her like I do.*

216

Caesar stops himself thinking, puts a gold pencil behind his ear and plays the tune. Might do an arrangement; lovely, dated old song. He sings it through again, and plays around with the theme for a while.

Childhood was much easier, wasn't it? He finds he is playing the melody of Dowland's 'Come heavy sleep', and he moves to the synthesiser to give it harmony and a beat, and all the time he remembers singing into a microphone in a BBC studio twenty odd years ago and feeling proud and happy at having caused a stir. Ten years old and a star. Sought after for his singing ability. Singing with Britten and Pears; singing at Sadler's Wells; singing at Covent Garden; praised, clapped, cheered — success success. Life was full of success. It was all so easy.

So what is all this striving about? He presumably has reached a certain status, hasn't he? So why strive? To go beyond? Or to stay where you were? But to stay where you were meant stagnation, surely? And stagnation is equal to death. Far too depressing to dwell on such thoughts, so back to childhood, quick, and the memory of Iffey there all the time, laughing and happy and proud because her son was a genius. Better than anyone else's son; everything she always wanted. She was always there to support him when he quailed, to soothe when performance was not perfect; to sustain when there was doubt. His rock; the womb he could return to. It was all so safe then. So why the anxiety now? With such a secure, sacrosanct childhood when life was a series of exciting achievements, he should surely have attained some sense of self-confidence in his adult life?

The telephone rings, dowsing him with the shock of being brought back to now. He turns up the sound to hear himself explaining his absence on the answerphone. "Sorry, I'm out. Leave your name if you want me to ring you back."

"Oh bugger you," says the phone. "I don't mind betting you're just sitting there listening and hoping it's a fan who's fought her way through security to get your number. Well it isn't, and I want you to take Scarlet and Simon for Friday and Saturday, because the au pair's taken off and I've arranged to go out. I'm sure their grandmother would be delighted to help you out, only she won't take kindly to me ringing her to ask. I'll bring them round at tea time on Friday, so please see there's someone there."

It's Lavender Corby exercising her rights, and Caesar listens to her indulgently, slightly guilty that he should feel condescension towards one who equally demands his respect. They have shared a large part of their lives over the past ten years, attempting, often without success, to retain the greater part of their separate personalities intact. Lavender claims the children, but it is impossible for Caesar to disclaim paternity when they both look so like Iffey. He enjoys paternity more than he dare admit but shrinks from the idea of the responsibility of bringing them up.

The phone switches off, with business-like clicks and whirrs and Caesar writes down the first bars of 'Come heavy sleep' with the words 'Don't change my life you girl of black-faced dreams' underneath the notes, imagining Sally as he writes, and being transported back yet again by the tune to the stifling excitement of being accepted by grown-ups as someone to be looked on as more of a master than an equal. Savouring the memory of the shocked and delighted respect with which he was regarded by those who heard him sing when he was ten. What security! But now . . . ? Now, anxiety that the next album may be a flop, and then what? This dreadful certainty that he is approaching black disaster and ruin.

He phones Sally again because she has induced a very strange excitement within him, and because he wants to talk about the past, to stay there, to pretend just a little longer. "I was thinking about those Cornish holidays."

Sally adjusts to the pleasure of being phoned twice in half an hour or so. "I think of them too. Sort of hang on to them when things are grim."

"That rock pool at Treyarnon; you remember?"

"You pushed me in when I couldn't swim."

"Only because I wanted to show off my life-saving technique."

"You nearly drowned me."

"And then we walked over to Constantine on our own and the mothers thought we'd fallen over the cliff."

"And I got terribly burnt that day."

"If only it had stayed like that Sally."

"Oh God. Why so morbid?"

"You reminded me of so much. Will you come back and stay with me for a bit *now*?"

"No. You'd only bring me down to your level of misery, and I'm trying to escape from misery at the minute."

"But you've had the most extraordinarily upsetting effect on me; can't quite put my finger on it, but it's probably love."

"Don't be so stupid." She laughs at the idiocy of the suggestion and at the same time feels a glow of satisfaction that he'd bothered to say it; good for the ego.

"Well can I bring two of my children to play with your children on Friday?"

"So that we can watch the little darlings with tears in our eyes and remember how we were?"

"Possibly."

"Then was then, Caesar, now is now."

"Stop making quotable remarks. I'll bring them to tea."

"All right. Did you mean it when you said you could get me a job?"

"Of course I meant it. I'll arrange for you to come for an audition the next time I get together with the group. I think it's Saturday."

"An audition? Oh God, will they all resent me?" She remembers the time when she met Andy's colleagues for the first time and saw her happiness collapse in pieces at her feet.

"They're not the resenting type. If you sound all right they'll like you. And anyway I'm the boss."

There is a short silence as Sally bites her nails.

"You're biting your nails, I can hear the snap crackle and pop."

"What shall I wear?"

"Stop fussing. Just be you."

"But they might not like me."

"This is an irritating conversation. You never used to be like this. Do we have to put up with self-doubt and can't-do-it philosophy?"

"You may have to, it won't do you any harm."

Caesar puts the phone down slowly and sits staring at it. Has she become as boringly indecisive as she sounded just then? When he saw her again after all those years, the proverbial something went zing in the way the strings of Judy Garland's heart went. All very childish and silly, because she's obviously turned into a boring old bitch and not a long lost soul-mate coming back to share his life; what a ridiculous idea. He doesn't feel in the least able or willing to cope with a dithering appendage at this or any other moment. It brings up visions of having to be responsible and this time he rejects it firmly; keeping Mum happy is all he considers he is capable of in that respect. But he feels cheated of a juvenile, nostalgic wallow, and he phones Iffey to be comforted.

"Hallo darling, just wanted to check that you're still alive or if I can collect my inheritance yet." He holds the phone away from his ear to receive the bellow of laughter that follows. "How are you, you old cow? And have you seen Sally yet? I think she's become boring."

Iffey settles back into her armchair, full of the pleasure of being in contact with Caesar. "Sally could surely never become boring," she says. "Embittered perhaps, depressed perhaps, anxious perhaps, but not permanently boring. And you're pretty boring yourself when you're depressed."

"I'm never boring," Caesar says, thinking how untrue that statement is. "I'm taking the children to tea with her children on Friday, you can come too and we can all be boring together."

"Does Rosemary know?"

"Probably. I'm feeling all nostalgic this afternoon. Remembering what a clever little boy I was and what a great time I had then. Thank you Iffey darling. It was mostly your doing."

"Nothing at all to do with me, I just followed your tiresomely precocious lead. Still do, come to that."

Just what she always had done — been an unfailingly appreciative audience. She and Sally had always been there, Iffey to applaud and Sally to bring him down to earth with her jealous carping. Without Sally's carping, he possibly would not have made the effort to improve.

"Listen to the new song, hold on and listen." He puts the telephone on top of the piano and plays the lead in: "Don't change my life you girl of black-faced dreams," he sings and then extemporises on for several minutes.

"I'm not sure," Iffey says when he picks up the phone again, "that I don't prefer the original Dowland."

"You don't appreciate me," says Caesar. "O.k. so I plagiarise a little here and there. But no one will recognise the original when I've finished with it, and it's such a great tune." He is childishly disappointed, and decides to scrap the whole thing.

"I love it," says Iffey, picking up his thought, "really I do. Finish it and play it to me then. You know I'm a push-over for everything you write anyway. You'll have to go elsewhere for an unbiased opinion."

"Who wants an unbiased opinion? I come to you for approval so that I don't get too depressed."

"Are you depressed?" Iffey's heart beats uncomfortably quicker. "Why are you depressed?"

"I'm not depressed, idiot lady; don't leap to conclusions. I'm as happy as Larry whoever he may be, and I'm in the middle of making a fantastic album which will bring me in lots of lovely lolly, and if Sally's any good I may take her on as a back-up singer."

Of course things are going well. Of course Sally isn't boring. Of course he is still a success.

26 *Productions: 1988*

So there they were, back at the beginning again, Iffey, Hilary, Rosemary, with appendages Sally and Caesar — Tim and Jonathan had, by this time, become foreigners who paid occasional visits and were entertained, but they did not belong. Rosemary and Hilary never did find out that Sally had not been abroad; Caesar did, but he didn't tell, not even Iffey, because he knew Sally would be distressed to be found out in such a lie when she had taken such pains herself to conceal it.

There was a great feeling of beginning with Iffey and Caesar and Sally, and a great feeling of ending with Hilary and Rosemary. Not that that necessarily drove them apart, though it did divide them a little into young and old, with Iffey being in the young group. A great deal of fuss was made over her eightieth birthday with national acclaim, television programmes and interviews galore. She delighted in the furore.

Six months earlier, Hilary had been equally fêted for the same reason, but in slightly more elevated manner.

"Amazing really," Rosie said, "how Iffey got almost as much coverage as you did. But I suppose she was always very popular with the general public."

"Meaning I wasn't?"

"No, of course I don't mean that you old silly, but when someone appeals to specialised taste like Iffey does, they don't seem to me nearly as important as people like you who's a national figure after all."

"I don't think I'm any more national than she is, my dear, and it's nice to think that we both appeal equally isn't it? You don't begrudge Iffey her popularity, surely?"

"How could you be so unkind as to suggest that?" Rosemary went very pink and angry at such a criticism. "It's just that I find it — well — a little unfair that you should not get slightly more kudos than she does, because I think you deserve it." She was angry with herself for not being able to explain her feelings better, and more especially with Hilary for not understanding at once what she meant. For some reason she was being shown up in a bad light, which was extremely unjust.

"Personally," Hilary went on, "I am delighted that I should be so celebrated for what I've done. I find it very gratifying. A flattering close to an active life I would say."

Rosemary felt a chill at the finality of the remark. "Stop talking as though you were dead," she said.

"As good as," Hilary reminded her.

On Iffey's birthday, Caesar and Lavender organised an impressive birthday party for her. "It's all very well having the nation celebrate your birthday like this," he said, "but I don't see why that should prevent us having a nice family affair as well."

"The family consists of you and me."

"Well — we'll ask a few friends shall we?"

"Better have it here at my place if you start asking your friends."

"They would tend to swamp my pint-sized hovel, it's true. But Lavender has decided she wants to organise the whole thing, merely to show how good she is at organising parties of course. So

I shall let her *think* she's doing it, but naturally, it will really be my show. You won't have to raise a finger."

Iffey was pleased. She enjoyed the company and plaudits of Caesar's friends and colleagues. "Don't know how you put up with them," Rosie once said to her, "always fawning around you and trying to cash in on your success, seeing what they can get out of you."

"But I get so much from them," Iffey protested. "Much more than they could ever get out of me, a tired old has-been."

"You a has-been? Iffey dear, don't be absurd. You are a star and they are just superficial upstarts."

Iffey was startled to hear Rosie apply the star title; she had never done that before. "Several of them are rather successful upstarts," she said.

"But they won't last," Rosie argued. "Here today, gone tomorrow, whereas you are still going strong. Just look how much acclaim you've had over the past few weeks, you shouldn't be swayed by the flattery of these pretentious clowns of the pop culture world."

Iffey realised she was having a dig at Caesar; poor Rosie, it must seem so unfair to her that darling, pretentious, upstart Caesar should have such enormous success.

"I know," she said. "It's impossibly immature of me to be so swayed. But I really do adore their flattery and the way they flirt with me and say I'm wonderful. It boosts my ego that they should bother. I love them for it."

Rosie shrugged impatiently. So undignified and silly of Iffey to waste her time with such people. And this party Caesar was organising, could she not see that it was entirely for his own benefit? She was so blind sometimes. "I don't think you ought to let them have a party here, Iffey, really I don't. I mean you know what their parties can be like with all the drugs as well as the drink. You're much too old to enjoy a party like that, it could be very nasty. I'm sure you'll regret it. Why don't you come over to us that evening and have a nice quiet dinner with Hilary and me? A special dinner I mean — why not?"

"But Rosie, it's *my* party — Caesar is organising it for *me*. I'm sure it will be a fantastic do, he's been working on it for weeks and it's going to be full of surprises for me I gather."

"Well I just hope they won't be more than you bargained for." Rosie had genuine misgivings. "I'm not sure if we'll be able to come, Hilary gets pretty tired these days you know. Can't take parties the way he used to."

What rubbish the woman talked, thought Iffey. Hilary was as strong as an ox and would enjoy the party as much as she did. It was Rosie who was not going to enjoy it. Poor old Rosie.

It goes without saying that Iffey was right; both she and Hilary revelled in the extravaganza which Caesar and Lavender had produced, while Rosie suffered silently and resentfully at the waste of money, the brash publicity, the noise, the riotous behaviour and the fact that she had been wrong in concluding that Iffey and Hilary would not enjoy it. She considered they both behaved with a distressing lack of dignity which showed them up as a couple of garrulous old octogenarians making fools of themselves. She was unhappily embarrassed for them.

"Darling Iffey," Hilary said breathlessly, as they made for chairs after dancing together, "how is it I seem to enjoy myself so prodigiously whenever I am with you? Even now?"

"Not so much of the even now. Why should we enjoy ourselves less because we happen to be old?"

"I would say that was obvious, you can't enjoy something if you can't actually do it."

"So thank your lucky stars you still can. There's no point in moaning because you can't climb Everest any more; who wants to anyway?"

"I seem to have lost a lot of the enthusiasm, not just for Everest, but sometimes even for existing. It's an effort to live these days."

"Stop complaining for God's sake and concentrate on the good things."

"What good things?"

"You and me for instance or had you forgotten us? I enjoy you as much as ever I did. The fact that the desire is perhaps rather more spaced out doesn't mean it's any less — better in some ways because it's not so frantic or so urgent and that means the pleasure takes you by surprise every time."

He took her hand in his. "Who says it isn't urgent?" he said. "Let's disappear upstairs, no one would notice."

"What and miss one single minute of my party? Not on your nellie my darling, you're not as attractive as that!"

The party seethed with celebrities; Rosie could be forgiven for suggesting that it might be considered Caesar's celebration rather than Iffey's, but then Rosie did not sympathise with, nor understand the simple truth that Iffey enjoyed Caesar's pleasure as much, and maybe a little more than her own. Had she realised that, the whole concept would have been to her yet one more instance of Iffey's absurd renunciation of herself in favour of her son, something Rosie considered destructive and dangerous.

She joined Iffey and Hilary, fighting her way through the thronged, gyrating crowd, away from the ear-splitting pop group sound, out of the alien mass of youth to the haven of the blessedly ostracised old.

She mustered a smile in order not to upset Iffey; must pretend to be enjoying it. "Too near the band," she shouted, keeping the smile fixed. "Being deafened."

"What?" said Iffey.

Hilary stood up and took Rosie's glass. "What sort of a drink?" he said.

Rosie shook her head. "No," she said, "I've had enough."

"Gin and tonic? Certainly," Hilary picked up Iffey's glass. "And the same for you?" He disappeared into the crowd.

Iffey laughed at Rosie's attempt to argue. "Poor old Hilary, deaf as a post."

"He's not as deaf as all that," Rosie said without smiling. "But he can't stand this sort of din any more."

"What?" said Iffey. "Can't hear a word through all this racket."

Hilary returned with the drinks. "Just met old Thingey over there," he said. "Haven't seen him for years."

"What?" said Rosie.

"You know, the chap who was in that play I did at the Globe, way back in the Sixties I think it was. What was his name?"

"Play at the Globe?"

"Yes, you know, had a wife called Phyllis or Philippa, lived down at — oh you know, the place on the river."

"You mean the ones we met when we went to — to — the ones we went on holiday with once?"

"No, not *them*, you're thinking of John — er — John — his wife's name was Daphne. No, no, this couple — Felicity, that was her name — they lived down near Bray, surely you remember?"

But Rosie had lost interest and was smiling grimly out at the mob all round her. Iffey heaved with laughter; what was she doing on this geriatric roundabout, for ever trying to remember names in conversations unheard, unheeded and unmemorable? This was one of the more calamitous and insidious vicissitudes of antiquity, this constant clutching at disappearing facts with the increasing knowledge that it will all come to nothing and that you will have to think up something else to talk about if you are not to seem senile.

Hilary caught her laughter. "I don't suppose it matters," he said. "I never liked him anyway, whatever his wife's name was — though she was rather nice I remember."

Caesar was instigating a drum roll in order to make an announcement.

"Apart from the cake," he said to a lulled rabble. "I want to announce my real present to my mother; it's a new song that I want her to sing in my monster, mammoth musical, that I now have the greatest pleasure in revealing to you all, and which is based very loosely on her fantastic career. Backers found, theatre booked, stars approached, auditions start next week and rehearsals immediately afterwards."

The announcement, and later the song, brought waves of riotous applause and much drinking of toasts to Iffey and the new production. She sat, as on a throne, all but drowned in tears and pleasurable emotion. Hilary was drunk enough to join in the rejoicing, but Rosie froze with embarrassment at Caesar's ill-bred lauding of himself and his mother on such a vulgar scale. It was unpardonable. And how could he imagine that Iffey could take part in a stage show now, at her age? It was an iniquitous suggestion and bound to give rise to ridicule and contempt. She was outraged at the thought of his letting Iffey in for such ignominy. The conceited, puffed-up little braggart. She watched, with continued displeasure, while Hilary led Iffey up towards the band.

"You can see I'm overcome," Iffey said to the multitude, wiping tears. "I think the only thing I can do is to sing to you one

226

of the corny old songs of the past." The roars of approval died down as the Jerome Kern romanticism flowed.

God . . . what was she doing? Rosie found it difficult to watch the spectacle. Was she making love to her son in *public*? Singing him a love song in public? She forced herself to look. But Iffey wasn't looking at Caesar at all. She was holding Hilary by the hand, and singing the song to him. "Can't help loving dat man of mine . . ."

Rosie's emotions took a leap forward and then appeared suspended in space as she took in the situation.

Iffey was in love with Hilary!

What an insensitive idiot I've been, thought Rosie. I never even realised, she must have been in love with him all her life and I never knew. Thinking all these things about her and all the time she was hopelessly in love. Oh my God — poor darling Iffey, yet another insoluble frustration in her life. Her sympathy for her friend welled up and engulfed all the feelings of anger and irritation with which she had previously been consumed. Iffey was once again the lame dog that it was imperative to help over the stile.

27 Show Down: Present Day

Caesar could never be certain of the exact time that he fell in love with Sally. There was a before-being-in-love period and an after-being-in-love period, but he could not decide when one ended and the other started. Quite strange really because the commotion it aroused within him was nothing like anything he had felt before, and he imagined it would have been easy to recognise when that sensation took over.

It was all so unlikely, anyway; there was no rhyme nor reason as to why he should have fallen for this unexpected remembrance of things past; because that was surely what it was.

"I suppose it's this dangerous feeling of superiority you give me."

"Thanks a million."

He sat down on her lap with his arms round her shoulders. "Don't be moronic," he said. "It's the infant feeling, not the adult one that I mean. You make me remember the baby confidence and belief I had in myself when I imagined that I could achieve anything; like if I jumped out of the window I could fly by just holding out my arms; that I could kill the baddie with one magic flick of my magic sword."

Sally found herself placed in the unprecedented position of nursing in her arms something completely dependent upon her. She flung her head back among the cushions in an explosion of laughter. "You idiot," she said, feeling confidently superior, and full of affection for this adorable infant on her lap. "Why do you persist in living in a non-real world?"

"Probably because the real one is far too unpleasant."

"Hardly unpleasant for you, surely."

"Superficially no, but this success, I mean, what do you do with it? And what do you do if it doesn't last? And where do you go from here?"

"Can't really tell you, being a failure myself, but place my feet on the bottom rung of the ladder, and I'll no doubt be able to enlighten you when I get to the top."

"Bargain?"

"Bargain."

He heaved himself off her lap and sat on the floor, taking off her shoes. "Hear that, feet?" he said. "I now hereby swear, therefore, to place you on the bottom rung." He kissed both her feet. "Always better to seal bargains with a kiss or kisses."

The kisses did not end at the feet. He was startled at the sudden intensity of feeling that unexpectedly knocked him, almost literally, sideways. Sex, that had always been a controllable and well-organised satisfaction before, at that moment became an explosion, over which he seemed to have no control at all. And to be so completely out of control was a new experience which he found surprisingly stimulating. Had he ever lived before this moment he wondered?

"It's important," he said, quite a long time later on, "to make absolutely sure that all bargains are sealed absolutely."

Sally was beyond speech at that moment.

★

228

In the weeks that followed, Sally and Caesar discussed when why and if they had actually fallen in love in any recognisable sense.

"You're so stupid," Sally said. "Of course it was that first time we did it. Oh God, that was something else, it really was. Jesus — it really did change my life."

"Well, yes, so it did mine, but is this, I ask myself, the true meaning of life? The be all and end all of existence? Is it nirvana or is it maya?"

"Don't be so tiresome you intellectual freak. You know I'm not up to that sort of talk. In more mundane language, I would say that sex is the great divide, and once you've got that under your belt and on a sublime level, everything else will fall into place automatically."

"Famous last words, my darling as you should know."

"Oh fish," said Sally, "if you're going to be insulting . . ." and she burst into song. "I'm in love with a wonderful guy," she sang, and waved her arms in the air.

"You're also miserably banal," said Caesar, "it's not even a good song. I suppose it could," he added, "have been that Wednesday when we were arguing about Iffey and her influence over me."

"But we are always arguing over that," Sally said. "I can't think that any one argument was different from another."

"You were being angry about putting Iffey into the show and I was saying that she was the whole point of it."

"We don't have to go through it again do we?"

"I thought it might remind me of why I fell in love with you."

"If you have to be reminded — I wouldn't have thought the fall was particularly significant."

"But it's deeply significant, can't you see? If I love two women who hate each other, I am bound to become a split personality. It never mattered with Lavender nor any of the other millions with whom I have slept because they weren't a part of me. We have got to resolve this somehow."

"I don't see why. I don't believe in love really — not *really* I mean — the word means nothing unless you quantify it. I just happen to fit in with your fantasies of the moment, because I need you, I want to be in your show — you want me in the show, we get on both in and out of bed, and there's a certain . . ." she hesitated and waved her arms about, "a certain magic, I suppose you could call it, about the relationship." She finished up rather sheepishly, with a near-smile on her face.

He grabbed her and locked his arms round her. "Magic? Love? Does it matter what you call it you stupid girl? I'm as much under your spell as I am under Iffey's."

She stiffened; "Nonsense, you're certainly not under any spell from me, and you simply haven't the guts to break away from your overbearing mother."

It had been a moment much like this one when Caesar had realised, with considerable force, that Sally would, in the future if she was not already, be a dominant part of his life. But Iffey seemed hostile. Surely it was not jealousy? Iffey wasn't the type. She had opposed Lavender, perfectly rightly as it turned out. Lavender was not a person to love, just someone to use as she had used him. Quite an amicable arrangement really, and it had produced two wonderful children, and the first steps of an extraordinarily successful career. Could he have done it without her? Possibly, but it would have taken longer and not been nearly so satisfactory. He realised that Iffey's disapproval was one of the spurs that had propelled him onward and upward with such obsession. Perhaps her disapproval of Sally would do the same. But he knew it wouldn't. It was different disapproval, something he could not quite fathom. It surely couldn't be the fear of the possible incest taboo? Could she consider that a problem?

"Why," he said to her later on that day, "don't you like the idea of Sally and me? I would have thought it was the ideal arranged match. Daughter of your best friend and everything."

Iffey looked at him and wondered if she should tell him. But why, for God's sake? It was merely an outdated taboo, invented to keep the community from interbreeding to excess, or even, maybe, to discourage the sexual abuse of children. And anyway, the chance was so remote, and he had always known of the affair with Hilary, he could perfectly well work it out for himself if he wanted to. She couldn't imagine that Hilary would ever bring himself to protest in public, however much the lurking doubt might disturb his conventional conscience.

The fact that she had never particularly liked Sally probably came from the old competitive spirit with Rosie in the old days.

Anything you can do kind of thing; all very sub-conscious at the time but none the less there, Iffey thought with the advantage of hindsight. But that did not mean Sally couldn't be absolutely right for Caesar now. She realised that she knew very little of Sally's character, so she could not afford to be critical.

"Perhaps I'm just jealous," she said. "You can't rule out that possibility."

"Never," Caesar argued. "You know perfectly well you don't have to be jealous of anyone. Are you worried because she might be my sister?"

Iffey smiled broadly. "And who told you that one?"

"Nobody told me, you old idiot. They didn't have to; it was an obvious deduction to all but those of plank-like thickness." It would have been far too unkind to add 'like Rosie'. The idea sped through both their minds simultaneously, and was drowned at birth. They both felt mortified by their malevolence.

"There's absolutely no reason to believe Hilary is your father darling." She laughed, "Well not much reason. It's just that I haven't got to know Sally very well since she's been back. But if you think you're right for each other, who am I to say nay? Much better than Lavender anyway. The only really good thing she did was to produce my grandchildren; I forgave her a great deal because of that. Does she mind?"

"Mind Sally you mean? Of course not, my drummer has moved in with her now. He's having a whale of a time and the kids love him. Sally's going to move in with me by the way, with her two; we're going to put some extra rooms on top."

So it was final then, all responsibility finished, off her hands and into his own life. Happy ending. And a soul-destroying gap left behind.

Caesar became blackly depressed and Sally reacted with fury. "God you're manic," she shouted at him. "Got absolutely everything going for you: all this money and backing and the musical coming along just fine except for bloody Iffey who can't sing in tune. What the hell's the matter with you?"

"I just feel a sod abandoning her like that. She shouldn't be on her own."

"But you haven't lived there for years, for Christ's sake. What do you mean — abandoning her?"

Caesar looked down at his feet. "I suppose I mean that I'm transferring to you, something I've not done before. I feel I'm killing her off."

"So it's about bloody time isn't it?"

"I wish you'd try to like her."

"So that we could be a comfortable little *ménage à trois*? No thank you. Lavender may have put up with that sort of thing, but I can't." She suddenly imagined Iffey as a mountainous monster-like creature, forever keeping her from Caesar. Her spirits drooped at once and she saw the whole relationship as hopeless.

Her voice wavered in spite of the aggression and Caesar heard her lack of confidence and trembling insecurity, and was torn between loving her for it and being angry that she wasn't really the strong, down-to-earth support he could lean on. He pulled her taut, resisting body towards him and held her in a tight bear hug.

"You sometimes make me feel like a big, strong protective male rather than a charmingly precocious little boy," he said. "Which means that you are very good for me even though I don't particularly like being the strong protective male. I suppose, though, that I should take continuous doses of you until I become a nice, normal personality."

"Keep taking the tablets," Sally said, kissing him, wondering whether she preferred the strong protective male or the precocious little boy, but realising, uncomfortably, that she loved them both.

"However," Caesar went on. "Reverting to my other favourite woman, I do think that Iffey seems to have somehow deteriorated these last few months, hasn't got the bounce she used to have. Must be my fault not having time to see her so much. But even if her singing is not quite up to scratch these days, the play is about her and for her and would be a travesty without her taking part."

"Her understudy is much better," said the strong, protective mother-figure he held in his arms at that moment, "and could sing far more songs than the one you've given Iffey to sing. It would be a more balanced show if you gave the character more to do, but of course Iffey's incapable of doing any more. It would be not only better without her, but you would do yourself a favour into the bargain. Everybody is just going to think you a sentimental nepotist if you let her wreck the whole thing." The brave words turned the monster Iffey in her mind into a helpless globular heap of abandoned detritus, in whose destruction she had been instrumental. What a shit she was.

"Leave off will you? She's in it, and that's final." Caesar shouted. The pain of suspecting the truth of the criticism was excruciating.

Hilary came racing round to Iffey's studio two weeks later.

"Sally says she's moving in with Caesar. Did you know this Iffey?"

"Yes darling; Caesar told me some time ago. Isn't that great news?"

"Why in God's name didn't you tell me? Why didn't you stop it? Why didn't you discuss it with me? We could have arranged something together. I could have got Sally on some tour overseas. What do you mean — great news? It's a disaster. It could be *incest*, can't you see that?"

Iffey felt the fury rising. "Stop dramatising, you dreadful old ham actor. I had no idea you ever seriously considered Caesar to be your son. *I* never did, and you haven't done anything during his life that caused me to think of you as his father. Why this sudden rush of paternity to the head? Perhaps a cold compress would cure it."

She put a drink in front of him with force, so that it spilt on to the table.

"This is no time to carp, Iffey. I realise I haven't acted out the role of a caring father; in the circumstances it was impossible; and anyway, you were vehement in insisting that he wasn't mine but entirely yours. I thought you wanted it that way — but darling, this is serious; if there's *any* chance of their being related, then we must stop it at once. God what a mess."

Iffey's exasperation collapsed into mocking amusement. "You are just too conventional to be allowed, dear old stick, and I absolutely and emphatically for*bid* you to throw your weight about in this absurd manner. Caesar is not yours, and you have

no rights to him and no hold over him. You are not his father —
understand?"

"How can you be sure of that?"

She took his hand. "I refuse to give my reasons, you're just
going to have to take my word for it."

"You swear?"

"Cross my heart and hope to die." Must get him out of this
ridiculous attitude. Must deter him from rocking the boat at this
late stage. What damage he could do, and all for some silly
convention. "It was Clement Brown," she said, inventing the
name as she spoke.

"Who the hell's Clement Brown?"

"One of my young clients of some thirty-five years ago."

Hilary was enraged. He felt suddenly empty and let down; a
great sense of loss. The whole thing was demeaning. She should
have had an abortion.

"Well, that's that then."

"Yes darling, that's that. I'm sorry if you're disappointed."

"Disappointed? What do you mean? I'm delighted."

Iffey laughed and pulled him towards her. "It would have been
nice to share him, I agree, but he is mine, you must understand
that, I could have shared him with nobody, and you have to let
me decide what is best for him."

"And what about what's best for my daughter?"

Iffey shrugged and got up to get herself a drink. "You will have
to decide that for yourself, my darling Hilary; so off you go home
and tell your story to the world and Rosie, if you really think that
the disaster of Sally and Caesar merits such confession. Perhaps
Rosie will be able to decide what to do. But I warn you, I'll fight
you tooth and nail every inch of the way with every cliché in the
book."

She sat down rather quickly, and took a large gulp of brandy,
feeling suddenly faint and ill. Could the situation be so
unnerving as to make her physically ill?

Hilary sprang from his chair. "Iffey, what's the matter? You
look ghastly. Does it really mean so much to you? Darling, of
course I won't fight you my love. How could I ever fight you?
You've promised me, after all, that my fears are groundless.
Darling," he put his arm round her and lifted up her glass, "have

some more brandy. Shall I call the doctor? I'm sorry I've upset you like this."

In spite of the painful unease she felt, amusement heaved inside her. What a good ploy to get round an impasse, she thought, as her heart pounded and the brandy made an effort to return from the stomach. If only it didn't happen to be genuine. The pain, that had been intermittent from the front of her body to the back since her birthday, returned with alarming intensity, and she clutched Hilary's hand.

"So you should be sorry, remember you're dealing with an octogenarian who has to be treated with extreme care and compassion."

"You're ill — I'll ring the doctor. Where's the number?"

Iffey drew a breath. Absurd how stress could affect one so physically. "I am not ill, angel, it was just the thought of all our worlds falling apart. Made me catch my breath for a moment, that's all. So absolutely no doctor; just the love and affection of my favourite lover for a few minutes and all will be well."

Of course all would be well.

28   Rehearsal

Iffey finally went to her doctor about four weeks later. It was stupid, she decided, to lie awake every night in an agony of fear, doubt and indecision. I don't really want to know, she thought, but I'm not going to be able to hide it much longer, so she made an appointment, underwent a series of tests, and came back to the doctor to have the knowledge she had nurtured over the past month or so, confirmed in the best possible taste.

"It's cancer isn't it?"

"Well Mrs Daly, there does seem to be some evidence — the tests do show, I'm very sorry to say; but there are many things we can do."

"Well if you're going to carve me up, then I would far rather you finished me off on the operating table. Can I rely on you for that?"

"Don't let's be pessimistic Mrs Daly; I don't think there's need for an operation . . . ."

"Too far gone you mean? But how could that have happened without me noticing it?"

"Unfortunately, this sort of thing doesn't always make itself obvious at the start. But our knowledge has moved forward in the last few years. So much can be done these days with chemotherapy."

"Suffer agonies, throw up all day and go bald you mean? At eighty years old? You must be mad. Good grief, and here was I expecting a heart attack or a nice fatal stroke because of my size. When I think of all that polysaturated fat I consumed in order to bring on some such thing; it's really most unfair. But take it from me, laddie, no way am I going to linger, I promise you that. How long do you think I've got?"

"Very difficult to say, Mrs Daly, until we know exactly how things are going to respond." Did he really have no sense of humour, she wondered, or was he just bored with dishing out all this unpalatable news all the time? "We should start the treatment straight away, my dear. I would suggest you come into hospital immediately."

Iffey stood up and towered over the small doctor, all but obliterating him. She was certainly not his dear. "No treatment, darling, apart from pain killers and exterminators. I'd rather die at home with the cat and the canaries and all my belongings. Couldn't stand all the clinical cleanliness of hospital, nor will I con*sider* tubes down my throat or up my backside. I may have been a fighter in life but I'm not going to fight death, not at my age. Just give me a good supply of dope and I'll manage on my own."

"I can only give you small amounts of pain killers at any one time, you must understand." He looked severe, like a headmaster.

The laughter rumbled up. "Oh perfectly, perfectly, dear boy. Avoid an inquest and a court of law at all costs."

Once home, she poured herself a half-tumbler of whisky, telephoned Hilary and tried to control the shivering. Extraordinary how it affected one, this inevitable news that you had awaited so long with growing resignation. Almost a relief that you don't

236

have to dread it any more; now you know, at least *that* anxiety is gone. Damnable that it hadn't chosen to come suddenly and unexpectedly. She had so hoped for that. But she bloody wasn't going to linger. Somehow or other she was going to see that she didn't linger.

"Got to start making plans," she said to Hilary as soon as she had broken the news. "You'll have to get me the pills; find out the best, I shall have to rely on you darling."

Hilary was stunned and not taking in what she said. Tears kept forming and making it impossible for him to speak, but he had to hold back because she needed support, not tears. But who was to support him? he wondered. The rock was being swept away.

Iffey was suddenly silent. "And then there's Caesar," she said at length, and she gave a long drawn-out moan of pain. "That's the worst thing; telling Caesar." She turned to Hilary, "I don't have the courage to do that. In fact it would be better if he didn't know; not yet, in any case. He doesn't have the stamina to take it." She became agitated. "Don't let him know, Hilary. Promise me you won't let him know before you've finished me off?"

Hilary was beyond remonstrating or even answering her and she was silent again for a moment.

"Whatever we do," she said slowly. "We mustn't spoil the show. I have to go before it opens, then it could be a grand memorial and make everyone sentimentally happy." She took Hilary's hands in hers. "You will fix it before it opens, won't you darling? Because it would be a real cock-up if I was petering out for weeks. No one would be able to concentrate and Caesar would be sure to cancel the production. But if I were to write a note and say it was my greatest wish that the Show Should Go On — in inverted commas — then no one would feel guilty, and it would be such a good thing for Caesar, give him something to do. Much the best thing. So we have to get on to it straight away — this week if possible, then it won't disrupt things too much; give everyone a chance to settle down before the first night. Good God, what's the matter with me? I somehow feel rather elated, isn't that strange? Oh my darling, don't cry, I didn't mean to make you cry because you have to be strong so that you can do all these things for me."

They lay on the sofa together with arms entwined, close together, like one person undivided.

"Darling Hilary, I have loved you so much for so long, in spite of all your infuriating habits and in spite of the bloody guilt complex that's been eating away at us both all this time. At least I'll be avoiding that running sore, though I suppose I'll probably be put through the tortures of the damned in Hell to pay me out for my self-indulgent wickedness. Thank God, darling, I have you in this world to help me out with the final job of speeding me on my way out of it."

Hilary turned his head away, quite unable to staunch the flood of tears. "Iffey, you don't know what you're asking me to do. How do you think I can just pop out to Boots and demand a fatal dose of strychnine or arsenic or whatever they supply."

Iffey rocked with laughter. "How can you be so out of date you funny old man. You're still in the Crippen age aren't you? I think it's bromides and alcohol these days isn't it? But there's probably a much better painless remedy by now. You have to find out from doctor friends, it shouldn't be difficult. They do say suffocating with a pillow is the least likely to show up in a post-mortem, don't they? But I shouldn't like that at all."

Hilary got up and walked away from her. "Stop it Iffey. I can't stand this sort of talk. Nor can I contemplate finishing you off in any way at all. I just could never do it, not ever. I'll be with you, nurse you, love you, do anything, but I can't shorten your life. You must go into hospital straight away and have treatment. It's more than likely that they can halt it. They do amazing things . . . ." He choked on the words, sat down with his back to her and cried, covering his face with his hands.

Iffey was shocked. She had not imagined he would refuse her this, but she had probably been silly to expect it. She had, after all, always been the one to take the decisions, do what was necessary, take the plunges. How could she really expect him to take over now? How could she expect anyone to take over now? After all these years of being self-sufficient, it was not possible to opt out of responsibility at the last moment.

"At least will you keep Caesar from knowing? Promise me you'll do that?"

"I'll try if you really think . . . but I'm not sure."

Hopeless, broken reed Hilary; could she rely on him? It seemed unlikely. Her world shattered a little further as she thought about Caesar and his reaction to any pain she might have to endure. How unlikely it was that he would be able to watch her deteriorating before his eyes.

Who else was there who could help her out? It was not conceivable that any of her other friends would oblige where euthanasia was concerned, even if they knew how; nor would they be likely to supply her with the means to do it herself. And it was not a job that could be done by just anyone. To ask one of her previous onetime lovers to do away with her would be little short of indecent, and not really fair on them. They might get into trouble for it. She thought of Rosie and was amused at the very idea.

It was imperative to do it at once, before Caesar could possibly suspect anything was wrong, so that the whole thing could be tied up and out of the way quickly. Otherwise everything could go wrong with his life; the production could collapse, and his first venture founder. Must avoid that at all costs. At the moment, she could not see the way out. What an old softie Hilary was.

She thought again of Rosie and her heart sank at the realisation of the propping up she was going to have to do in that direction. Poor, silly Rosie would come and weep all over her, and make all sorts of clichéd comments, and bring her grapes, and probably want to sit with her all day so that she shouldn't be left alone. Heaven forbid, she was not sure that she was up to that.

"You mustn't tell Rosie yet," she said. "She's bound to over-react."

"I shall have to tell her," Hilary said. "I can't take it on my own."

Iffey looked at him with some surprise, and then realised that one's own death is less traumatic than that of a loved one. Supposing this had been Caesar's imminent death they were discussing — what then? The idea of such a thing seized her heart with such pain that she gasped. How unthinkably worse that would have been. Poor, wretched darlings, all of them, what unhappiness she was putting them through.

"Come here, my lamb," she said to the weeping Hilary. "And let me give you a great big cuddle." Just like she used to do to Caesar when he had suffered some childhood disaster. Just like that it was. She would have to invent some story about the doctor

supplying her with things to keep her alive and splendid pain
killers that meant she was never going to suffer, right up to the
moment when she could think out a way of getting hold of the
materials to finish it off herself. That's what she had to do.

"*Cancer?*" Rosie felt herself drained and stricken. "Oh *no!* Far
advanced? But how can it be? Why didn't it . . . ? I suppose
she's been in pain for ages and never said anything. How *awful*."
She sat down, her elbows on the table, her head in her hands, and
she cried unrestrainedly. "So much a part of my life," she wailed.
"I can't imagine living if she's not there."

Hilary sat beside her, reined in and controlled, but with tears
running down unchecked. He put an arm round her shoulders,
awkwardly. Perhaps he should have kept the whole thing to
himself. Such a coward to think he needed support.

Rosie's storm of weeping did not last long. She sat up and blew
her nose. "No use collapsing," she said. "We must make plans.
So much we can do to help. Does Caesar know?"

"Iffey was particularly insistent that he shouldn't. Swore me to
secrecy."

"Not tell Caesar? But how ridiculous, of course he must be
told. That's so typical of Iffey — only thinking what will save *him*
distress rather than considering her own predicament. Of *course*
he must be told."

"Rosie, I promised her . . . ."

"He would never forgive us for keeping it to ourselves — I
would never forgive myself. There are some things, darling, that
one knows are right. Iffey may think she's doing what's best for
him but, more likely, she is just trying to live his life for him in
the way she always has. She doesn't realise that it's important for
him to be able to care for her when she needs him. He has so
much to repay, he should be given a chance to do so. But you
don't have to worry, I'll do it; I'll tell him."

All sound, good sense, but Hilary was racked by the certainty
that he was betraying his beloved. And to let Rosie do it was even
worse. She had no real sympathy for the boy and this would
obviously betray itself in the telling. Almost like a vindication of
her attitude to both of them; not that Rosie would ever realise
this herself. But her telling him would mean that he, Hilary,

would not be breaking his word to Iffey. The slight glow of relief pushed aside the hypocritical context without his having had time to notice it was there.

To say that Caesar took the news badly would have been a travesty of an understatement.

"Caesar dear," Rosie settled herself as comfortably as possible in the Rennie Mackintosh chair, because it was higher off the ground than any of the others and had a firm, supportive back. She had rehearsed what she was going to say, as well as the pauses for his expected answers, and had a plan of action for his expected hysterics.

Caesar gave her a gin and tonic with ice and lemon, and remembered that he had not yet written his Keats-Milton type lyric about bubbles winking at the brim. What on earth was old Rosie going to lecture him on this time? 'You are not a fit person to marry my daughter' perhaps? Or more subtly 'I think Sally should be given a little more time to be on her own Caesar dear; do you think it wise . . .' et cetera et cetera. Well, never mind, he would agree whole-heartedly in any case with everything she said, and send her on her way rejoicing.

"Caesar dear, I have some very sad and shocking news for you . . ." and he knew immediately that Iffey was dying, had not wanted him told, and that Rosie had betrayed that trust. What a *shit* the woman was.

"I know Rosie." Ice-cold calm crept through his body from the frozen heart and solar plexus outwards to all extremities. "Iffey is terminally ill. She didn't want you to tell me, but you considered it your bloody business, you warped old harridan. Tell the truth and shame the devil — honesty above all, no matter how much it hurts." Keep going at all costs, and then the message can be stifled for a little longer. But it wasn't true anyway; neither true nor possible; a silly, impossible lie that did not have to be faced, nor even brought into the conscious mind.

Rosie was thrown into confusion: "But I didn't know . . . but how . . . " How did he know all that? Of course he was upset, didn't know what he was saying . . . but so vindictive and unpleasant. All the sympathy she had wanted to pour out dried up and was forgotten.

241

Sally came flying through into the room, having heard the exchange, and put her arm round Rosie's shoulders, ushering her gently towards the door.

"I didn't know . . . I thought he should . . . ."

"Of course you did, and it was brave of you to tell him."

"Ridiculous not to tell him . . . ."

"Yes, quite ridiculous; but now he has to be left alone." They reached the front door. "I'll deal with the situation."

"He had to be told . . . ."

"Of course he did." She pushed Rosemary, quite gently, out of the flat and rushed back to Caesar, who was sitting as she had left him, staring at the floor.

She slid her arms round his neck and rested her cheek against his. "I apologise for my mother. Did you actually know about it?"

"No inkling until she said sad and shocking news, and then I immediately knew everything."

The realisation had still not surfaced. The news that his mother was dying lay there unattended and unadmitted, like some discarded litter. He was able only to deal with the emptiness that filled his head at that moment until at last rage surged in to destroy the vacuum.

"She had no *right*, Sally, no *right* to spoil Iffey's and my last little drama together. How dared she spoil that? We would have played out the whole thing in the pretence of it not really happening — how *dared* she take that away from us?"

He started to cry very suddenly and very helplessly. Long, uncontrolled sobs that brought both Ben and Emily into the room, wide-eyed and afraid at the sight of funny, grown-up Caesar, who had just been playing tag on the Common with them, crying like any baby would cry, in their mother's arms. This was unacceptable grown-up behaviour.

"Poor Iffey is ill," Sally told them. "And that has made Caesar very unhappy."

"Hasn't it made you unhappy?"

"Yes, of course." Had it? Was she really in any way unhappy? Hadn't she actually felt a wave of relief when she heard the news?

"But Iffey is Caesar's mummy so it's specially sad for him."

"Is she going to die?" Ben asked.

"Yes, I'm afraid she is."

Emily started to cry because of the unaccustomed atmosphere and Ben moved towards Caesar. "I would cry very much if Sally was going to die," he said.

Caesar took his hand and brought himself back to life. "So would I," he said. "But luckily Sally isn't going to. It usually only happens when you are very old and tired."

The effort of considering Ben's anxiety helped to stem the collapse into despair and self-pity, because it was, after all, himself he was crying for, and for the guilt he felt in having been a possible cause of the disaster. She had obviously deemed herself no longer needed, and therefore able to give up living.

Iffey and Caesar came through the anguish of their first encounter in the shadow with the conviction that nothing could ever be more agonising than that particular experience.

"Silly old bag, thinking you could keep it from me."

"Silly old bag nothing. I knew perfectly well you'd know as soon as you saw me, but I wanted you to realise it your*self*, so that you could decide how to react. You could quite easily have decided not to admit to it, and we could have acted out a lovely little Mimi-Rudolf production."

"Rubbish, we never could. Your tiny hand isn't frozen at all, it's hot, clammy and extremely large. And how long do you expect me to put up with this brinkmanship? It's as bad as saying goodbye at a railway station, pretending you're not aching for the guard to wave his little green flag. Most embarrassing."

Iffey heaved with laughter. "Not fair," she groaned. "It hurts when I laugh."

"Shall we kill Rosie for spoiling our fun?"

"She can't help it, darling. She has to have everything cut and dried and above board. She is depressingly honest and good and full of kind thoughts. All the things I am not."

"This is true, you wicked old battleaxe, and you're worth ten of her."

"Only ten?"

"Well, twenty if you insist."

She hid the pain from this much loved creature, sympathising deeply with his grief. How much more difficult to hide was grief than pain. No way could she ever ask him to finish her off. That would be far too cruel.

"Two people," Caesar told Sally afterwards, "trying to comfort each other for something that was completely beyond comfort. There was not even relief in the fact that you forgot your own grief in trying to assuage the other's, because the very thought of the other one's problems was far more devastating than one's own desolation. I don't think I can live through the things she is going to have to suffer."

Sally was torn between a kind of hopeless misery at witnessing his distress and an anger at his desire to opt out of the situation.

"That remark could be construed as self-centred," she said after a pause. "Like me saying I can't stand your distress so I'm going to take myself off."

"But I can't stand pain," Caesar shouted. "So I'm self-centred, so I'm a coward. But I want to die now, immediately. I can't stand the pain. I can't see her in agony and taking months to die — I can't live through that."

His outburst steeled Sally further and further into an icy seclusion of resentment; against Iffey for dying, for daring to prevail upon Caesar to this extent; against Caesar for hysteria, over-loving and being out of touch with reality.

"So give her the kiss of death," she said. "Put her out of her misery now, at once, before she can destroy your life any further."

"What do you *mean*? What are you saying? Are you some sort of monster?"

"Possibly. But if you really can't stand the thought of her suffering and dying a lingering, painful death, I would have thought it would be sensible to help her out of it."

"But I couldn't possibly do that; how could you imagine . . . ? No way could I do that. Do you think the doctor . . . ?"

"No, not her doctor. He came and saw Ben the other day and

244

he's a typical old-school Tory-type reactionary. It's against the law remember. He might fill her full of drugs so that she doesn't feel so much, but he'd never pull the plug out."

"You're talking about her as though she were a thing."

"Well if she were a cat you wouldn't hesitate."

"She isn't a cat."

"Oh all right; so you haven't the courage to do it so forget it."

"No, I haven't the courage, because I would never be certain I didn't do it just because *I* couldn't stand the horror or because it would be tidier and better for everyone else if she were to be put away quickly. How could I ever be sure about that?"

"I don't suggest you ever could, but if you were just thinking of her, that shouldn't bother you. So your antipathy is a selfish reaction, isn't it? You're thinking of you, not her. You're just worried about your own feeling of guilt."

Caesar found himself shivering violently and uncontrollably. "You're a cold-blooded sod," he said. "Would you do it?"

"I think I could, but I wouldn't, because if I did you'd never forgive me. You'd say I did it out of spite and because I wanted to get rid of her quickly, without having all the bother of the suffering and the dying. And it would probably be true, particularly when I see what her lingering death will obviously do to you and your plans for the future."

"If you mean the production, well that's obvious anyhow, I would have thought. There's no way I could even think of it now, not in the immediate future, not even in the more distant future either. At the minute, I can't imagine that I would ever be able to think of it again; far too many connections."

Sally turned away, angrily. "You're going to let down a lot of people."

"You mean I should go blithely on with the show with Iffey dying in the wings?"

"Of course. She'd be furious if she thought you were throwing everything up on her account."

"You surely can't imagine I could carry on?"

"Of course you could carry on if you weren't such a weak, self-centred drip."

Caesar squatted down on his haunches, his head on his knees, his arms locked behind his head.

"Help me, Sally, help me. Please don't abandon me too. I can't cope alone. I'm a very incomplete person."

Sally knelt down beside him and stopped his rocking. "Who said anything about you being alone?" she said.

29   Finishing Touch

Rosemary puts her knitting at the bottom of her shopping bag, adds the tastefully packaged bunch of muscat grapes she had bought that morning from Harrods, a bunch of flowers from the garden, the current copy of *Country Life*, the small, insignificant package from the young doctor to whom she had recently been recommended by one of her more advanced thinking friends, and sets out on her daily visit to Iffey.

Her life has taken on new and far deeper meaning than ever before. She feels a little ashamed that this new sense of fulfilment has only surfaced because of the tragedy of Iffey's illness. Almost as though she is thriving on the misfortune of others. Her mind clouds with the unpleasantness of the thought and she wishes it were not so private and shocking, because otherwise she could discuss it with Hilary. He would be able to put her mind at rest that her reaction is in no way selfish or vicious. She is sure, in her own mind that it is not, but is not able to work out the rational explanation as to why her feelings of — well — satisfaction you could call it, she supposes, why these feelings are not at all immoral but might, indeed, be looked on as considerate and without thought of self.

She becomes confused with the various niceties of what is and what is not self-consideration and self-approbation. The effort to rationalise her doubts is altogether too much for her and has to be shelved for the time being. In any case, it would not be relevant for very much longer and would soon be swamped by a much deeper and more serious question of morality.

"Just going to see Iffey," she calls out to Hilary before she opens the front door. Just as though it was a normal day, she thinks, and the significance of the everyday remark momentarily paralyses her on this far from normal every day.

"Ah," Hilary appears in the hall, surprisingly suddenly, she thinks to herself. "Does she — are you sure she — er — is she up to — I mean she might find daily visits a bit of a strain don't you think?"

"What *are* you saying?" Rosie laughs at his foolishness. "I'm not completely insensitive you know! I don't think I could be accused of forcing myself upon anyone!"

"No of course I didn't . . . ."

"She needs company now Hilary. You must understand, she needs support and comfort. I know how difficult it is for you to deal with terrible situations like this. You're much too sensitive. Somehow I think perhaps I can be of help to her in this awful period, now that her condition is deteriorating." More than you know, Hilary darling, more than you know. "Perhaps I shall be able to get her to go to hospital to be properly looked after, or get her to employ a nurse." At least have another go at her for all the good it would do. "Caesar is worse than useless, poor boy; can't control his emotions even when it upsets poor Iffey so. I'm really the only one she can rely on at the moment."

Hilary retreats in a bleak despair and finds himself cursing Iffey for not consenting to die like anybody else, neatly tidied away in hospital or hospice, safely and peacefully, cared for by kind strangers who know how to deal with such things. For a moment he feels rage at her lack of consideration for everyone all round her, before he pulls back his anger in shocked guilt.

Iffey hears Rosie's key in the lock with a sense of dread. Rosie, who had had a key cut for herself so that Iffey should not be bothered with answering the door every time she dropped round — sometimes twice or three times a day, any time she was passing. "And of course you only have to telephone whenever you feel you want me," she had said. "I can be there in five minutes darling; please remember that."

Iffey remembers it only too well, and steels herself not to show pain, not to show irritability with kind, loving Rosie, who only has Iffey's best interests at heart. Rosie who is her best friend and whom she has deceived over the whole of their adult lives. It was

247

surely possible to keep up the deception a little longer; shouldn't be all that difficult. She swallows another pain killer — even though it is a whole hour too early — and organises a smile.

"Hallo darling." Rosie comes softly into the room and moves about it with maddening silence and sympathy, throwing out yesterday's flowers and replacing them with the ones she has chosen particularly from her garden, straightening pillows, tweaking at curtains, and — worst of all — smiling continuously. Iffey feels murderous; if she had the strength she would hurl a book at her. Thank God she had made her will before she became ill, because there were times . . . .

Rosie places the grapes on a plate and takes her knitting out of the bag, "I'm getting on, aren't I?" she says. "It's for Ben. I hope Sally will like it. He chose the pattern himself, but you never know these days, the young change their minds and their fashions so quickly, and Sally has such definite ideas about what they should wear. I have taken quite a time over it."

Because the shock of Iffey's illness had put paid to any sort of normal occupation for some considerable time after she heard the news, Rosie had found it difficult to continue with the mundane things of life like sewing and knitting. It was only the deliberate resolve she had made to carry on as normal that has made it possible to take them up again.

Iffey doesn't speak. It's all so pointless somehow. She wants to make a joke of it by suggesting that Rosie should start knitting a black sweater for him instead, but that would be cruel, wouldn't it? Mustn't be cruel to Rosie; not any more that is. She feels childishly petulant that she should have to be considering Rosie's feelings when her own at this time are particularly wretched. Time is moving fast and relentlessly, and so far she has made no progress in her efforts to arrange for her own suicide. It's this apathy she finds difficult to contend with. The illness has somehow seemed to sap her resolve and fill her full of indecision.

But isn't it really because she is too afraid to take any decisive step? Isn't she just as much of a coward as everyone else? There is something in her of the 'see what happens tomorrow' attitude; the tiny flicker of hope that things will be better tomorrow; they could have made a mistake; quite often she felt almost well. Silly to go before it's absolutely necessary.

She hears Rosie talking to her and tries to blot out the words with thoughts of her own. But it's no use, she is like the wedding guest in the Ancient Mariner and feels like quoting ' . . . hold off! Unhand me grey-beard loon!' but it really wouldn't be very appropriate, Rosie doesn't have a grey beard. She starts to heave with silent laughter and feels a little better; if only Rosie had a sense of humour, they could have shared that moment. But humourless old Rosie is obviously holding her with her glittering eye and the patient is listening like a three years' child while Rosemary has her will. The humour still bubbles inside Iffey as she quotes on to herself other bits she remembers. There were those creepy crawlies 'Yea slimy things did crawl with legs upon a slimy sea!' What a splendid piece of poetry that is . . . .

". . . and I do think you should, Iffey," says Rosie. "For the sake of everyone you love."

"What?" shouts Iffey, coming to with a jolt. "What should I do?"

Rosie looks at her, full of gentle understanding for her difficulty in concentrating on what is being said. "Let us arrange for you to go into a nursing home darling, where you could be properly looked after and cared for, and perhaps cured. It's not fair on all of us round you not to do everything in your power . . . ."

"Shut up Rosie," roars Iffey. "I'll not listen to another word about that taboo subject. As none of you have the guts to do me in, I am at the moment in the process of finding someone who will supply me with the means, and then I'll trouble you no longer. I am not, repeat *not* going gentle into that good night."

Rosie is silent. At least she has tried; couldn't ever accuse herself of not making every possible effort. So there is no alternative it seems.

"Another thing I wanted to say," she says as Iffey sits smouldering with the fury of the last conversation.

"Not on that subject then."

"No, not on that subject, it's quite different. I wanted to tell you how grateful I am about you and Hilary."

Iffey could have sworn that her heart stopped at that moment.

"What do you mean, grateful?"

"Well — well I only realised a short time ago how much you

249

loved Hilary. I mean I realised that you have presumably been in love with him all your life and I'm so dreadfully sorry that you should have had to suffer in silence like that for so long. I feel almost guilty that Hilary should have loved me and not you, because I realise how awful that must have been for you all those years. I just want to say how wonderful I think you are, Iffey, for never trying to take him away from me. I don't think I could have been so strong and I don't think I could have gone on being friendly with someone who had what I wanted so desperately. I'm sure I should have felt jealous and vengeful and vindictive and you never did. Or at least if you did, you never let it spoil our friendship did you? Darling Iffey, you are a friend indeed. I just want you to know that."

She gets up from her chair and turns her back so that Iffey shouldn't see the tears and think her a sentimental idiot. "If ever I had lost either of you," she says, "my life would not have been worth living. I would have killed myself."

She picks up the bottle of whisky that is on the table beside Iffey's chair. "And now I'm going to mix us a drink," she says in a voice that wavers noticeably, and she takes the bottle and glasses and the small packet she has recently obtained from the young doctor into the kitchen. Must remember to bring back the empty package. Had to look as though she'd done it herself. A wave of heat flushes through her at the thought of the deceit. Something so alien to all her beliefs. To pretend something is just as despicable as lying, just as immoral. The guilt is stifled as she enters the kitchen; this is, after all, the final retaliation she is offering her old and trusted friend; the final helping hand.

Blessedly alone for a short moment, Iffey deplores the fact that a self-destructive weapon is not immediately to hand; she might even have overcome her horror of blood and guts to use a sharp knife on herself. Instead, she sits, shaking and speechless, listening to ordinary sounds like the tap being turned on, the clink of glass, Rosie's footsteps, the unscrewing of the bottle top, the slurp of whisky in the glasses, and the hiss of soda. Each sound has a little life of its own in the cold void of Iffey's mind. Thought is dead, only the body throbs on relentlessly and unnecessarily.

Rosie returns with the drinks on a tray, hands her the whisky and raises her own glass. "What was it they said in that film?" she says, smiling into Iffey's eyes. "Here's looking at you kid."

Iffey finds herself laughing at the absurdity of such a toast coming from Rosie. The whole situation seems somehow hilarious. Even Rosie starts to laugh.

Iffey clinks her glass against Rosie's. "Play it again, Sam," she says, and drinks the whole draught in one go.